To Face the Universe

Mutiny

Starship
Book I

BRIAN MICHAEL HALL

Mutiny is a work of fiction. All of the characters, places, organizations, and events portrayed in this novel are either the product of the author's imagination or are used fictitiously.

DEDICATION

To my glorious wife Leticia – words cannot express the gratitude I hold within my heart for you during the many times you put up with my computer tapping when I should have been doing something else!

CONTENTS

ACKNOWLEDGMENTS

This book was made possible by the many Authors I grew up reading (you know who you are) and it is my solemn hope that one day you too might pick up this book.

I believe that my children were instrumental in my desire to share my stories with others; hence this first in hopefully many publishing's. I thank my Daughter Lillian and her Husband Jeremiah for being my sounding board s, and my Daughter Mary for being an undaunted artist extraordinaire.

I also thank Author Stan Nelson for the most encouragement in pursuit of this labor of love. Your turn; ATC my friend!

THE MUTINY

1

"I'm telling you Edwards; you are essential to the whole operation!" Lt Frederick Song Ha said in a low voice. He was quite adamant about the proposed mutiny he was about to get involved in. He current mission was to convince the ship's Quartermaster, Ensign Ken Edwards, to join or he would personally have to dispose of him. His was not a violent man, being a Xenologist by profession, but he was a Marine and his Commanding Officer was quite clear on this one point. Edwards was looking pensively toward the main stage where, among others, sat the ship's Captain, the First Officer, Doctor Kuremoto, and Princess Shirae. The Emperor's own daughter was here to christen the starship *Iwakina* for its maiden voyage on the morrow. The First Officer began his opening remarks. Song Ha bent a little closer to the QM who shared the chair beside him out on the fringes of the crew section.

"Without your help we are all doomed. You want off this awful rock as much as any man; surely you can see the benefit in this plan..." he had been giving the details of the plan in hushed tones, the numbers involved, what was required of Edwards, and the timeline, without naming any of his coconspirators since the ceremony began. Edwards looked at him directly for just a moment, and Song Ha could not read the thoughts on that face. Edwards had turned back toward the ceremony. Song Ha continued, "Look, I don't know what the future holds for us, but if we pull this off, no one can touch us, and we'll be able to get rich, all of us!" Song Ha was absolutely out on a limb here; he had no idea what the Boss's plans for the future were, but he was in this knee deep already. He was sure that Edwards was the sort of man that would be lured in by the thoughts of big numbers in his bank account. Edwards was needed because he controlled the ship's storage codes at the moment. Without those, the Marines aboard ship could not move the munitions stores out of reach of those not involved in the mutiny. *If only this guy was a Marine…; what honor was there among the thieving Supply Corps? Enough.* Song Ha was pulling out his last ditch plea, "Look, we'll have the Princess as insur-"

"I'm in." Song Ha was cut off mid-sentence by Edwards's acceptance. He saw Edwards turn back toward the ceremony. Song Ha pulled out a handkerchief and wiped the sweat off his brow, slumping a little in his chair. He watched the Princess give her remarks and lift the ceremonial bottle of wine to smash it against the hull of the dull black ship. It simply bounced off. She tried it twice more before the Captain graciously offered to smash the bottle against the hull using his sword.

* * *

Third Officer Darren Jones woke up in time to catch Third Meal at the base dining facility. He resented the fact that he had to miss the after party for the *Iwakina's* christening. There were many important people with connections that he would have liked to have met. He had a job to do though, if the *Iwakina* was to makes its maiden voyage in the afternoon. He performed his last looks at the calibrations being done on the bridge before heading off; inspecting each deck along the way to the cargo hold to check supplies. On his way through the ship's gray strip lit corridors he saw several groups of Marines scurrying about. *What could they be up to at this time of night?* He mentally checked his ship's schedule through his neural-network. No Marine activities were evident there. After verifying all cargo was aboard and secure, he headed back toward the bridge. To skip heading down to deck six again, he used the tube from the cryo-storage area to deck 5A. When he opened the tube access room's hatch to the corridor, he startled yet another group of Marines, who knocked over a cart they were wheeling, spilling weapons onto the deck. The Marines snapped to attention.

"What are you Marines up to?" he asked them, expecting some crazy hazing ritual was afoot. "We are transporting these weapons to the Arms Room for inspection, Sir." was the reply of the Marine who seemed to be in charge.

Jones cocked an eyebrow. "I have no scheduled weapons maintenance on my list..."

"Captain's orders, Sir." Was the Marine's flat reply while he motioned for the rest of them to get the weapons back on the cart. Jones bade them carry on and continued toward the bridge. As an afterthought, he stopped the lift at deck 3A and looked for more Marines. Sure enough, he caught another group transporting weapons with the same excuse as before, "Captain's orders." This confounded him as he lifted to the bridge. He checked to make sure all systems were good to go for the ship's launch all the while wrestling with thoughts of bringing his observations to the Captain. He mentally checked the time; it was 0240. He verified the Captain was aboard on his manifest. "*Iwa*, locate the Captain, please." He queried the *Iwakina's* Artificial Intelligence. Such pleasantries were not required, but he always felt like he was speaking to a real person. An angel's voice tinged with honey responded that the Captain was in fact in the Captain's Quarters. Surely, he was sleeping off whatever concoctions the local Commander could conjure up for alcohol on this God forsaken outpost. Again, he hesitated; he was told Captain Saitow could be quite cross when disturbed from sleep, unlike the former Captain, *God rest his soul.*

He couldn't help but ponder other dissimilarities between the two. The new Captain was young, ambitious, and sometimes rash, while the later had aged gracefully, was calculated, and of calm demeanor. He made up his mind, and after delegating authority to the Assistant Watch Officer, headed down to the Officer's Billeting deck. He paused outside the Captain's hatch and steeling himself, swiped his wrist past the hailing pad on the bulkhead next to it. His token ring activated the panel and would inform the Captain of his presence. He heard the muffled bleating of the hail through the hatch. There was no response. He waited another minute and hailed the Captain again. He again received no response. All the thoughts of foul play that he had been harboring came to a head, and with another swipe of his wrist, he used his Command Override authority to open the hatch; it swished open to the darkness within. As his eyes adjusted to the dimly lit room, his senses were on level one, ready to move his body to respond to anything untoward within. What met his ears was a heavy snoring that could surely wake the dead. He keyed the illumination control panel to raise the lighting of the room to a useable level and had the hatch close. He scanned the room and found no intruders, only the Captain with his boots and jacket off snoring loudly and sprawled upon a lounger. As he approached the man, a strong smell of exotic alcohol assailed him, and he stepped back a moment to contemplate his next move. Should he awaken the man in poor spirits, he would surely get a tongue-lashing the likes of which he had never endured, even at the Academy. However, his suspicions were much too important to contemplate pulling out now, so he gingerly approached within speaking distance and softly called for the Captain's attention. He received a renewed bought of deep snoring for his trouble. Taking a new approach, he tapped the Captain's shin lightly with his foot. That did the trick as the man sat bolt upright and groggily peered around blinking his eyes. Jones stepped back a pace or too. "Jones?" the Captain squinted his eyes in Jones's direction, then grabbed his head with one hand and pointed toward his desk with the other, "Stims...In the top left."

Jones found the box of stims the Captain had motioned for and handed it to the man. He counted out two with difficulty, but managed to get both into his mouth. The Captain sat back in the lounger with his eyes closed as the stims took effect. A minute later, the Captain got to his feet, seemingly as if he had been completely sober to begin with.

"What's going on Jones, is the ship on fire?" the Captain seemed rather sarcastic to Jones, but not as hot tempered as he was led to believe.

"Sir, no sir. I just had some observations while pursuing my duties which I thought you should be aware of. Something odd is afoot."

5

"This something better be pretty damn good to disturb me out of a drunken slumber at three in the morning."

"Yes, My Lord, I believe that it is." Jones spelled out his encounters with the Marines to the Captain in minute detail. He then told the Captain of his suspicions on what he thought was really going on given that the operation was not on the events listing and occurred at such a late hour. "Sir, I believe that the Marines may be staging a mutiny."

The Captain appeared to be aghast. "A mutiny you say? Hmmm..." Jones couldn't help feeling there was a tinge of the sarcasm he had heard earlier. "We'll have to deal with this at once. Who else besides the Marines is aboard?" Jones told him about the Assistant Watch Officer and the engineers on the bridge, and the Chief Cook's assistant who was inventorying food stock on the Mess Deck. He checked the manifest again. No one else was aboard. "OK, we have contingencies for such an occurrence. The local MPs are on standby and as soon as I send the code, they will take about 20 minutes to get here. We'll stay put until they are five minutes out, then head down to Access and let them in. They can deal with the Marines." The Captain was gazing steadily at Jones, which gave him an eerie feeling. The Captain then looked up as most people do when addressing the Ship's AI.

"*Iwa*, implement Code 37-Lima." An acknowledgement hail sounded, and then the room seemed deathly silent as the two stared at each other. Jones was unaware of any such code.

"So there went the call. Do you play Darkats, Jones?" it was an old game played with rectangular cards; he'd heard about it and its addictive gambling qualities, but never played. He avoided such vices as much as he could. It seemed he was about to have to learn this one.

"No sir. I suppose you could teach me given that we have time to kill."

"Great. Move that table over here under the overhead lighting."

Jones moved the table and a couple of chairs to the designated place while he watched the Captain go over to the illumination panel and bring the lights to an agreeable level. He stepped toward Jones and the table, which was now at center of the room in front of the main hatch. Jones noticed he seemed to pause for a few seconds, and then he veered around to compartment side of the desk. After watching the Captain's hands disappear behind the desk, he saw the man pull out a box from somewhere in there and he headed back to the table. The Captain moved his chair so that he faced the main hatch and gestured for Jones to move his chair opposite. With both men seated at the table, the Captain opened the box of cards and, pulling them out, began manipulating them into stacks of ten or so it seemed to Jones. Just then a hail sounded from the hatch. The Captain stood up, said "enter", and before Jones could turn around, two heavy bodies were on top of him, one quickly placing a neural-net scrambler around his neck.

"I guess they got to us first, Jones." The Captain said in that sarcastic tone of his. "Confine him to the brig. Use the tube access behind my desk. Do not be seen by anyone." Jones heard him tell the Marines as a chem-bag was placed over his head. He lost consciousness quickly.

*   *   *

Captain Glenn Saitow watched as the Marines disappeared with Jones into the tube access behind the mural behind his desk. He stood for a moment contemplating the Imperial crest embroidered upon it. That won't be there for very much longer. He would replace it with his family's crest – a blue tiger's head. He crossed the room and slumped down into the lounger with a sigh. He thought about how this all started in the first place. If he hadn't been such a rash young man at twenty-four, he wouldn't have even been in the military, much less the Captain of a top-secret Imperial starship at thirty-eight. Surely, he'd have been running the family business of starship trading and manufacturing at this point. However, he didn't regret spurning the business back then and didn't have much desire for it now. Since he was so head-strong in those days, they sent him on deliveries, helming sometimes illegally armed personal yachts with skeleton crews to planets far away from his homeworld of Roseglade. He was on such a delivery when, coming out of hyperspace, he emerged dead center in the midst of a battle between the new Imperials who were outgunned and some unknown fleet, who turned out to be pirates. Quick thinking had saved him, as he immediately laid into the pirates with his ship's weapons, and with the element of surprise on his side, turned the tide in favor of the Imperials. His ship was badly damaged in the fight and easily boarded by the victors. He and his crew were given aid, but his ship was then seized and he was forcibly recruited to serve in the Ros'Loper Imperial Navy, from which his family tried extracting him to no avail. He couldn't have cared less. Let the family squirm and wring their handkerchiefs over him, he was living the excitement of military service; they just wouldn't understand.

It had taken him many years of distinguished service, first as a fleet officer up to Captain, fighting against pirates and independent world navies, then several desk jobs at Imperial Headquarters, to land the slot as Lord Captain of this very special project. It didn't hurt that the former Captain had come to an untimely death during an off-world excursion. Now he could get back at those self-righteous brothers of his by showing up with the grand prize, not only of the *Iwakina* and its many wonders, but also a princess by his side, which he would make his own. He would also have the satisfaction of sticking it to the rotten Imperials whose policies and practices had turned his stomach on more than one occasion. He checked the time on deck. He had better say something to the Assistant Watch Officer in case Jones had told the man he was coming here. He checked the ships manifest and duty logs. "*Iwa*, Bridge." A 'communication connection established' signal sounded. "Bret? This is the Captain. Jones has fallen ill and has been escorted to the hospital on base. Can you cover the remainder of the watch?"

"Aye, Lord Captain." The man responded tiredly.

"Good. Carry on." Saitow closed the link with a swish of his hand and settled back into his lounger once again. Later today he would also finally be free of this accursed dust bowl of a planet he and his collaborators loathed so much. He was soon snoring away in that manner of his that would surely rattle furniture.

* * *

Goh Takagawa waited patiently in the *Iwakina*'s martial training room. Being one of the Assistant Engineers on the ship, he naturally surveyed the room and its contents while he waited. On one end was a cabinet with several lockers for training equipment. The opposite end held the entrance. On the right long wall hung a long banner which reached from floor to ceiling in the center of the wall. The banner held the Tenets of Training in Standard Codex English. Prominent in the center and in bold it read, "The heart is the engine of the body; the brain is the engine of the mind. The two must work in unison to be enabled in the way of order. FOCUS is order." He thought that seemed pretty profound. He heard the entrance hatch slide open to reveal his best friend Kintaro Sagura similarly dressed in loose training clothes.

"Poles today?" Kintaro requested in that high pitched voice of his. Goh nodded his head and moved to the equipment cabinet and retrieved two poles from inside. He tossed one to Kintaro. He bowed and observed a return bow from his opponent. Each then moved to the ready position. Goh just barely got his pole up in time to block Kintaro's first blow. He knew that Kintaro was better than him when it came to martial training, but the guy was getting more and more ahead of him in their daily sparing matches. Although he was leaner and taller than his peer, he felt he would soon be calling the slightly chubby and shorter man Sensei, meaning a superior to be learned from, in the ancient Old Imperial language.

"OK, ok, you have got to teach me how you got that momentum going for that first strike."

Goh listened intently as Kintaro explained the

mechanics involved, taking it all in earnestly. Once they both agreed that he had it down they continued to spar for the rest of an hour.

"Phew. Time's up." Goh reminded when the timer's chime sounded throughout the room. Kintaro went to put the poles back in the cabinet. Goh wiped the sweat off his brow and marveled at Kintaro as he watched the man put the equipment back. It seemed as if Kintaro never sweats during their sparing matches.

"See you on the watch." Kintaro said as he went out the door. Goh headed out the hatch himself after swiping his wrist's embedded token ring over the light panel. The room went dark.

*　　*　　*

Sanae approached the cabin of Kintaro Sagura, entered and secured the room. She checked various tells she had set up to detect if anyone had been inside while she was away. Satisfied that all was well, she deactivated the personal Transmutor device that gave her the outward appearance of Kintaro Sagura, Navigator. She quickly wiped all the sweat off of the device and placed it on the bureau. She was sure she detected a bit of perplexity on the face of her only friend Goh; perhaps he had wondered again about her outward lack of sweat, although she was drenched in it now. Goh was getting better at martial training and soon might be good enough for her to go all out on him. Perhaps in a few more weeks of their infrequent sparing bouts she would have some actual sport. She undressed out of the loose training clothing, stepped out of her underwear, and removed the wrap that compressed her average breasts. She stepped into the shower. She wondered what to do about this new set of predicaments. She was a spy for the Imperial Court, who had assigned her here under suspicions that there were some criminals among the crew. Who would have guessed that the criminals were led by none other than the Captain himself! Then there was the fact that an Imperial person in the form of the Emperor's only child was to be aboard during the ship's maiden voyage. It was her duty to protect the Princess at all costs, although she would need to do so covertly or else risk blowing her cover. So, when she was approached by Goh to join the mutiny, she had no choice but to accept. She would need to find out when the mutiny was to occur and report her findings, but the plan was only known to the top criminals. She could only ensure the safety of the Princess and wait for the right time to send her dispatch on the special equipment she had hidden in her cabin. When her shower was done and she had dried herself off, she rewrapped her breasts with fresh cloth and donned her tight mercenary suit. She tapped a hidden panel on the bureau and removed a terminal unit from inside. She plugged the Transmutor device into the terminal and programmed it for Kintaro's duty uniform. Once finished, she put the terminal away, reset those tells that she had disturbed, donned her Kintaro disguise, and headed out the cabin. She went down one deck on the lift to the ship's galley. As usual for this time of day the galley was deserted. As was her routine, she made herself a sandwich, leaving a friendly electronic message for the Chief Cook on the main countertop, and headed back to her cabin. Once there she could eat without the spectacle of shoving food through Kintaro's face; the Transmutor was good, but it still had its limitations. She had the rest of the crew believing she could only eat in solitude for religious reasons. Even the ship's Priest stopped pestering her to attend services. Her training had no room for actual religion, only duty.

*   *   *

Saitow woke with a start. He checked his internal clock; still plenty of time before the big show. He lumbered out of the lounger and headed toward his private bath. As he stripped and proceeded to shower, he contemplated the machinations that led up to the day's main event. He'd known and served with his First Officer, Victor Soto, and his Medical Officer, Kimberly Rosel, for many years. He had personally recruited the Commanding Officer of his Marines, Lieutenant Yusef Simpson, and trusted the loyalty of all of the Marines on board. They would do whatever needed to be done as long as their commander ordered it. Saitow hoped they wouldn't have to get too serious. He brought his personal cook Bonifacio along as well. The man who was in charge of the whole project that the ship belonged to, Doctor Edward Kuremoto, and the ship's Priest, Stephen Jing, who represented the interests of the Universal Church, were the roughest recruitments. All the other players that were needed were the responsibility of the Marine officers.

A few weeks ago, he had approached the laboratory of the ship with Bonifacio in tow pushing a serving cart. His cook was not only useful in pouring the tea he was bringing to share with Doctor Kuremoto, but also in reading the Doctor's mood. They took the lift up which was the only way of access. He hailed and waited for the Doctor's approval before entering the lab.

"Greetings Doctor, I was wondering if you could spare a few moments for a break..." Saitow motioned toward the serving cart.

"Why yes, Captain. I was meaning to discuss a few things with you as well." Kuremoto tapped a couple instructions into the countertop input and swiped the holo-display away with the swish of his hand. He motioned for Bonifacio and Saitow to join him across the room at a lounge area of the lab. Bonifacio served the two men seated across from each other and withdrew to an adjacent chair out of earshot. Saitow and the Doctor exchanged pleasantries for a few moments, and then the Doctor broached the subject of his time.

"Captain, you have known me for some time now."

Saitow nodded for him to continue.

"I have been stuck here on this God-awful planet for several years now with not one week of vacation time; not *one* I tell you! If only I could get off this accursed rock for just one week, I would be forever in your debt." Surely the man was exaggerating. However, this played perfectly into Saitow's plan. He tested the waters a bit.

"Doctor, do you have some pressing off-world business to attend to?"

"Glenn, actually there is a pressing matter of some research that a friend of mine needs my help with and I need the time to collect materials and equipment for the work." Kuremoto looked at him apprehensively. Saitow wondered if the man was being straight with him. He glanced at Bonifacio who sat with one raised eyebrow; a sure indication that the Doctor was leaving something crucial out of the equation.

"What pressing matter would be of more import than the loving care of your baby here?" Saitow made a sweeping gesture indicating the ship itself. The Doctor often referred to the *Iwakina* as his 'baby'; he *was* the chief scientist who broke the code on Pruathan technology and trained the bulk of the crew.

"Well... Are you aware of the situation on Uprising?"

Saitow thought for a moment then remembered that the bulk of the inhabitants on Uprising were afflicted with some rare disease. Such epidemics were almost non-existent nowadays. "I believe there is some kind of outbreak of disease there?"

"Yes. As you know, besides my current engineering expertise, I have extensive experience in Xenology and biological chemistry. My friend is there on Uprising trying to get to the root of the disease. He has asked me to help him if I could." The Doctor looked quite earnest to Saitow.

It was time for his end run. "Doctor, this equipment you need probably costs a good deal of money, right?"

"It is expensive, but I have saved quite a bit of MU over the years I put into this project. I just need the time to put together a lab and do a bit of the research for him. That is all I am asking." Kuremoto looked pensively down at his tea cup.

"Doctor, I would like to ask you something." Saitow was taken aback a little as the Doctor's eyes concentrated at him; his attitude change was so abrupt. "If you were free, say tomorrow, from this project what would you do then?"

Saitow watched intently as Kuremoto looked contemplatively around the lab.

"Well... I suppose that I would take my vacation, but it would not be long before I was missing my Pruathan experimentation and this ship."

"Well Doctor, I intend to set you free." Saitow grinned inside at the Doctor's shocked reaction.

"But... that's impossible! You don't have the authority to allow me to just leave the project. I am only asking for some time off..."

"OK, Doctor, I will make you a deal. I will only set you free to take your leave of absence if you agree to work for me. I am offering the financing to do your biological research as long as you continue to spend at least 80% of your time working on Pruathan tech. You can even continue to use this lab as long as you can guarantee that none of the crew will be exposed to any exotic diseases. I will double the poor salary that the Imperials have saddled you with and you will continue to provide Doctor Rosel and I with Rejuve as needed. These are simple terms are they not?" Saitow watched as the shock on Kuremoto's face changed to deep thought as the man sat back in his lounger.

After some minutes of contemplation, the Doctor finally spoke. "You know, Captain, this offer has the trappings of treason attached to it."

"Yes, Doctor, you are quite right. As you know in a few weeks this ship will make her maiden voyage. Many of her crew wants escape from this awful dust hole and to get out from under the heel of a tyrannical empire that cares little for its citizens and military. I am under the impression from our years of contact that you are inclined to feel the same."

"They will hunt us down like ursine on Calestra." The Doctor seemed skeptical.

"We have ways of staying a few steps ahead of them. I assure you Doctor; we will have many adventures and explorations, together with your 'Baby'."

"What guarantees do you have that we will stay a few steps ahead?" was the Doctor's next response.

Saitow did not want to give up the whole ghost before he had this man in confidence. He hesitated, but then let out his biggest secret to the whole scheme.

"Doctor, you know my family. We have resources throughout the quadrant. We will be operating under the full protection of the Saitow Conglomerate, independently of course." Saitow threw that last little bit in, although he knew when it came down to it, he would have to answer to the family for every action he took. They were fully funding him after all.

Doctor Kuremoto raised an eyebrow and let out a sigh. "I see. Well, I guess changing task masters from a tyrant to a matriarch could have its advantages. How is your mother these days?"

"She sends her warmest regards. Shall we discuss the details of your vacation Doctor?"

Kuremoto gave him a wink and simply said, "Lets."

The two men smiled and continued to enjoy their tea.

* * *

Stephen Jing was a touchy matter. Saitow knew he would have to have some assurance of non-interference from the Universal Church, or all was lost. When the Rangelley Empire finally collapsed, it was the Universal Church which had kept most of the systems from total chaos and their fleet is the envy of all political entities. They have agents everywhere, especially where there were adherents. His own crew had a few and with them came the Ship's Priest. He went to the chapel to find him in deep meditation. Saitow sat in a rear pew studying the man. He sat crossed-legged in front of his alter, seemingly oblivious to Saitow's presence. Saitow found this man's appearance to be very contrary to that of the priests of his youth. Stephen wore none of the flowing robes and greying hair of those men. He was clad all in black, wearing military trousers, an empty utility vest, and sleeveless shirt. Only the band around his neck was white. That was mostly concealed by his long straight jet-black hair, which framed a somber yet foreboding face aged beyond his thirty-five years. That odd discoloration on his left cheek, which some say was the wing of an angel, paler than his own skin, was barely visible in the dim lighting of the chapel. Saitow cleared his throat, as much to alert Stephen of his presence, as to get over the uneasiness he felt seeing Stephen in this way. Stephen opened his eyes, focused quickly on Saitow and rose.

"Captain, what brings you hence? I had thought that our daily training session was postponed due to your having inspections today." Stephen said as he approached. His cool smile instantly put Saitow at ease. They were very old friends and trained in the martial room daily.

"You're quite right, Stephen. There is just a pressing matter that I need to discuss with you. Have a moment?"

"Shall we retreat to the sanctuary?"

"Sure. Where's Gunter?"

"Ah, I sent him onto base for a few errands."

The two men sat in comfortable chairs in the large room. It was filled with books and quite a few artifacts from around the planet. The room served as the Church's 'office' for lack of a better word.

Saitow surveyed the place. "It would serve you well to get this stuff packed. Lord knows how effective the inertial dampeners will be when we leave the ground."

"Gunter's next task, assuredly. So, what pressing business requires a personal visit from the Captain?"

Saitow wasn't sure if Stephen was chiding him or being serious. Did the priest know what was going to happen already? Saitow attributed it to his friend's wry sense of humor.

"Saitow began in earnest, "Stephen, you and I have been friends for, what, these last ten years or so?"

Saitow confirmed his friends attempt at humor when the man's face became even more somber than usual. The priest replied, "Certainly."

"We've often discussed the Church's view on what goes on within the Empire. Now do me a favor. Take the fact that I am an agent of that empire out of the equation and tell me what the Church's true views are."

"Glenn. I have always been forthright with you in expressing the Church's views, regardless of your stature within the empire. The Church exercises complete neutrality with regards to all of the political entities within the quadrant as long as the current state of Church operations is unhindered."

"Right. I know church doctrine. However, think for a moment. What would the Church's position be with regards to say, a rogue entity emerging from the Empire, with no allegiances whatsoever, but in no way contradictory to church operations?"

"Hmm. What size entity are we talking about here? If it were a planetary rebellion then the church would only get involved if adherents were being persecuted by either side. Otherwise, the church's doctrine of neutrality would be strictly enforced. Why such a sudden interest in church doctrine, my friend?"

"Curiosity killed the feline, eh?" Saitow tried to sound nonchalant, but his friend seemed to know better. He decided to just come out with it. He had known Stephen Jing from his days at Imperial Headquarters, where Stephen had served as an aide to the Church's representative. He believed that the fact that the Church had assigned Stephen to the *Iwakina* when Saitow took command was no mere coincidence. He was determined to learn the truth now.

"Stephen, I need a fair and truthful answer to my next question: Are we truly friends here, or were you attached to me for the purpose of extra attention from the church?" Saitow immediately regretted his question as he watched his friend visibly flinch.

The priest stood up and moved over to a cabinet at the back of the sanctuary. Saitow watched as he poured himself a drink from the decanter inside. He turned and said amicably, "Care for a drink Captain?"

Saitow nodded and the priest returned to offer him a glass of what appeared to be wine after taking his seat. Stephen sat back and took a good swig from his glass before beginning, "Glenn. It is true that I was assigned to the *Iwakina* to keep an eye on its pretentious Captain; their words not mine. The circumstances of the former captain's demise and your appointment beyond the norm did not escape the eye of the Church's extensive network. Yes, I was assigned to the *Iwakina* to keep an eye on you for the very fact that you are my friend. But, my friend, the things I have learned from you and to know that you are nothing like the Church's initial assessment of you has only strengthened the bond of friendship between us." Stephen took another gulp of wine. He looked genuinely taken aback by Saitow's confrontation.

Saitow sipped at his wine and let the moment sink in before responding, "Stephen, my friend. I do not mean to judge your friendship; of that I am certain. I merely wished to learn the truth of the Church's motives. Have I done anything that remotely goes against the wishes of the church?"

Stephen thought for a moment, "Not a thing." He sat back once again with what appeared to be a smile of bewilderment.

Saitow thought it time to come clean. He would need assurances from his friend that the church would not interfere. "You said yourself that the Church would not meddle in the affairs of politics so long as Adherents were not threatened, correct?"

Stephen nodded and leaned forward in his chair.

"You know as well as I that the Empire is as oppressive as it is unconcerned for its citizens. The very ship that we are on now represents an advantage over those other political entities within the quadrant that the church holds dear. I intend to deprive the empire of such an advantage." Saitow let this sink in for a moment. Stephen seemed to regain himself and stood up once again, "Another drink?"

Again, glasses were exchanged and the two men were once again sitting comfortably.

Saitow continued, "I intend to take the ship and keep it out of the hands of tyrants. I am telling you all this because you are my friend and I want you to join us. Rest assured the portion of the crew that does not go along with this plan will be treated humanely. We will be dropping them off where they will easily be found and rescued. I only ask that you send Gunter with them when the time comes and only inform the Church through him. What say you?"

Saitow knew that this was the very moment that would make or break his plan. If Stephen could not be trusted, all was lost. Saitow sipped on his wine while he watched the man mull things over.

After a long moment that seemed like an eon to Saitow, Stephen spoke, "So Glenn, you are fully intent to have a peaceful mutiny on the *Iwakina*, and will guarantee the lives of all crewmembers... and you wish for me to join your Mutineers? You do realize that I will be required to report to the church at every opportunity that presents itself?"

"Yes. But I am hoping the opportunity will not present itself until after we are underway from dropping off the non... 'Mutineers' as you say..."

Saitow did not want to use his last trump card; the fact that he knew the Church had been using Pruathan technology for decades. He would certainly be able to persuade the priest that it is in the best interests of the Church to get this technology out of imperial hands.

Stephen seemed to have made up his mind, "I will join you my friend. Now tell me the details of this grand plan of yours!"

Saitow was a little taken aback by the joviality of his friend's acceptance of it all. "I'm afraid I can't tell you anything beyond what I already have. It's a technicality really...Not all the pieces are quite in place as of yet. I will give everyone the details once we are underway. You do understand, don't you?"

Stephen had regained his ever-somber look. "Yes, of course, my friend."

Saitow held up his almost empty glass, "This isn't..."

"Lord, help me, no!" Stephen smiled the biggest grin Saitow had ever seen him smile.

* * *

The *Iwakina*'s Security Officer Nanami Oliver was very excited. It was going to be a very interesting day; the day she got to coordinate mutiny against the hated Imperials. As she slipped out of her camisole and headed toward the bath, she contemplated the events that led to such a magnificent occurrence. It was just a few weeks ago that she had been summoned to the Intelligence Corps Adjutant's office to receive an answer to the request she had submitted for an assistant and command override access to the ship's computer core. Such things were standard when flight missions were about to commence. She was denied both requests. There simply were not enough Intelligence personnel on Euphrosyne to spare, and due to the mission's nature, only the top brass had command access. Saluting briskly with the standard right fist to left shoulder, she about-faced and left, heading down the corridor and out the usual double hatch found on all military buildings on this horrible dust bin of a planet. The drastic rise in temperature that assailed her further darkened her mood. What if something went wrong or the Captain went rogue? She surely wasn't expected to accept that the First Officer would take command; she was Intelligence after all. She would take pride in killing them both and taking command. However, this Captain was quite different than the general scum of the Imperial Officer Corps. She was the one who made it possible for him to command in the first place. Because of her circumstances she hated the Imperials so much that she infiltrated their elite, and had orchestrated the untimely deaths of no less than five officers; one for nearly every member of her immediate family that the Empire had ruthlessly slaughtered. The last had been the former Captain of the *Iwakina*. It had taken only a year here and a little push from an anonymous donor of a large sum of MU to get her to act. She had made many connections on her way up the ladder and she had called in some very precious ones.

Nanami toweled off and pulled on her uniform while checking some reports from the *Iwakina* AI's direct feed to her neural-net. It seemed everything was going as planned. This made her recall her confrontation with the Captain that led to her being reluctantly recruited. It was the same day that her requests had been rejected. She high-tailed it back to the ship on a gravibike and headed up the long ramp that serviced the ship. There were a lot of odd crates in the cargo hold. She had checked her neural-net for a manifest, but not one of them showed up. She had confronted the Quarter Master about it after stowing the bike, and he only replied, "Captain's orders." shaking his head. There was also an inordinate amount of food stocks. This was just too much for an Intelligence Officer to swallow, so she had decided to confront the Captain about it.

Nanami made it to the Captain's quarters in seconds flat. She straightened her uniform and sent a hail. An answering hail sounded and the hatch slid open with its audible whooshing sound. Inside she found the Captain seated behind his desk. The Ship's Doctor, Kimberly Rosel, had just risen from a chair in front of the desk. Nanami stood to the side as the Medical Officer stepped out of the door, giving her a cursory nod. The hatch whooshed closed.

"Have a seat Oliver." The Captain said as he sat back in his chair.

"I'd rather not My Lord. I come on urgent security matters." Oliver approached the desk and stood to one side of the chair. The Captain nodded at her to continue. "Sir, I have just come from Headquarters. My requests for an assistant and the regulation command computer override authority have been denied. Furthermore," Nanami paused and bent over the Captain's desk in order to touch a few activation panels controls there. This brought up a holographic real-time view of the cargo hold. "These items here, here, and here are not on any manifest for the ship. The Quartermaster says they are extra food stuffs for the voyage, but why aren't they on any manifest? These are serious breaches of security, Sir!" She stopped there awaiting the Captain's response.

"Nanami, how have you been? It seems you've been under a lot of stress lately. It's unfortunate that Command doesn't have the personnel to spare out here. I'm afraid command protocols are a bit different for this experimental vessel. You see? As for the extra cargo, well, I thought it prudent to have extra rations in case something goes wrong. It is this ship's maiden voyage after all. We don't have to have every little piece of bread on a manifest, do we?" The Captain put his hands together in front of his face as if trying to appear like some father contemplating a nagging child. Nanami didn't like this one bit.

The Captain continued before she could object, "Nanami, I think you have vacation time coming up, right? Why don't you take a cruise to the Grand Mar? I hear the beaches there stretch out forever."

"Captain," Nanami had turned a lighter shade of pale. "You cannot be serious. This ship is about to face its first voyage and you want me off the ship!? Who will do security? There will be a royal person on board for Christ sake! I cannot leave; I have to get to Juliana..."

"Oh?" interrupted the Captain. He leaned forward in the chair and his attitude went from father figure to imperial inquisitor in the flash of a second, or so it seemed to Nanami. "Got sights on your next target?"

Nanami was taken aback from the implication of those words. It was true that she had assassinated the former captain so that this one would be in command when the *Iwakina* took its first breath of space in eons. Did he know of her plan to kill the fleet admiral at

Juliana? It would be her final vendetta and she would go out with quite a bang. She sensed that he could see right through her at this point.

"Look Oliver, you are one of the finest officers that I have ever had the pleasure to command. However, sometimes your attention to detail is just too fine. I'm having a little bit of a trust issue with you. Can I confide in you something?" The Captain sat back once again in his chair waiting for her to respond.

"Captain, I am your most loyal officer; you can count on that. I am not quite sure what you mean about a target, Sir..."

"Nanami, you and I both know that I would not be here if it weren't for you. I know all about your, well, I certainly cannot call it a *little* secret. Your real name is Sakura Nechenko and your entire family was murdered by Imperials while you were away on business. You managed to change your whole persona, enlist in the Imperial Intelligence Corps and rise in the ranks while secretly killing off several Imperial officers, the last of which opened this very seat for my promotion." The Captain must have seen that she was visibly shaken and offered her the seat in front of the desk. This time she sat. "Now tell me, Nanami, why I should not send you on vacation and off my ship? Because you need to go to the Juliana Naval Base? Ah, but I am afraid this ship is not going to Juliana."

Nanami Oliver felt like a mouse backed into a corner by a feral cat. She needed time to absorb all of what the Captain was saying. She instinctively thought of the sidearm in its plastic holster at her belt. However, this man was the means for her to continue her personal mission. But didn't he just say that the ship was not going on its maiden voyage?

"...not going to Juliana?" Nanami repeated the Captain's words almost inaudibly to help them sink in.

"Yes, Nanami, this ship is not going to the Juliana Naval Base."

Nanami looked up, still bewildered, "No maiden voyage?"

"Well, there's that. The *Iwakina* will sail, just not to Juliana. If you take your vacation, all will be forgotten, or at least unreported."

The full realization of what was happening hit Nanami like she had been shot with an AK on full-auto. She had always been quick to put things together, but this time the enormity of the situation had shocked her senses.

"Captain, you are going to mutiny! You don't want me around because I am dangerous and you think that I am a liability." Nanami saw it all now. If she could stay aboard the *Iwakina*, she would not have to throw her life away meaninglessly in pursuit of vengeance. She could be a part of something far more damaging to the Imperials she hated so much. She needed to get back in the Captain's good graces.

The Captain shifted a little in his seat. "Like always, you are catching on quickly. You see Nanami, I have struggled with how I should deal with you. I sympathize with all you have gone through and once again, if it hadn't been for you, I would not have been able to pull this off... at least not with a ship of this magnitude. The Imperials cannot be allowed such an advanced piece of equipment. They would surely turn it into a war machine. So, I will be taking it somewhere other than Juliana."

Nanami pondered for just a moment, then said her piece, "Captain, you know my history. I'm talking about my record within the Intelligence Corps. I have been an exemplary officer from day one. Given that you know my true history, I can only request that you keep me on as Security Officer. You know my capabilities. What you don't know is that, now that I know your mindset, you can be assured that my loyalty to you goes far beyond that of subordinate, I am also loyal to your cause. Taking this ship will do far greater damage to the Imperials than my own petty machinations. Let me stay on, Sir, please."

The Captain sat silently for what seemed to Nanami as an eternity before giving her an answer, "Very well, I will contact you when it is time to brief you in on the plan. In the meanwhile, it's business as usual. I do not have to stress the severity if this comes to light; but then again, you *are* very good at keeping secrets, aren't you..." Nanami almost felt as if this was the outcome the Captain expected all along.

"Aye, Sir." Nanami turned for the door, and just barely noticed what sounded like something metal being slid into something plastic before the whoosh of the door caught her attention. She paused at the door and looked back at the Captain who only grinned at her sitting back in his chair.

*   *   *

Haruka Koritsu had been assigned to Princess Shirae for almost ten years now. Her longevity was only surpassed by that of the Chief Retainer who had served the court for thirty years. However, she was the only one permitted to attend the Princess aboard ship. She had inspected the temporary cabin that was assigned to them and brought a few items to keep the Princess amused and properly dressed. It wasn't a matter of whether she liked to serve the Princess or not; all she did was for her betrothed. She was a Pure Blood, raised in a family that was a holdover from the days of the Old Earth Empire. At the end of this year she would be released from service and free to marry her fiancée who was also a Pure Blood in service to the Emperor. This was the only way they would be allowed to be together; the new Imperials frowned upon those that sought to keep their bloodlines intact. When the time came for them to attend the first flight of the *Iwakina*, she escorted the Princess, who seemed quite awed by the ship, which was quite different than any starship they had previously voyaged on. There were very few of those. Before this year, the Princess had only been to various sequestered palaces and moved between those in the Emperor's personal yacht escorted by a fleet of swift military conveyances. Recently the Emperor decided that in order for the Princess to rule, she would have to see the galaxy. Attending the maiden voyage of the *Iwakina* was but the first step on such a journey. It was one of those conveyances that had brought them to this God forsaken desert planet. At least she felt that the Princess was happy to have her as company. Princess Shirae often complained about having too many servants, but always requested her presence when she was expected to go anywhere. To Haruka there seemed to be an ominous foreboding in the somber gray passages of this ship. She halted the Princess outside the lift which they would take up one level to the bridge and checked her raiment one last time.

* * *

Sanae was on the bridge disguised as Kintaro Sagura at the navigator's station. Kintaro's assistant navigator, Hanako Quan, was in the hospital having come down with a nasty stomach virus. Such illnesses were rare these days given the general populace's enhanced immune systems, but still cropped up on dirt-water worlds from time to time. It was just as well; Sanae didn't want her involved in the mutiny and didn't want her getting in the way either. She had just finished last minute checks on the integrated navigation systems which took the Grand Pruathan Schema and added the Imperial databases of worlds. She always marveled at the way it was synced to real-time movement of the entire galaxy. It also allowed for addition of new information gleaned from future voyages. She surveyed the bridge. Most others were doing last minute checks as well. The Captain and First Officer were circulating among them making small talk. Doctor Kuremoto was lounging in the temporary chair they had mounted for him to observe the launch. Just then the lift doors opened and a strong looking woman entered the bridge. She seemed to survey the bridge with the air of a military agent, assessing threats and options. The woman cleared her throat and said, "Her Imperial Highness Princess Shirae."

From behind the strong woman stepped a demurer yet confident looking younger woman. At the sight of her, Sanae almost dropped the stylus she was holding. She was astonished and shocked with disbelief at the same time; how on earth did this Imperial family member have the same face as herself? The air around her felt electrified and she suddenly realized that the strong woman was intensely gazing straight at her at the same time that she realized everyone else on the bridge were in a deep bow. She quickly did the same.

"Thank you all." the Princess said, and everyone straightened up.

Sanae realized with certainty then that the Princess *would* be involved in the mutiny as well; most assuredly without her knowledge. Sanae had yet to be briefed on the timing of the mutiny. She had made assumptions about a royal having been present at the Christening, but had not been sure that the Princess would also make the maiden voyage of the *Iwakina*. It was her duty to serve the Princess while she was aboard ship and now while she was assuredly to be involved. She could not, however, approach the Princess directly; she would have to meet with the strong woman once the ship was underway to whatever destination the Captain would divert her to.

The Princess then gave a few short words of encouragement to the bridge.

2

Captain Saitow sat in his command chair half listening to the obligatory calling off of the *Iwakina*'s instrumentation. A smile crossed his face; it was go-time on the bridge. The *Iwakina* would make its maiden voyage and the Empire would be stunned by his audacity. Everything should now be in place. Most of the crew was in the General Mess watching the event on a view-screen; absent the Marine contingent. They would have no clue that anything was afoot until the mutiny was over. A squad of Marines would be loading the Princess's luggage into the modified billet that he had designated. By now, Goh Takagawa should have programmed a door between two of the soon to be former officer's quarters; it was amazing what the man could do with Pruathan nonotech. His First Officer had made arrangements for the goods to be picked up after the Princess's retainers were taken to a remote area to watch the launch. He glanced at the man, seated to his left. He seemed calm as ever, almost to the point of annoyance. Doctor Kuremoto fidgeted in a seat to his right. Ahead of him were the various bridge stations that operated the ship. Each had a seat for the Chief of its station and its next ranking assistant. The assistants were doing all the work. Well this was it. Just a couple of jumps and then he would-

"Lord Captain." The First Officer broke his reverie. He focused and found everyone staring at him.

"Right." He glanced behind to see the Princess seated on a raised dais, her personal retainer standing by.

"Proceed Captain." She said, a little too

energetically. She seemed a little too enthusiastic to him. Nodding to her he turned back toward the bridge.

"Commence launch."

"Aye, launching the *Iwakina*." Navigator Sagura said as rehearsed. His station doubled as the helm during maneuvers. The distinctive dull hum of the Gravipulsion Drive started up and slowly faded as it stabilized. The forward view-screen appeared displaying the ruddy desert landscape of Euphrosyne from above as the *Iwakina* rose into the atmosphere. Once free of the planet Sagura stepped into the middle of the bridge and displayed a holographic plot of the course the *Iwakina* was to take to the Juliana Naval Base, where a reception for the crew and Princess awaited. Saitow would miss the flavorful wine they would serve. Three easy jumps. When the presentation was over and Sagura returned to his station, the Captain ordered, "Maneuver to Jump Point One."

"Aye." responded the helm. After a minute the First Officer stood up calling, "All rise." The entire bridge, including the Princess, rose as the image of the planet on the forward view-screen was replaced with the visage of Emperor Ros'Loper.

"Bow." And everyone bowed to the view-screen. Saitow knew this was a recording, but played along for the sake of appearances. The Emperor began his speech by allowing everyone to sit. He then went into a lengthy speech about glory and achievement and blah blah blah; at least it killed the hour it took on Impulse to reach a safe jump point. Saitow couldn't help but smirk at the part when the Emperor thanked him for his service. The Emperor would be cursing him soon enough.

They reached the jump point in good time. Communications Officer Pinero keyed up a feed on the view-screen from a scout ship sent ahead of them to record the event. The *Iwakina* looked like a pregnant, triangular-headed, hammerhead shark from the scout ship's angle. Saitow ordered the first jump, and as the Jump Vortex Drive initiated, he felt that tell-tale queasiness as the gravity systems inertial dampeners kicked in. On the view-screen everyone saw the black ship disappear in a shimmering wave as they entered Hyperspace. They returned to real-space less than a minute later almost fifteen light-years away. They would wait five minutes for the jump drive to fully charge for the next jump. Sensors reported no contacts. Engineering reported no structural anomalies. Navigation reported no errors in positioning and keyed up the next jump sequence. Saitow acknowledged each report as it came. He turned his chair toward the Princess who had an awestruck look on her beautiful face. He smiled at her; she hadn't been out of court for very long. He had received a personal missive from the Emperor himself, detailing his plan to show her the galaxy in order to prepare her to rule in his stead. Saitow would show her the galaxy all right. She must have noticed his smile.

"It is astonishing Captain! I have never seen a ship enter Hyperspace before. It was beautiful."

"Yes, Your Highness, nothing quite like it."

When the drive was fully charged the ship went through the process and once again jumped through Hyperspace; this time not quite ten light-years. This is when things would get interesting.

After the prerequisite charge time, Saitow checked his internal clock; less than a minute to go before the final jump. He looked around to see Doctor Kuremoto happily chatting with the Princess. He nodded to the First Officer and looked nervously at Takagawa. The Assistant Engineer who easily outpaced his supervisor in intellect, glanced quickly at his boss, and then gave the Captain thumbs up. The program was in place. Saitow activated his command console and punched in the agreed upon set of numbers and letters that would put his plan into action. The report came of the fully charged drive being ready for the next jump.

"Initiate jump." Saitow commanded with a huge grin on his face.

*　　*　　*

Lowey Jax wasn't happy to have been roused from sleep to attend the ship's maiden voyage in the General Mess. He *was* happy to have the opportunity to fleece some of his shipmates from other shifts playing Darkats. He was a legend among Third Watch and they avoided playing with him when any wagers were involved. When the view-screen of the Mess suddenly went blank it was none of his concern; he was about to score big. However, suddenly all was lost as he was thrown from his chair with a force that seemed as if some unseen assailant had hit him in the chest with a full sack of rice. Before he lost consciousness, he saw his winning hand dancing in a shower around his head and heard two claxons sound with the ship's eerie voice, "Warning, jump drive initiation failure..."

*　　*　　*

When the shock wave came from the inertial dampeners momentarily kicking in with nothing to dampen, the Marines were ready. They had received the signal from the ship and their training kept them from succumbing to the effect. Once the failsafe kicked in, they sprang into action. Sergeant Rionosuke "Rio" Watanabe led half of the Platoon to the General Mess to subdue non-mutineers there. Corporal Indra Kanesh led the squad that was to search the ship for stragglers. Lieutenant Song Ha took a squad to take care of the bridge. Lieutenant Yusef Simpson was overseeing all this through the military-only neural-net modification each Marine had in their heads.

*　　*　　*

Saitow picked himself up off the deck as the double claxon wailed. He glanced over to where the Princess was and saw that she was dazed but unharmed. His only real worry in this whole mutiny thing was how much trauma the inertial dampeners' momentary activation would cause. Doctor Kuremoto was helping her retainer guide the Princess to his Ready Room as they had agreed upon. Once there she would be isolated until he could deal with her. It would act as a convenient sound proof holding cell. It seemed as if for the most part that those involved in the mutiny were much better off than those who were not; his Chief Engineer was unconscious.

"Report." He commanded. Sensors reported that the ship was adrift in Hyperspace. Good, that's exactly where Saitow wanted her to be. Engineering reported that minor structural damage caused by the inertial dampener activation was being repaired by the ship. Saitow marveled at the fact that the Pruathan nano-technology allowed the ship to repair itself. Navigation reported no change in position other than the ship now being in Hyperspace.

Although he had reports from Lieutenant Simpson over his neural-net and a squad of Marines was nearly outside of the bridge, he felt he should keep up appearances for the benefit of the ignorant. He walked the bridge, checking on his crew, the First Officer accompanying him.

"Get this man on a stretcher." He commanded, indicating the unconscious Chief Engineer. He motioned to Sagura and Communications Officer Kent, another mutineer, to take the man to the Medical Officer. He then opened an intercom channel.

"Attention all decks. This is the Captain. Report all injuries."

A hail came back almost immediately.

"Lord Captain. This is Medical Assistant Marishima reporting from the General Mess Deck Three. We have two crewmen unconscious and a number shaken up but no internal injuries. Things are being tidied up here." Good. *Things being tidied up* meant that the Marines have captured the main part of the crew that he had gathered there for that purpose.

"Received, attend to any wounded."

"Aye aye, Lord Captain."

"Lord Captain. This is Corporal Kanesh on Deck

Five. We have one casualty; a crewman Barnes. We are headed to the Medical Bay, injuries unknown." Damn. Barnes was a decent man. He'd do his best to notify the man's family.

"Very well, keep me posted." No other reports were forthcoming.

As the lift doors were closing on the litter bearers, the rear bridge doors whooshed open and a squad of fully armed Marines entered. Saitow stepped aside to get out of their way. His First Officer followed. His Intelligence Officer Nanami Oliver directed the Marines toward their astonished charges, the remaining officers on the bridge.

"Shackle them all except this one." She pointed dubiously at Takagawa.

*   *   *

Things had turned out better than had been expected. All of the crew were accounted for and most had only minor injuries, although there was one death caused by a jumpy Marine finding a couple of crewmembers where they shouldn't have been. Crewman Barnes's as yet unknown partner was strapped into a medical bay gurney and highly sedated due to shock trauma. She couldn't be identified by the Marines for obvious reasons. Perhaps Barnes had died with a smile on his face. Saitow shook the morbid thought from his mind. Quartermaster Edwards had a nasty cut on his scalp, but that was his own damn fault. He was sleeping in his office instead of being where he was supposed to be. Jones was still secretly tucked away in the brig. Saitow had sent Takagawa to check on him. Princess Shirae was still locked away in his Ready Room. He was sure that Doctor Kuremoto was keeping her company. He felt it was time to address the crew. He queued up a video feed.

"Crewmembers of the Imperial Starship *Iwakina*; an imperial starship she is no more. I apologize at any rough treatment you may have received from my Marines. If you haven't yet figured out just what is going on, I'll tell you. It is mutiny. The Imperium is far too corrupt to wield the power that this ship represents. Its range, exotic technologies, and capabilities are far too advanced over those of other governments that I fear a return to the empires of old. We must not allow such an advantage to fall into tyrannical hands. I will ask each and every one of you to consider this and join those of us who have taken this burden upon us. In the weeks prior to this historic day, select key crewmembers were recruited for the task of this undertaking. Although we have control and can take this ship wherever we wish to go, we still need more loyal crewmembers to fully operate, so I ask you to speak up if you wish to join us. I cannot guarantee that the road ahead will not be a rough one. I can guarantee that it will be a profitable and adventurous one. I will also guarantee that those of you who do not wish to join us will be treated without malice. Please consider your choice carefully and those of you who wish to join, please make your choice known to the nearest Marine."

* * *

Lowey Jax was not a happy man. Having lost consciousness right when he was about to make a killing at Darkats, he has now awakened to find himself shackled and seated uncomfortably on the deck. He looked around to find the majority of his crewmembers in a similar state; a couple of Marines armed with assault rifles guarded the lot. The all-call sounded and the view-screen at the front of the General Mess once again lit up; this time with the visage of the Ship's Captain looming large upon it. Jax listened to the Captain's speech in disbelief then immediately brightened. He, like many of his peers, was a conscript forced into service to the Empire, just for being one of its more intelligent yet poorer citizens. Here aboard the *Iwakina,* due to the nature of the project the ship belonged to, there were only a few conscripts and he was their unspoken leader. He looked for them around the room. A couple of them made eye contact and he nodded to them. He hoped like hell they understood his meaning in that nod. He wanted no blood on his hands. He heard the starboard hatch whoosh open and looked to see Security Officer Oliver enter. She was taking in the scene and Jax looked away quickly. He had never seen the woman so intense. She looked like a tigress hunting for prey. He felt an ominous presence at his front and looked up to see Oliver's steely gray eyes taking him in.

"You're Jax, leader of the conscripts?"

"Yes Ma'am."

"Will you join us?" She bent over him and beamed with an enthusiasm that further shocked him.

"Yes?"

"Excellent, and your compatriots?" She asked as she

went around to his back, unshackled him, and brought him to his feet. He looked at each of the conscripts and each nodded in agreement.

"Wonderful!" Oliver motioned for a Marine Jax had not noticed until now had been by her side to accompany him and unshackle those he indicated. As Jax did so, he glanced at Nanami Oliver from time to time as she went along the rows of crewmembers. She stopped to speak to just a few, had three or so released, and shook her head sadly at a few more. He and his compatriots were led to the Crew Mess and were left there with an armed Marine to await further instructions. Just a few more crewmembers joined them after a short time. Jax passed the time bewilderedly contemplating his new-found admiration for this woman Nanami Oliver.

*　*　*

Doctor Kuremoto was doing his best to keep things amicable in the Ready Room. He was quite successful in engaging the Princess in small talk; her particular area of interest being the ship itself. His only worry was the Princess's retainer, whom the conspirators had given the codename Dog. He detected that she was becoming antsier as the minutes passed; she was continuously pacing the room and had checked the hatch for access several times. It was only a matter of time before she suspected foul play. That moment came sooner than he had wished.

"Honored Doctor, what is going on here?" Haruka Koritsu spoke at last.

"Ah, well, something important must be happening, otherwise the hatch would not be secured." The Doctor did his best to diffuse the situation. It had been a good twenty minutes since he had led them here.

"Haruka-chan, surely the Captain has important reasons for keeping us here." offered the Princess. Kuremoto was not surprised to hear her use an honorific from Ancient Imperial. The *Japanese* language was all the rage among the royals these days.

"Oujo-sama, this situation is below Your Highness's station. Surely you see this? We should not be stuck in a room as are common prisoners." Haruka was apparently not copasetic to the current situation. Kuremoto then remembered that the Dog was a Pure Blood, tolerated only because she pledged her service to the royal family. They did their best to keep their Japanese heritage alive. Kuremoto kept his scorn to himself. He detested Pure Bloods.

"Now, now, I am sure the Captain has the Princess's safety in mind. Perhaps some untoward incident has occurred within the ship and it isn't safe for your personage to be about." offered the Doctor.

Just then a hail sound filled the room and the hatch to the bridge slid open with a whoosh. In the door stood the Captain surrounded by a group of armed Marines.

"Please accept my apologies Your Highness. It seems that we have a saboteur aboard ship. My Marines will escort you to the safety of your cabin." the Captain motioned for the women to exit the Ready Room.

"Captain, tell me more of this saboteur." requested

the Princess.

The Captain responded while directing them to the lift, "In due time Majesty. Be assured that my Marines are taking care of the situation." The two women were surrounded by four Marines inside the lift as the lift door closed.

*   *   *

Princess Shirae was at her limit of excitement. She had never felt such adrenaline as she felt now. She was aboard a starship like no other under the command of a superior officer of the Empire, and some unknown danger was afoot. This was far better than any fictional video she had ever seen or even the combat training she had endured as a member of the royal family. The Marines brought her and Haruka-chan down one level and straight to their cabin. They were escorted inside and told to remain there until the Captain called upon them. This seemed to agitate Haruka-chan who paced about like a wild cat with no prey in sight. Haruka became even more agitated after checking on things inside their cabin. Shirae had only been here for a short time hours ago, but it felt like things were completely different. She noticed almost immediately that on one wall where there had not been a door before, one now stood, and Haruka went straight for it. Haruka disappeared through the door for a moment and emerged with an even more disturbing look on her face than before.

"Shirae-sama, we have been deceived." Haruka held up the Princess's most prized possession, a stuffed lion that had been given to her by her father the Emperor; a stuffed lion that should have been left with her retinue, to be returned to the palace at Algaia for her eventual return. "All of your possessions are here in this second room, as well as a full bath." Haruka checked out the hatch that led to the corridor. She found that it was secured just like the Ready Room had been. "It appears that we are prisoners Oujo-sama." Shirae didn't quite know what to think about this situation. Her excitement slowly turned to disdain.

3

Lieutenant Denton Bret was a loyal officer of the Imperial Navy. He had been assigned to the *Iwakina* after graduating top of his class at the Imperial Academy. It perturbed him just a bit to have been assigned to Third Watch these past few months aboard ship. Now this day, he had been slightly upset to have been roused from his duty rest, and then became extremely angry at being tossed into the midst of enlisted sailors as a prisoner of the Captain. On top of that, that bitch of an Intelligence Officer had ordered him shackled! He set his mind to do something about this mutiny, but what he could do at this time he knew not. The General Mess had been fitted with some sort of neural-net scrambler; he could not access any of the ship's systems. He sat up and eyed his surroundings. He noted there were heavily armed Marines guarding each of the hatches that led out of the Mess. The Bitch was nowhere to be seen. He searched for his Watch Officer Darren Jones among the prisoners, but only recognized most of the engineers from his watch among others. There were probably thirty to thirty-five prisoners in all. Suddenly, an All-Call sounded from the view screen and the dubious face of the Captain filled the screen. He addressed those assembled in the Mess.

"Imperial Officers and enlisted of the *Iwakina*. Consider yourselves relieved of duty. It pains me so, but you were unfortunately not chosen to continue in service to this fine vessel." There were some hissing and other noises from those gathered, but Bret raised his voice to call them to silence as the Captain continued, "Fear not. I am not a murderer, nor a sadist. You will all be treated humanely and fairly until such time as you can be dropped off in a neutral location for the Imperials to rescue you. But be warned..." the Captain's amicable tone changed to deathly seriousness, "any attempt to resist the instructions of those put in charge of you will be dealt with swiftly and unequivocally." The Captain sat back for a moment and straightened his coat. "Enough un-pleasantries. Shortly this ship will set down in a safe location, leaving you with enough food and water to last until you are rescued. Be assured that most of you have done a fine job in these last few months and may God be with you."

Bret clenched his teeth for most of the Captain's speech and cursed under his breath at the man's audacity. To not only mutiny, high-jacking the Empire's most prized starship, but to also kidnap the Emperor's only daughter... he almost harbored a thought of admiration, which he quickly replaced with a determination to thwart the Captain at every turn. *How to do it, though?* What could he do, shackled as he was and guarded? Surely, they would have to move them to either an exterior hatch or down to the shuttle area. He would formulate a plan and wait. It was all he could do for now. These enlisted dogs would be of little use to him. Some even seemed quite relieved and in good spirits. They were all fools.

*   *   *

The Captain had his bridge team assembled. All the major players that were needed to operate the *Iwakina* were present and manning their stations. He would lead, of course, and his First Officer would command when he was off the bridge. Kintaro Sagura sat at

Navigation and controlled Maneuvers and Sensors. Goh Takagawa sat at Engineering and also controlled Weapons and Shields. Nanami Oliver sat at Protocol and controlled Communications and Damage Control. This would do until he got his augmentation from the Company. He just hoped his instincts about these people were sound. Dismissing any negative thoughts, he ordered Sagura to pull up a holograph of the current sector.

"Takagawa is everything put back together?"

"Aye, Lord Captain." Takagawa had ensured that the protocols had been removed and the ship was completely under Saitow's control.

"Oh no, that won't do at all. I am sadly now a criminal of the Imperium, so let's drop the Lord bit, shall we?" the Captain said with a snicker.

"Aye, Captain." Takagawa replied smiling. He seemed to relish this whole adventure.

The Captain stood from the con and pointed inside the holo, "Sagura take us here. It should only take one jump."

Sagura captured the coordinates and punched them into the nav-control panel. "Jump ready, Sir."

"Away we go." was all the Captain said as he quickly took his seat just in case Takagawa had been wrong about fixing everything.

* * *

Bret felt the tell-tale sign that the ship had made a successful jump. The fact that he had slept through a staged jump malfunction had not even occurred to him. Soon they would be in orbit over whatever God forsaken hell-hole the Captain was going to drop them at; no doubt nowhere near any civilization. He figured out that there were only three possible routes to exit the ship; two, if they didn't use the shuttle and flat out landed the *Iwakina* somewhere. One was down the lift to deck five, through access tubing to the cryo-unit maintenance and then the Cargo Bay. The Cargo Bay had several access hatches to the outside. They most likely would avoid taking prisoners through the confines of the access tubing. The second was the forward lift to deck six, then the center lift to the Cargo Bay. If they used the shuttle, they would still need to switch lifts on deck six. He knew of several weapons caches along the way to thwart boarders and he had the codes to all of them. As long as he could cause a distraction to divert their escort's attention, he could get at those weapons. This all relied on them re-shackling him in the front when they moved him, which was standard procedure after all.

*   *   *

Sanae sat at the controls to Navigation disguised as Kintaro Sagura. She had observed the Captain address the non-conspirators, and then choose a destination from the holographic display of the navigation system. Mine 213 was a depleted precious metals planet deserted by the Rangelley centuries ago. The database designated it a temperate world teaming with jungle and not much else. There was plenty of water and the atmosphere was thick and barely breathable. The last information in the database was decades old. They were now in orbit over a substantial abandoned complex. What made the Captain choose this sight to drop the remaining crew? It seemed to her that the Captain's plans were well laid out and he quite possibly had outside assistance. Sanae would have to find a clandestine moment to relay her findings to Contact Sigma.

The Captain was standing over her looking at the view-screen. "Ah, to see the beauty of green again! Sagura," the Captain stabbed at the holographic navigation controls in front of her, spreading his fingers wide to zoom in on the complex. "Set her down here."

"Aye, Sir" Sagura replied and keyed in the parameters that instructed the onboard artificial intelligence to land at the designated spot. The sublight engines engaged for a moment, and then the Gravipulsion Drive took over for atmospheric assent to the planet's surface.

*   *   *

Nanami Oliver returned to the General Mess to see that all was going according to plan. She had been given temporary command of the Marines in order to see that the remaining crew was safely removed from the ship. The supplies to be left had been disembarked to a sheltered area not far from the ship and crewmembers were to be escorted off the ship in groups of no more than five at a time. Once they reached the Cargo Bay, they were fitted with respirator kits and escorted off by Marines in Combat Suits. The only touchy part was getting them from the Mess to the Cargo Bay. Lieutenant Simpson assured her that there would be no problems; his Marines had escorted prisoners on numerous occasions.

*   *   *

Lieutenant Bret was in one of the last groups to be taken. He was sure he could pull off his little plan, but began to have doubts as to what good it would do. In the end he decided that it was worth the attempt to thwart that damn traitor or die gloriously for the Empire if his plan failed. He was placed in the front of his group of five. Each was fitted with a neural-net scrambler. They were taken down to deck six as he suspected and there would be several weapons caches along the way. For his plan to work he needed to be in the middle of his group. He feigned tripping on something and was slow to get up letting the two behind him pass. He apologized profusely to the Marine escort, asserting that he was getting too old for this type of thing. When he finally chose a weapons cache to exploit almost half way toward the center lift, he feigned again this time stumbling into the man ahead of him when he had just passed his target. He spun around quickly and rushed into the man behind him causing that man to hit the one after causing a domino effect into the Marines behind. He then whirled once again, keying in the code to open the cache and grab a pistol from within. He became quite bewildered when his hands found no such weapon; the caches having been emptied by Marines the night before. He stood up and suddenly felt a sharp pain in his jaw as the full force of Sergeant Rio Watanabe's rifle butt impacted his face. The last thing he heard before he lost consciousness was Watanabe saying, "Idiot Imperial. You two, drag this dog to the lift."

*　　*　　*

Stephen Jing had kept Gunter busy praying in the chapel for a safe voyage. Neither of them was hurt by the jump malfunction, but the Sanctuary was now a mess. Papers, books, and religious artifacts were strewn about in all directions. Stephen had purposely left off packing to give his assistant something to do while the mutiny took place. Once Gunter had gotten the place cleaned up, they were already landing at Mine 213. Stephen sat him down and poured the two of them wine from the cabinet at the end of the room. Stephen almost winched at the look of grave concern on Gunter's face. When they had both had a few sips Stephen spoke.

"Gunter, I hold you in utmost confidence. God has chosen you for a greater mission than to remain as my assistant." He noticed that the man squirmed a little to be praised so. The task he was about to get would require a strong resolve. "We have just landed on a deserted planet. There has been a mutiny on the ship and the former crew is to be dropped off here for eventual rescue. I must remain with the ship to further the cause of the Church. I need you to accompany these people and deliver a message for the Holy See from me. You must be the spiritual guide for them." Stephen took Gunter's hand and touched the man's token ring to his.

"You must report to the Officer Nanami Oliver in the Cargo Bay. Now go, and God Speed."

*   *   *

When Lieutenant Bret came to, he found his Watch Officer Darren Jones standing over him. Jones turned suddenly and looked out from under some sort of roof. Past the man Bret could make out the *Iwakina* lifting off as it started to rain in a torrent.

*   *   *

Because the offload of the former crew would take some time, Sanae, as Kintaro Sagura, got permission to take her evening meal. The Captain had apparently called ahead because Bonifacio was in the kitchen holding a sandwich and beaming at her. She quickly headed to her cabin, scarfed down the sandwich, and then pulled a communications terminal from the hidden compartment in her bureau. She attached the communications terminal to the ships terminal port in the wall and sent an encrypted coded message through the ship's communication's system. Unfortunately, it would not be sent by the ship until they passed a GCN node. It would probably be logged, but could not be deciphered by anyone other than the holder of the key, Contact Sigma. She had programmed her terminal to transmit via a random terminal elsewhere within the ship. The message simply read: SPARROW 64 TO CONTACT SIGMA: IWAKINA CAPTAIN MUTINED. CURRENT POSITION MINE 213. CREW OFFLOADED; SEND RESCUE. SPARROW REMAINS WITH SHIP. DESTINATION UNKNOWN. ROYAL ABOARD AND SAFE. WILL PROTECT.

Just then, a communications hail filled the air startling her. "Sagura, return to the bridge." It was Goh. She keyed her own comm terminal, "Sagura, on my way." She stowed her equipment quickly, fixed the tells she had disturbed and headed to the bridge.

* * *

Things were going quite well Saitow figured. There was that annoyance with Bret, but the man was a textbook Imperial; couldn't be helped. At least all the former crew had been dropped off without incident and Quartermaster Edwards had gotten the timed distress beacon deployed in orbit above them. That would start transmitting in less than an hour. It was time to put this ship through her paces. He had Sagura bring up the Nav-holo again. "Sagura, let's see what this baby can do. Set course for the Jumpgate at Saragothra. fifty light-year jumps, automatic." Sagura seemed to look up at him with fear in his eyes. "Just do it. I know what this ship is capable of, no matter what the manual says. Don't worry."

"Aye, Sir. Setting course for Saragothra; fifty light-year jumps, automatic. Sequence: 47; Time to destination: approximately four hours, forty-one mikes." Sagura keyed the inputs into the AI and the jump drive kicked in. They were now fifty light-years away from Mine 213 and charging for the next automatic jump.

"Well, people we've got four hours to kill. It's time to relax. Return to the bridge when the all call sounds." Saitow got up from his chair and stretched. Nanami Oliver stood as well and gave him a cursory nod. She would be giving the Dog a once over soon.

*　*　*

Nanami left the bridge and headed down to deck three. She looked in on the General Mess to find the remainder of the crew getting things back in order. Then she headed up to deck two. She went down the corridor to find the Princess's quarters guarded by two Marines. They stepped aside as she approached. She spoke to one of them briefly and brushed her token ring over the hatch controls. The door swooshed open and she stepped inside to find the Princess and her Dog lounging on a divan. The Dog was fanning the young royal. Nanami made a show of bowing to the Princess. When she stood, she spoke directly to the older woman. "Haruka Koritsu, please come with me."

The Dog stood up and took a step forward, "What is the meaning of th-"she tried to speak but was interrupted by Nanami.

"You are here to protect the Princess, correct?" Nanami's tone was quite cold. "I have word of today's incidents that I must impart to *you*. Please step outside."

55

Nanami was happy to see the woman was somewhat unnerved by her presence. She hated the Imperials for what they had done to her family. Haruka stepped gingerly toward the door after looking back at the Princess, who just looked at both of them as if in a daze. When the Dog was outside and the hatch had closed, one of the Marines grabbed a hold of Haruka while the other checked her for weapons. Nanami was pleased to see that she had a dagger hidden in her waist coat. Nanami took in the sight of this woman. She was only slightly taller than the Princess, but looked to be as strong as Nanami herself. She bore the distinct features of a Pure Blood; jet-black hair, yellowish skin and almond shaped dark-brown eyes. Her whole being was in opposition to Nanami's tallness, blond hair, and gray eyes.

"Bring her to Temporary Holding." Nanami instructed one of the Marines and followed them a little way down the dim gray corridor to one of the disposed officer's quarters. It had been cleared and only two chairs facing each other remained. Nanami took the larger chair and offered the other to the Dog.

"Let me make one thing perfectly clear..." Nanami began, "You are only here at the pleasure of the Captain of this ship." She let those words sink in before continuing. She could see a fire beginning to burn in the Dog's dark eyes.

"The Captain has decided that he can no longer serve the Empire. He has also decided that this ship, if it remained in Imperial hands, would give far too much of an advantage to them, and therefore has removed this advantage by mutiny. It is unfortunate that the Emperor chose the maiden voyage of this particular ship to introduce his only daughter to the galaxy. However, it plays nicely into the hands of the Captain that she is aboard as insurance in case the Empire would rather destroy the ship than let it be stolen." Nanami paused looking for some other reaction than anger, but found none. "*You*, must do your best to keep the Princess occupied. I would suggest you make something up to disguise what has actually occurred and keep the Princess from panic. It will be quite some time before the two of you will be allowed to leave the ship. The Captain will do his best to treat the Princess as befits a royal person. However, this is no longer a ship of the Imperium, and resistance to the will of the Captain will not be tolerated. Am I clear?"

Nanami wondered what venom the Dog would spit at her, but was sorely disappointed at the woman's lack of fire. Something of her demeanor actually started to bother Nanami.

"Yes, you have made yourself perfectly clear." was all the response she received.

*   *   *

When Haruka was returned she found the Princess on the verge of tears. She knew Her Highness could be a little immature, but hadn't figured that she would break down so easily. Haruka went to a casket and retrieved a new dagger from its contents. She quickly hid it in her clothing. She sat with the Princess and consoled her for a while before the young lady spoke. "Haruka-chan, what has been happening? My first real adventure in space and I am stuck here in my room as some sort of prisoner? Who was that scary woman that took you away? Why was her uniform devoid of any

Imperial decoration? What in my father's name is going on?" Princess Shirae choked back a sob.

Haruka considered all that Nanami Oliver had spoken to her and then the state the Princess was in. She knew the Princess was stronger than this; perhaps some factor unknown to her was influencing the Princess's chain of thought. Surely it was one Haruka must dispel. She sat next to Shirae and began to speak earnestly. "Oujo-sama. You must be strong. Events are not as bad as they appear. You are safe and have me by your side. Your things are all here and in order. You are taking your first real voyage through space, even if it will take you far from your Homeworld. Is that not what your father commanded of you? We will only be confined within these chambers as long as it takes for the Captain to sort things out with the events that have taken place. It has required him to take the ship far out from the intended course, but I am certain that things will be alright. Please, Oujo-sama, calm yourself." Haruka saw that the Princess was doing just that. Uncharacteristically, the Princess laid her head in Haruka's lap.

"Haruka-chan, what kind of man do you think Captain Saitow is?"

Haruka was caught off guard by the odd request. She almost let slip the whole truth of the matter, but softened her tone to keep the Princess calmed. "Oujo-sama, I believe the Captain to be odd. It would be wise to be cautious in dealing with such a man. Has he yet seen to your Royal Highness personally since this ordeal began? No, he has not."

"He must be very busy having an entire ship to look after; especially with some harrowing incident afoot." the Princess offered. Haruka began to suspect just what the thing was that was distracting her charge. "Oujo-sama, if I may ask, what do you think of this Captain?"

"Oh, I do not quite know what to think, so I will think of him no more. Haruka-chan, please fetch me a book... on... astrophysics." The Princess said nonchalantly.

"At once, Your Highness."

* * *

Princess Shirae sat back and pretended to read the book Haruka-chan had fetched for her. She didn't want her attendant to know what she really felt about the Captain. It was very odd indeed that she would find this older man attractive. Of course, he was a hero of the Imperium, and had won great accolades from the court and her father, but what was it that made her excited to the point of almost being giddy? Now she was in even greater conflict due to the fact that something untoward had occurred on the ship and Haruka-chan wasn't about to let her know about it for fear of panicking her. She didn't want to give Haruka-chan any hint that she was stronger than she let on to be; it would make Haruka feel bad to know that she wasn't really needed after all. She would talk to the Captain sooner or later and get to the bottom of her feelings and what was going on with the *Iwakina*. She sighed, and settled back into catching up on her astrophysics.

4

Goh Takagawa lay idly on his bunk listening to the latest techno music he had acquired. His room had been modified by the ship's AI to provide the best acoustics. He half listened to the rhythmic beats while contemplating the reasons for him having joined the mutiny. It wasn't that he resented the Empire. After all, the Ros'Loper Empire had stepped in and helped the rebellion he was a part of to throw off the shackles of those who would take advantage of the long-lasting power vacuum created by the fall of the Rangelley. They had helped his family and community rebuild their winery and businesses after decades of neglect. That was the sole reason he had joined the Imperial Navy in the first place. His admiration of what the Empire stood for was great. This Captain had changed all that. He had shown him personally, some of the atrocities that had been perpetuated by the current Empire, both covertly and overtly; all done in the name of Ros'Loper. However, that was only the seed that started him down this path. It was his desire to be reunited with his one lost love that kept him on the *Iwakina*. To find and reach that mysterious world he had visited many times through the screen behind the mirror in his Grandmother's attic, he would have to maintain access to Pruathan technology. This ship might be the very key to his quest. He had been studying hard under Doctor Kuremoto, learning to decipher the Pruathan language and symbols in order to delve into the depths of their technology. He almost knew this ship like the back of his hand. He could easily program any sort of modification barring those beyond the laws of physics. He was on the verge of learning how the Pruatha had thwarted some of those as well.

What had made him suggest to the Captain to drag his best friend Kintaro Sagura into the mutiny? Hanako Quan had already been recruited for the task of piloting the ship. When she became ill, he had jumped on the chance to recruit Kintaro. It was probably the fact that Kintaro was his only real friend. He had learned so much about the martial arts and how to read starmaps from the man. Sure, he had his quirks, like that religion thing, but he was a great comrade to be around. Goh was glad that his friend had agreed to stay on with the ship.

Goh closed his eyes for a moment and concentrated on the lyrics to the random tune that queued up next, *"I'm sick of all the insincere, I'm gonna give all my secrets away..."*

* * *

Saitow knew that the fake registry entry his family had devised for the ship would work. What annoyed him currently was the fact that they still awaited clearance from the New Rangelley Alliance to access the Saragothra Jumpgate. It didn't surprise Saitow that there were still noble families that clung to the old ways. He was pretty sure that they were now close to the seat of the last Rangelley Prince Sheenid, who had his capitol at Askelon. The Jumpgate was a magnificent sight; it was like a huge metal ring with interspersed gravitic stabilizers that looked like Christmas bulbs all along it. A control station orbited half a kilometer away lest it be warped by the gravitational wave generated by a forming wormhole. Once a ship entered it would travel over half a sector in the time it took a Human to cross a quarterdeck.

He had sounded the All-Call to the bridge as soon as they had exited hyperspace from the final jump. He had Sagura pull up the nav-holo again. Saitow confirmed to himself that they were in fact deep in Alliance territory, as Askelon was only a few light-years from Saragothra. A couple of Alliance cruisers were stationed close by to the gate. Goh told him that Sensors indicated a shuttle craft was bearing down on them from the gate station. A hail sounded and Saitow nodded to Nanami to open a channel. "This is the Captain of registry 56973-0. What can we do for you, approaching shuttle?" the Captain tried to be as friendly sounding as possible.

"Ship registry 56973-aught, we require that you let us board your vessel for inspection before you are cleared through the Jumpgate." came an authoritative voice-only response. Saitow almost cursed, but held his tongue. He had come too far to let some backwater old Imperials kill his gambit.

"Very well, our escort will meet you at the starboard hatch."

*   *   *

Francis Parham was a very observant officer of the Alliance. Having received a report from one of the Alliance cruisers that a ship awaiting access to the Jumpgate had sensor blocking technology, he formed a boarding team with hidden equipment on their uniforms and headed to the ship. Its registry had checked out; it belonged to the Taibor resident Saitow Starliners, and was designated a Cargo Ship. The Captain was supposedly one of the immediate Saitow family heirs. His Majesty Prince Sheenid would surely want intelligence on this ship and he intended to provide it. Parham's shuttle was docked to the starboard cargo hatch and his team was met by a small group of crewmembers who appeared to be just a bit too military for his liking. The one who appeared to be in charge addressed him.

"My name is Lieutenant Simpson. How can we help you gentlemen?" the leader said. Parham thought him to be a little too cut and polished for a mere cargo ship officer.

"I would like to see your Captain while my team inspects certain areas of your ship."

"I'm afraid the Captain is indisposed at the moment. He bade me show you whatever areas you would like to see. We are an honest trading company after all."

Parham didn't find a need to anger one of the larger and more powerful of the Alliance's business partners. He was on the move up and knew a thing or two about when to make waves and when to smooth the waters. "Very well, we require all access to this cargo area, the engineering section, and the bridge."

The leader of their escort thought for just a moment, and then indicated Parham's team follow them inside. Parham was impressed by the amount of cargo space the ship held, which was mostly empty, exempting an inordinate number of foodstuff containers. He noted quite a few more storerooms below decks, and an extensive medical facility on the way to Engineering.

There he noted that the ship was powered by a standard Captured Hyperspace Anomaly Reactor or CHAR, but wasn't quite sure of the ship's FTL capability. When he asked Simpson what it was, the man merely shrugged and apologized for his ignorance. When they arrived on the bridge, the First Officer was attending the con.

"Ah, Commander Parham, I am First Officer Soto. How goes your inspection? I pray everything is in order?" this man was as gracious as Simpson.

"Ah, yes, everything seems to be in order. I just have a few questions about the engineering of this ship. You understand the safety of the Jumpgate is my main concern."

"Yes, of course. I have a detailed explanation of the engineering systems right here on this tablet..." the First Officer handed Parham a handheld computer which appeared to have financial information rather than engineering schematics on it. "The Saitow Family is rather adamant about sharing their proprietary interests with their allies." The First Officer indicated an entry box to Parham. It was labeled ACCOUNT FOR DEPOSIT. Parham noticed the figure to be deposited and looked up at the smiling First Officer. It was true that Parham was an observant man. However, there were times when observant men must look the other way in the interests of relationships between powerful entities. His Prince would get his intel, while Parham would have a sizeable retirement account to fall back on. Just in case. Parham smiled back and entered his secondary MU account number. It could not be traced by anyone he did not want to know it.

"That's very impressive." Parham said as he handed back the tablet. "Please have your escort direct us back to our shuttle. You will be cleared for jump once our shuttle has reached a safe distance."

On the way back to the Cargo Bay, Parham ran his hand along the wall of one of the passages they traversed. He felt an odd sensation as if the texture of the wall was like that of the tongue of his pet cat.

*   *   *

Sanae, disguised as Kintaro Sagura, stayed at her station awaiting orders. She had no idea how long the New Imperials would be aboard ship, but she knew that this might be her only chance to get another message to Contact Sigma letting the Empire know the whereabouts of the ship in time for them to act. She had managed to program her comm terminal to interface through the ships systems to her Navigation console. She quickly typed out a message and sent it via the Galactic Communications Network. The GCN allowed near-instantaneous communication throughout the developed areas of the Quadrant. Contact Sigma should be monitoring the GCN signals that she had been ordered to use. This time the message read: SPARROW 64 TO CONTACT SIGMA: CURRENT LOCATION IWAKINA – SARAGOTHRA JUMPGATE. AWAITING INSPECTION BY NRA FORCES. TIME FRAME UNKNOWN. POSSIBLE WILL REMAIN FOR ONE HOUR. ROYAL STILL ABOARD AND SAFE. AFTER JUMPGATE DESTINATION UNKNOWN. She dared not send more information than that. She could almost feel the Intelligence Officer staring at her as if she were being licked by the woman's eyeballs.

*   *   *

Parham and his inspectors cleared the ship and disembarked in their shuttlecraft. It would be just a matter of a few minutes while a MU authorization passed through Protocol and the ship would enter the Jumpgate. Commander Parham instructed the shuttle pilot to move off a bit while his team got some extra video of the exterior of the ship. The Prince would most likely be very interested in what information they could provide. The *Iwakina* was surely a hybrid of Human and Pruathan technology; something the Prince had been seeking for quite some time. Parham had felt that tell-tale texture only once before when he was shown a piece of Pruathan technology that was found near his homeport very long ago. The team stayed taking video all the way to the point where the *Iwakina* passed through the Jumpgate's wormhole event horizon, then headed back to transmit the data.

*   *   *

Once they had exited the KV Jumpgate and circled around for reentry, Saitow found it much easier to negotiate with the Kyrovalkirii. The Kyrovalkirii Confederation was a very loose confederation of territories controlled by various houses of the mixed Xane races. There were seven types of Xane, each species genetically altered from their Xane ancestors thousands of years ago by the long dead Mechanismoans. Trading was in their blood *these* days and Saitow's family had contacts among them everywhere. He noted the gate fees were a bit steep, but this was no time to bicker; especially when he was so close to getting home. Once they exited at the Taibor gate, it was just a matter of a few short jumps to his Homeworld Roseglade and he could finally relax.

Once they were in orbit over Roseglade he excused himself, giving the First Officer the con, and asking everyone to standby for further instructions. He had a bit of business to take care of planet-side before he came clean with those that had helped him get this far. He took one of the ten Ethla Class fighter craft down to a pre-designated area of Saitow property near the family estate. He was met by gravicar and brought straight before the Matriarch herself, his mother. They exchanged pleasantries and some wine. He was given his instructions and bade enjoy the estate as long as he would care to. He didn't quite like being kept on a leash, however loose that leash may be, but his family was paying for his little adventures to come. No doubt he would be paying them back sevenfold.

He returned to the ship on a shuttle followed by two more which were destined to replace those ridiculously outdated Imperial ones currently taking up space in their berths on the *Iwakina*. The shuttle docked at a cargo bay hatch and the augments for the crew that his mother had saddled him with came aboard. He had Nanami assign them billets and he would divvy out jobs for them soon enough. Two of them were not to be staying. They were only there to take the old shuttle craft back planet-side. His two new pilots were flying the new craft up with more augments.

* * *

First Officer Victor Soto sat uncomfortably at left of the head of the conference room table. He had known his good friend Glenn Saitow for many years and was more than eager to join him in this endeavor for good or for bad. They had served on numerous ships together and seen some of the worst of the Empire's treachery. What made him uncomfortable now were the reports of extra personnel being assigned to the ship; personnel he knew nothing about. It was true that the Saitow Family's backing was needed to pull off this little stunt of stealing a ship out from under the Imperial's noses. However, at what cost would it eventually come to? He was drawn out of his thoughts by the whoosh of the main hatch as the Captain entered. Everyone made to rise, but before they could get to their feet the Captain bade them keep their seats, and then sat down himself at the head of the table. The Captain gave everyone a good once over before he began the meeting. Soto noted that, besides himself, only members of the inner circle of conspirators were there; Doctors Kuremoto and Rosel, Lieutenants Simpson and Song Ha from the Marines, the Quartermaster Ken Edwards, and the Security Officer Nanami Oliver. The Captain handed each of them a tablet. This one was thinner and lighter than the ones on the bridge. The Captain began with a snicker, "This is the latest technology coming from the family. On it you will find a list of all the personnel my family has saddled us with and what billets they are to either be trained up for or fill outright. I have my own small network of spies within the Conglomerate. What little background information they could dig up on these people is in their files as well." Soto noted that Oliver was about to speak, but the Captain cut her short. "I *know* that it seems a bit *odd* that my family is so involved with this endeavor. However, this would not be possible at all if it wasn't for the backing of the Saitow Conglomerate. Now we will be able to operate independently and funding will remain available as long as we hold up our end of the bargain."

It was an agitated Doctor Kuremoto who next spoke, "And just what sort of bargain are we involved in?" Soto stifled a snicker at the way the old man could deftly raise one eyebrow just so.

"It's very simple." The Captain continued, "As I mentioned when I recruited you Doctor, we are after Pruathan technology. We will be searching out such technology elsewhere in the quadrant under the guise of a ship-for-hire; all the while using your Pruathan sensors to detect it. The Princess will remain with us for insurance against any ambushes the Empire might devise. Any head on confrontation can be easily avoided with our jump capabilities." The Captain seemed to look everyone in the eye to see if there were any more interrupting opinions. There were none so he continued, "Also on your tablets are the assignment of chains of command for each of you, to include who I wish you to keep a keen eye on."

It seemed to Soto that Lieutenant Song Ha was somewhat perplexed and the Captain had caught on to this as well. He addressed the man directly, "Lieutenant Song Ha I am well aware that your specialty is in Xenology. However, I feel that you are a man who can do any number of things once you put your mind to it. I need an outstanding Third Officer and you are the man for the job. Consider it a well-earned promotion. Now everyone go to the last page on the tablet; I am sure you all will be pleasantly surprised by what you find there."

Soto did as he was instructed and found a balance sheet from a new MU account in his name. He instinctively brought his token ring to the edge of the tablet and verified the balance noted there by neural-net. By the look on the faces of the others around the table, he was now the First Officer of a well-paid crew.

"Ok, I believe I have covered enough for tonight. Song Ha, you have the bridge. Be sure to read up on the ship's specs, alright? Good. Vic, here are the tablets for your charges Sagura and Takagawa. Simpson, maintain a watch schedule of your Marines. The off-duty folks and everyone else can go planet-side on the shuttles for the evening. My estate will meet them and provide for their needs. Make sure they get their own toiletries; no more freebees from the service. You can relieve the detail on the Princess. I'll be inviting her to dine with me this evening. Oh, and Vic, make sure Song Ha learns how to lock the front door. I don't want any of these new personnel running off with my ship."

*   *   *

Saitow ordered Bonifacio to prepare a fitting meal for his new charge. While he waited, he sent a dispatch to the Imperial Headquarters via the GCN. It read: CAPTAIN SAITOW OF THE IWAKINA TO HIS ROYAL HIGHNESS ROS'LOPER II: URGENT DISPATCH. THE SHIP'S CREW HAS BEEN COMPROMISED. TYRANNY AND IMPERIAL INTRIGUE HAVE TAKEN THEIR TOLL. SUCH ACTIONS HAVE TURNED MY STOMACH TO THE POINT THAT I WILL NO LONGER SERVE UNDER SUCH. YOUR DAUGHTER IS SAFE AND

WILL TRULY SEE THE GALAXY AS YOU
ENVISIONED. HOWEVER, SHE WILL SEE WITH
CLEAR EYES OUT OF REACH OF IMPERIAL
INFLUENCE. WHEREVER I GO SHE WILL GO.
FEAR NOT, FOR SHE WILL EVER REMAIN SAFE
AND COMFORTABLE WITH ME.

Once that was done, he retired to the Captain's Mess.
He saw that Bonifacio had already made use of his new
staff in getting the dinner setting together. Saitow
admired the man's skills very much. He just hoped that
having to address a royal wasn't too much for his old
heart.

* * *

Shirae had almost gotten her head wrapped around
wormhole mechanics when a hail sounded and the
hatch to her cabin whooshed open to reveal an aged
bald man. He bowed deeply and meant to start
speaking when Haruka-chan sprang in his direction. If
she had intended to do the man any harm, it would not
have mattered, as he had deftly maneuvered to avoid
her advance.

"Haruka! Let the poor man have his say!" Shirae
almost snapped the words, and Haruka knelt quietly
between the man and herself. Shirae nodded to the
man to continue.

"Please pardon me, Princess. I am Bonifacio, the
Ship's Cook. I have prepared a meal for your attendant.
However, the Captain wishes for you to dine with him
this evening."

Shirae saw Haruka's head begin to quiver and the woman practically shouted, "Her Highness will not be havin-"

"Haruka!" Shirae snapped and Haruka fell silent once again. Shirae was getting rather angry with her retainer. However, she knew the strain of the situation was getting to them both. She wanted answers and dining with the Captain seemed like her only option to getting to the bottom of what was to be her fate.

"Bonifacio was it? Yes, please inform the Captain that I will dine with him tonight. My conditions are that my retainer be allowed to kneel outside the door." Haruka gave her a sharp look; one she returned with equal sharpness. Haruka looked away toward Bonifacio once more. "And once the guard has escorted us there, they will guard us no more. Please tell him. I await his response." Shirae saw the old man crinkle his brow. He was apparently not used to conveying parley between persons of high stature. Whatever made her consider the Captain of high stature just then? She would get to the bottom of what was going on with the ship and with her own emotions soon she hoped.

The old man bowed and replied, "Of course, Princess." He then wheeled in a cart with Haruka's meal on it. The he bowed once more and retreated through the hatch which whooshed closed.

"Haruka-chan, eat your meal at once." Shirae said and turned her back on the woman. It pained her to treat Haruka in this way. However, she needed subordinates who would *obey* her; at this time more than ever.

* * *

Saitow had agreed to the Princess's terms and had them conveyed via the Marine escort. However, Haruka was once again relieved of her hidden dagger. She was allowed to remain kneeling outside the Captain's Mess as requested. When the Princess entered, he was struck by the small woman's beauty; her long dark hair and radiant eyes that were a little too wary made her all the more attractive. However, he did not have her brought here to woo her. He did need to get her on his side; to have her see why this mutiny was necessary. He rose quickly and moved to manage the seat for her. She allowed it and he took his place opposite at the small table. He motioned a porter to pour them wine.

"I hope you enjoy the wine. I had it taken from my family's personal stock. I also took the liberty of having my cook, whom you've already met, prepare your favorite meal; at least I hope I got it right." He did his best to get her to feel at ease, but he wasn't quite sure he was succeeding. She was nonchalantly nibbling on the appetizer that was set before them.

He figured he had best just come out with it. "Princess, no doubt you are curious as to why we have not reached Juliana. I must apologize to you about the bit of indiscretion I placed upon you when last we spoke. There was no saboteur aboard the ship. In fact, the ship is in proper working order." Saitow noted the Princess's wide-eyed glare and continued, "You see, we have taken it upon ourselves to right a very serious and dangerous wrong. We have stolen this ship in order to keep it out of the hands of the Empire." Saitow did his best to remain serious in spite of the fact that

Princess Shirae had almost spewed the mouthful of wine she was sipping. He had expected her to respond angrily at this point, but aside from a slight tremor in her eyebrows over the napkin she patted her face with, she seemed far too calm. Maybe she was smart enough to see the futility in opposing him. He continued, "Do not fear, dear Princess, I will continue to follow the one order your father the Emperor gave me that I feel must be followed: I *will* show you the galaxy. However, this ship cannot remain in the hands of tyranny and oppression. It is far too advanced and would give too great an advantage to an Empire that preys upon its very citizens." Oh! That seemed to get the young girls temper up. Saitow sat back to watch the expected fireworks. He doubted that even the roasted bird; *what was it called again...Chicken*? Shirae's favorite dish that was being served to them now would hold back the tempest. At least she calmed herself enough to wait until the service was completed.

"Captain Saitow. How dare you spit on the very government that brought you to such stature and renown. My father holds you in the utmost regard, as such that he would entrust his only daughter and heir to the Empire. My father even awarded you the Imperium's highest award for valor, the Silver Embellishment, and this is how you repay him? My father is a just ruler and the people love him!" Shirae had not even touched her roast bird; her sincerity must be without question. Saitow couldn't believe that she could not have heard of or seen the atrocities that were being perpetuated by the regime. Perhaps as the only heir to the throne she was being sequestered and truly didn't know what was going on. In that case, it made even less sense that the Emperor would entrust her to Saitow, ordering him to show her the galaxy. Surely, he would have known she would have seen what was happening in her own territories. He glanced back at her to find she was greedily devouring her main course. He took a bite of it himself; like all of Bonifacio's dishes it was quite good. They continued to eat in silence until the dessert had been served. It was something called *strawberry tart.*

Saitow took a bite of his, followed it with some more wine, and continued to try to get the Princess to see reason. "I will tell you this, Princess. As long as you are aboard this ship you will be safe and well taken care of. I have servants of my own family who will be attending to your needs within reason. We will be taking this ship to wonderful places that you cannot even imagine. It will just take some time for us to trust in each other."

"Trust? You wish for my trust? You have stolen Imperial property, misled an entire starship crew, kidnapped an Imperial person, shall I continue?" Shirae was showing some spirit this time around. Saitow leaned forward and placed his elbow on the table; his chin in the palm of his hand. "Please do, Princess."

"Oh Captain, I looked so forward to this journey, but you have turned the whole thing upside down! How can you possibly call my father a tyrant? The Empire is strong and may hunt us down like animals to the very corners of the galaxy. Mark my words!"

Saitow thought that this was enough for the Princess to know for the time being. He excused himself and headed to the service entrance to the Mess. Before he keyed the hatch to open, he spoke once again in order to get the Princess to act. Perhaps she really was innocent in all that had been happening within Imperial territory.

"You may not believe my words; of this I have no doubt. But from this moment I grant you full access of the ship as long as you are escorted by someone in my crew. Ask them to take you to a Multimedia room. Then ask them to key up the Galactic News. You will find atrocities happening in a variety of systems, the majority of which you will find within your own precious Empire!"

5

Sanae, in her disguise as Kintaro Sagura, made her excuses to Goh when he invited her to join him planet-side. She had things to do aboard ship; things that she didn't want Goh to know about. Once the majority of the old crew had left the ship and those of the new arrivals had settled in, she excused herself from the bridge and went directly to her quarters. There she sent another coded message to Contact Sigma via GCN relay telling of her status and the ship's location. She also indicated that she would contact the Princess's retainer. She was puzzled as to why she had yet to receive any response to her dispatches. She was also plagued by thoughts of the collaborators and the audacity of Captain Saitow. She decided to take a walk to clear her head and work out the best way to approach the Princess's retainer. She covered the corridors of deck two, and then descended to deck three on the forward lift. Rounding the corner at the Captain's Galley, she noticed the very object of her deliberation kneeling at the entrance to the Captain's Mess; the woman's back was towards her. Sanae quickly ducked back around the corner and considered her options of approach. She decided that the best course of action was to beckon to the woman from inside the VIP Head which had its entrance directly across from where the woman knelt. It seemed puzzling to Sanae that she was no longer guarded. Perhaps the Captain did not see her as an immediate threat. Sanae doubled back and accessed the VIP Head via the maintenance space at the center of the rear corridor. She disabled the lighting, opened the hatch, and silently beckoned for the woman to come to her. The woman almost caught Sanae by surprise by swiftly rising and leaping at her, a knife in her right hand. Sanae dodged, turning into the woman's advance and grabbing her extended right arm, using her momentum to pin the woman against the back bulkhead. The Hatch swooshed closed. The room was dimly lit by emergency lighting.

The woman cursed at her in Japanese; a sure sign that she was Pure Blood. Sanae tried to calm her while keeping steady pressure on her to remain against the wall.

"My name is Kintaro Sagura; I have no intention of harming you. I am an agent of the Empire and I will do everything within my power to help you. Please be calm. If you drop your weapon, I will release you."

The woman let go of the knife and Sanae released her, but not before sending her with momentum toward the left bulkhead away from the weapon. Sanae quickly retrieved it. Keeping her eye on the Princess's retainer, she keyed the door to lock and activated the lighting. The woman was against the left bulkhead, poised like a cat ready to pounce, but apparently aware of Sanae's skill. Sanae found it amusing that the conspirators had given this woman the codename of Dog; she was more like a feral cat. The Dog spoke, "How does a small chubby man like you move so swiftly and with such power?"

"I have been trained by the best in the Empire. That matters not; what may I call you besides the Princess's retainer?" Sanae didn't know whether to take the woman's statement as a compliment or insult.

"I am Haruka Koritsu, Attendant to Her Royal Majesty Princess Shirae of Ros'Loper. You may address me as Koritsu-san. Will you help us escape?"

"I will have to formulate a plan. However, it will take some time to contact the Imperials in order to facilitate a viable escape. I will make liaison with you once escape is possible. You had best get back to your position." Sanae keyed the lighting back to emergency settings, unlocked the hatch, and after checking the corridor, offered Koritsu her knife at the exit.

"May the ancestors be with you, young man." Koritsu offered as she went out the hatch.

*   *   *

Goh Takagawa had just finished purchasing stuff he needed for an extended journey aboard the *Iwakina*. He even bought some long sought-after music and an upgraded interface for his neural-network with his new-found wealth. He also picked some things up for Kintaro; he wondered why the man hadn't joined him Planet-side. It wasn't surprising that he might be acting strangely since the mutiny began; this was all new to both of them. He stepped out of another music shop into the thoroughfare of the massive shopping complex and watched the other shoppers as they hurried by. He probably looked pretty damn out of place with only his backpack. It seemed that swords were all the rage here. Only the security goons he saw infrequently throughout the crowd carried projectile weapons. He snickered a bit at that. He had briefly been on a team researching particle beam and directed energy weapons. With all the technological marvels of his time, no one could find a proper power source capable of sustaining a lethal level or one that was small enough to be useful. Those weapons remained the purview of starships. The blasters he had seen in old fiction vids were still a notion of the future. Goh had taken a few steps down the walkway when he noticed a group of three people walking straight toward him. At their front was a plainly dressed woman. She was looking right at him. Goh turned his head away then back to find the woman still looking his way. Behind her were two men, also plainly dressed, one of whom tapped something under his coat with the clear intention of letting Goh know he had a weapon. Goh just stopped and waited for them to reach him. The woman tapped a tablet she held and addressed him. "Hello, I am Vanessa Orchard. Can I assume that you are Goh Takagawa?" she showed him his own image on the tablet.

"Yes. Yes of course." Goh stated while sizing each of them up.

"We are from the Saitow Conglomerate. Please follow me." The woman led them to the nearest exit. There, a gravicar waited. Goh was a little anxious, but these people worked for the corporation that the Captain's family ran. Perhaps the Captain had recalled the crew sooner than expected.

The gravicar took them to the Saitow estate and he was escorted to the main dining hall of the residence. Surprisingly, he was seated to the left of the head of the table. Wine glasses for two were brought. A few moments later, a stately woman entered through an inner door followed by a couple of aides. The aides remained at the edges of the room and the woman sat at the head of the table. Goh instinctively rose as the woman approached then regained his seat after her. He was of noble birth after all. The woman spoke as wine was poured for them. "Goh Takagawa, you must tell me news of your grandmother." The woman could not have been a day older than the Captain, perhaps a sister of his.

"I'm sorry my lady. You have me at a disadvantage." He said to explain the puzzled look he was surely giving her.

"Oh dear, forgive me! Your grandmother and I have been friends for ages. I am Regina Saitow, your dear Captain's mother." The woman swirled the wine around a bit in her glass and sniffed its bouquet. Goh took a sip of his to hide his astonishment. He was even more astonished to find the wine he was enjoying was his own family's vintage. Regina Saitow noted his surprise and continued, "Yes, my boy, this is from your own family's winery. I have them commissioned regularly." Regina took a sip of her own.

"Pardon me, Madam. Unfortunately, I have not been in touch with Grandmother in quite some time."

"Yes. Yes, you have been learning all about Pruathan technology aboard the *Iwakina*. Do you miss the family business?" Regina seemed very friendly and easy to be around. Not quite the stuffy noble that Goh had expected to be in charge of a galactic corporation.

"Well, as you probably know I was unavailable to help rebuild the family wineries after the civil war on Calliope. Because the RL Empire had liberated us, I enlisted immediately. I did visit on occasion, but I have been out of the loop for a long time now. It is wonderful to see my family's work appreciated this far from our homeworld." As was usually the case, his family's wine was making Goh talkative.

"Oh dear, again I must ask your apologies. You must be famished. Won't you join me for dinner?" Regina beamed at him. Goh had had a quick bite to eat at the complex, but even the expertise of Bonifacio would pale at the chance to dine as a noble once again. Goh accepted eagerly begging her pardon for his lack of suitable attire.

After the main course had been served, and Regina Saitow had entertained him with a few stories that his grandmother probably would not want him to know, the woman got down to business. "Goh, please tell me. What do you think of Doctor Kuremoto?"

"Doctor Kuremoto is well respected and very intelligent. He is the foremost expert on Pruathan technology." Goh wasn't quite sure where this line of conversation was going, but he had his suspicions. He hadn't been in the inner circle, but he could tell who was pulling the strings and funding the whole operation. The ship's orbit over this particular planet said as much.

"My question is, can the man be trusted? He may be the current expert in Pruathan technology, but I see a far younger and more enthusiastic up and comer in that department right before my eyes." Before Goh could speak, she continued, "Please do keep an eye on him for my son the Captain, alright? Good. Now if you'll excuse me, I have pressing business to attend to. Do send a message to your grandmother; the poor dear worries so." With that they both rose and Regina Saitow exited the room, aides in tow. Orchard returned to escort him to suitable quarters; apparently, he was staying overnight. The next day he had instructions for reporting his observations of Dr. Kuremoto.

* * *

When the hatch to the Captain's Mess swooshed open, Haruka placed her head on the deck; her hands in a diamond shape before her. Princess Shirae emerged and bade her rise. Haruka led them to their quarters. There were no more guards at the hatch. Haruka keyed the hatch open and checked the room. It was the same as they had left it, but she felt an uneasy feeling. She requested the Princess rest on the divan once more while she checked out the other room. Haruka entered and keyed the hatch closed behind her. There, between the bath and the Princess's bed, were two women kneeling on the floor in the same submissive position Haruka had taken when the Princess came out of the Mess. One was to the left and back from the other. She didn't quite know what to think so she just said, "Who are you and what are you doing in Her Majesty's quarters?"

The two women raised their heads, but still remained kneeling with their hands in their laps; again, a sign of submission. The lead woman spoke in perfect Japanese, "Oujo-sama, I am Ran Tsureyama and this is my assistant Amane. She cannot speak. We are here to serve."

Haruka replied to the woman using Japanese as well, "Why do you address me so? Who are you here to serve?" she was very confused at this point, and was already contemplating the knife still kept hidden.

"It is well known that among the Pure Blood, Oujo-sama is Oujo-sama. We are here to serve you, and through you the Princess of the Empire." The other girl nodded enthusiastically. Just then the hatch behind Haruka swooshed open and Shirae came in yawning. "Haruka-chan, what is taking so long?

Please draw my...bath?" Haruka just noticed herself that the bath had already been drawn, vapors rising lazily from the water. She turned once again to the two intruders who had once again placed their foreheads to the deck. Ran Tsureyama repeated the introduction she had said to Haruka a minute ago, this time in perfect Codex English.

"Haruka?" the Princess was even more perplexed than Haruka had been.

"It seems that you have been assigned more retainers by the Captain." Haruka said as she removed her hand from the knife she concealed.

*   *   *

Doctor Kuremoto was not a happy man. He not only had been assigned several engineers and two biologists from the newcomers, but two of the engineers were Pure Bloods. When he checked the rest of the list of newcomers, there were quite a few of them that were Pure Bloods. He went to the Captain's quarters at once. This could not be tolerated. He hailed and was allowed in. He saw the Captain had stripped from his evening dress and was slouched in his lounger, a wine glass in one hand.

"Ah Doctor! Please, join me in a drink." The Captain motioned toward a recess in the back wall where there were plenty of spirits.

"I'm afraid I did not come here for a social visit. Glenn, when you asked me to join this endeavor, I had no idea I would be giving up one *task master* for another. I suspected that you would need some sort of backing, especially with the generous salary you offered, sure. I even resigned myself to my position, with the chance to do good for a change, I could put up with a little bit of restriction." Kuremoto began. He went ahead and poured himself a drink anyway before continuing, "However, being saddled with these unfamiliar crewmembers; did you know there are so many Pure Bloods among them?" He didn't let the Captain reply, "Pure Bloods are a scourge I tell you! There are two among the engineers I have been assigned. They could sabotage the ship for God's sake!" Kuremoto gave the Captain that wide eyed look he always used for emphasis and finally let the man reply.

The Captain seemed to consider his words carefully then began, "Edward. Why all the fuss? I realize that my family has stepped over the line just a bit with all these extra crewmembers, but I am still the man in charge. The Pure Bloods have been around forever, and have served my family well for generations; freely, not like those indentured Imperials, mind you. What would make you hate then so much?"

Kuremoto took overlong to sip his drink while trying to come up with an appropriate answer. His hatred of the Pure Bloods ran very deep, but the reason was a secret he could not divulge to anyone. It was that in a sense he was a Pure Blood himself. His father had been a just man, but died in exile away from the Pure Blood commune, leaving him, his mother, and siblings in poverty and despair. This occurred because his father had chosen to pursue science renouncing Bushido, the way of the warrior. He had vowed and succeeded to follow in his father's footsteps, but not without harboring a deep hatred for the rest of Pure Blood society. What of all this would the Captain understand?

He was a noble of mixed blood and probably had never even heard of Kuremoto's homeworld of Oedo. He decided to play it safe. "I have good reason not to trust the Pure Bloods. Believe me Captain; you do not want them on your ship."

Kuremoto thought he saw a glimmer of mirth cross the Captain's face, but when the man spoke, he was very serious, "Edward. I cannot for the life of me fathom what makes you so vehement toward these Pure Bloods. Sure, *some* of them may look a little odd. Sure, they like to speak some long dead language besides Standard Codex. But the majority of them are good people who are just treated badly because of prejudice." The Captain seemed to pause to let his words sink in while he sipped his wine. Kuremoto didn't reply so he continued, "By the way, you never told me about your time babysitting our Princess. Please share."

Kuremoto thought for a moment before answering. He wasn't quite sure where the Captain was going with the conversation. Was he trying to change the subject? Kuremoto wanted to find out. "I am not sure what that has to do with the Pure Bloods in the crew, but I'll tell you. It was a fairly nice but long-lasting chore. The Princess chatted with me about the ship, while her retainer seemed rather uptight."

"There." The Captain interrupted. "Besides her being upset, was there anything else odd that you observed about the Dog?"

Kuremoto smiled at the codename. "Well, no not really. She seemed like any other bodyguard of the royal family. What has she to do with my reservations?"

"She, my good man, is a Pure Blood and you didn't

notice." Kuremoto almost winched at the look of satisfaction on the Captain's face. Kuremoto thought back on the whole encounter. Sure, he had noticed, he had been briefed even, but it just occurred to him that it had not bothered him as much as these assignments. In hindsight he could pick out the familiar features. Of course, he could not have encountered all the possible blood lines, so that point was moot. Her attitude was very servile, yet strongly protective toward the Princess. Outwardly, she was nothing like the proud and haughty Pure Bloods.

The Captain continued, "So you see you cannot determine every Pure Blood's disposition just by stereotyping them. I don't know what beef you have with them as a whole, and I sympathize. I will remove the two engineers from your employ and put them under Takagawa. However, the rest of them are just as much crew as our own people. Unless you are provoked by one, there is no reason for you to be alarmed. Trust me. Now pour yourself another drink and have a seat. I want to hear about your vacation plans." Kuremoto thought for a moment then did as he was asked.

6

Wallace Horatio Aisou stood on the balcony of one of the spires high above one of the many summer palaces of the Imperium. He was hard pressed to suppress a grin from forming at the thought that this would soon be all his. He thought it ironic that he of all people could supplant the Emperor, but it was certain to occur. He had all of his Special Service troops positioned and they were doing their duty terrorizing the loyalists, there were so many of them, into submission. He had already assembled a shadow government that would step in and take the places of the many noble families that operated within the Imperium. All this he did under the very nose of the Emperor as Chancellor, best friend, and advisor. If all went well, he would find a way to dispose of the old fool while avoiding suspicion; with his only heir in the hands of a rogue officer on the run, it would be up to him to fill the void. Then the rest of the Empire would learn to respect him and there would be no more gossip behind his back. Family Aisou would finally be vindicated. His family had come into the nobility far later than the norm, having discovered vast amounts of precious metals on an 'officially' uninhabited planet. They no longer had to scrape by doing salvage and exploration. He and his brothers had not been introduced to Rejuve, the anti-aging drug, until very late in life. Therefore, they stood out among the younger appearing older nobles. He still curried favor with the Emperor, gaining his trust, and has served as Chancellor to the Empire for over fifty years now. It was true that the old man was still beloved of the people, but *his* people were changing that world by world; soon he would not be missed.

*   *   *

The transport vessel that carried the survivors of the *Iwakina* mutiny was about to land and 'official' news of the *Iwakina*'s taking was about to be spread. Chancellor Aisou had news of it days ago of course, because he had received the dispatches from Sparrow 64 and the Captain's message to the Emperor. No doubt Sparrow 64 would be confused at the silence of Contact Sigma. Aisou stood by on the platform as the crewmembers were escorted off the ship. He beckoned for one of his Lieutenants that had been checking names against a roster on his tablet. "Who is the senior officer among them?" Aisou inquired. He would bring a scapegoat before the old fool of an Emperor.

"Lieutenant Commander Darren Jones, The Third, my Lord." replied his subordinate.

"Interrogate him separately, and then have him waiting for Imperial audience at 0900 tomorrow morning. The rest of the crew should be segregated by billet and interrogated thoroughly. Oh, and find the Third Officer's family, they should visit and see that he is well."

The Lieutenant keyed some input into the tablet. "We are in luck my Lord; the man's family resides in the town below."

"Well, well, that is good news. I so hate wasting resources. Carry on." With that the Lieutenant relayed directions to a group of servicemen, who in turn hauled Officer Jones out from the group of crewmembers. Good news indeed.

*   *   *

Darren Jones was very tired. He had been interrogated non-stop for several hours; his interrogators only stopping because they felt he had told them all there was to know. He had been assured that the rest of the crew, although they were to be interrogated like he had been, would be reassigned to other service. The military officers were to be demoted, but allowed to continue service at the Emperor's pleasure. He however, being the senior non-mutineer, was to have an audience with the Emperor himself; surely to be met with some punishment for his lapse. He was only given a couple of hours of sleep, when he was aroused by the sound of children. When the door to the palace holding cell was opened, he barely had time to raise himself to a sitting position before two young bodies collided with him, that of his five-year-old and seven-year-old daughters. His wife entered behind them and the door was closed behind her. His smile at the sight of his children vanished instantly at the look on the face of his wife was quite grave. She spoke in hushed tones. "Darling, I am overwhelmed to see you; the children and I missed you so much." His wife sat down beside him and the children. Hugging him, she whispered as to not be heard by the guards or any sensors in the cell, "Darren, your life is in danger. Rumor has it that the Emperor is quite mad. Oh, Darling what will happen to us?"

Jones did his best to reassure her. "Sweetheart, God will see us through this. I must take responsibility for the loss of my ship. Surely the Emperor will be just."

Jones's wife turned away to hide her tears. He held her closer, while the children squirmed in his lap sensing distress. Just then the cell door opened and a guard stepped in. "Mrs. Jones, it is time to go."

Before they parted, Jones kissed each of his family members on the cheek and bid them farewell.

*　　*　　*

Emperor Ros'Loper the Second sat lounging on the throne of the grand court hall in his favorite summer palace. He distractedly flipped through some holographic video of the court's business; no doubt constructed by his Chancellor's advisors. He rarely got a glimpse of the actual news via the GCN, but that was to be expected. These things sorted themselves out. Oh, how he missed the company of his beloved daughter Shirae. However, he knew he had to groom her for her turn on this very throne, so she was off on an adventure among the stars; not too far away from home he hoped. Soon another day would begin full of business from the locals and intrigue from the nobles of the court.

A hail sounded at the court's side entrance and the head caller cried, "His Lord Chancellor W.H. Aisou."

Ros'Loper looked over the man as he approached the throne and bowed deeply. He was somewhat older in appearance than most nobles. His Chancellor had an air about him of warmth and compassion, but it seemed tainted by something the Emperor could not quite put his finger on. No matter, he had served well as friend and advisor for some odd fifty years or so.

This was a man he could trust.

"Your highness I come with the gravest of news." Aisou stated bluntly.

"Come. Take your seat here beside me and share this news."

"Your Majesty, I come hither from the spaceport where news of a treachery has reached us that the great ship of the Pruatha that we had pinned so much hope for in turning the tide of stalemate among the Human worlds has been stolen by none other than its Captain."

"The *Iwakina* you say? And news of the Princess?" The Emperor could not have heard graver news.

"Sadly, Your Highness, she was aboard and is feared kidnapped. There are a number of non-mutineers that were left abandoned on a deserted mining planet. Our fleet discovered them when a distress beacon was detected in orbit there. We learned of this news from them and verified that the *Iwakina* never arrived at the Juliana Naval Station. We have the senior officer among them awaiting your audience. A suitable punishment is advised my Lord."

"Yes, yes. Bring the man before me." Ros'Loper was very agitated and thought that someone must be punished for this breach. To think his only daughter was in the hands of traitors? *Oh God in heaven.*

Aisou continued, "Before he is brought forth, my Lord, there is one more issue you must know. The princess's twin sister is also aboard that ship as our spy disguised by the Transmutor device. As you know, she is part of the Sparrow Project." Ros'Loper was astonished by this news and almost caught a slight glimmer of mirth in his Chancellor's eyes, but he dismissed it. Not only was his true heir on the stolen ship, but her abandoned twin, who had been taken at birth for one of Aisou's 'projects'. This news was grave indeed. It had taken ages for scientists to enable his wife and him to conceive. When his wife died giving birth to twin girls, he had given one to Aisou with the assurance that she would never know her birthright. The fertility treatments he had been given were a one-shot deal; he remains sterile to this day. "How could this be? You assured me yourself that the two would never come in contact with each other!"

"Your Majesty, I assure you that it was a fluke that she would have been assigned to the *Iwakina,* a top-secret military project, and that you would chose that ship of all the ships in your fleet to place the Princess on..." Aisou seemed to let the thought sink in.

"No matter; I am sure if she has been trained by you, she will realize the seriousness of her mission and prevail without revealing herself to our daughter." Ros'Loper knew from reports early on in Aisou's projects that the man took a personal interest in training his 'special assets' and that they would die before revealing themselves as what they truly are. He shuddered at the thought of being anything other than this man's friend. "Bring forth the senior officer."

"Very well, my Lord."

Darren Jones was brought into the court hall flanked by two armed officers. Ros'Loper questioned him at length about the *Iwakina,* his daughter, and Captain Saitow. He inquired as to whether the man had a family and found out that they were here at the palace. The Emperor passed sentence on the man of 100 days hard labor in the local mines, then to be stripped of military rank and privilege, and returned to his family to live out the rest of his life contemplating his failure. His family would be given his pension to live on. Jones was then led out of court.

Aisou smiled at the Emperor as the court nobles began to filter in for the day's business. "A just sentence, Your Majesty." He said and then posted to his normal space in the hall.

Ros'Loper resigned himself to the couple of hours it would take to be rid of them.

* * *

Aisou headed leisurely down the palace corridor. He was in no hurry. The old fool had too much confidence in his 'training techniques', but it was just as well. He had trained Sparrow 64 as he had the rest of the Sparrow Project. However, he knew just what would break that training and sow the seeds of doubt in his operative. It was only a matter of time before she would be questioning her own existence and looking to those around her for answers. His plans were going quite well at this point.

He went through an automatic door and down a much narrower corridor to the holding cell area. He found his lieutenant waiting outside Jones's cell as instructed. "Take the man in this cell off-world and kill him, but not before you reunite him with his entire family. We can't have so many lives relying on a pension, can we?" the Lieutenant saluted and Aisou strolled off, grinning from ear to ear.

7

Captain Saitow had just returned from negotiating with the family about Doctor Kuremoto's vacation. The man had been quite adamant about getting this done; so much so that he pledged to lead the Saitow conglomerate to a major Pruathan prize: a complete but slightly damaged Pruathan Jumpgate. Saitow didn't even know that the Pruatha *had* jumpgates, let alone one within the former Rangelley Imperial territories. Nevertheless, Kuremoto's gate was deep within Didier space. The Saitow family had a significant interest in trade with the Didier, mostly in precious metals for technology. They should be able to negotiate rights to the gate with the trade of a destroyer or two. The Didier is a peaceful species. However, even peaceful species have to defend themselves. Part of the negotiation included reassignment of the two engineers that were Pure Bloods to the gate project once rights were obtained. For the life of him, Saitow could not figure out what reasons Kuremoto had for disliking - even hating - them. He came to the realization that he really didn't know the man as well as he would like. He had an extensive file on all of his people, but nothing in the Doctor's indicated his odd behavior toward Pure Bloods. Training of new personnel and the sweeping of the ship for Imperial fail safes would take two to three weeks. He would have some investigation done in the meantime.

*   *   *

Doctor Kuremoto sat in the main lounge aboard a loaned corporate yacht sipping a rare Taibori wine. He was given the loaner in order to make the jump to the KV gate; Nanami Oliver and her goons were on the bridge awaiting clearance. The plan was for the yacht to traverse the jumpgates, and then meet up with a Conglomerate cruiser, the *Kurumi*; a ship much too large to use the gate system. The yacht would be taken aboard and then the cruiser would FTL to Didier space, where they would begin negotiation for the Pruathan gate. Kuremoto had been around a long time. He knew that the Rangelley had discovered the gate, found it didn't power up and was damaged, and abandoned it as unworthy of salvage. They really hadn't had the technical expertise to reverse engineer it. Actually, they couldn't spare the expertise; constant war kept their people rather busy. Kuremoto came across all the information they had on it and then some when he was assigned to the *Iwakina* project. If he had been assigned to *that* project, the Rangelley Empire might have spanned the entire quadrant. It was probably a good thing that he hadn't been. Now he would be leaving that to other engineers; he had pressing issues in other areas. Once the gate was located and accessible, he would be allowed to use the loaner yacht for his vacation; provided Oliver and her goons accompanied him. They weren't needed to fly the ship. With its state-of-the-art onboard AI, it practically flew itself. He knew they were there for insurance, although their official role was his personal 'security' or something like that. There was a minimal support crew to serve meals and tidy up. He could have easily gone on his own. Oh well, as long as they kept out of his way, they were but a minor nuisance. He had more important matters to think about.

*   *   *

Sanae entered her cabin and instantly knew something was amiss. Several of her tells had been disturbed and there were items that had been moved and put back into place. Her training prevented her from panicking. It did not surprise her that the scheduled sweep of the ship for fail safes included personnel spaces. She checked and found that the secret compartments in her bureau had not been found. They weren't using the proper scanners that she would have. She got out the Transmutor terminal and programed some varied outfits for her Sagura disguise. The crew had taken to ditching their uniforms in favor of more comfortable clothing. When she finished, she put that terminal away and pulled out the comm equipment. When she keyed it on an indicator immediately began flashing red, so she quickly keyed it off. The engineers, probably Goh, were scanning the ship's systems and her non-system terminal would have been detected. She put that away and tended to the sandwich she had made herself while contemplating the day's observations. She had come across the Princess and her retainer who had two more retainers in tow. *The Princess conveyed herself with such grace*, she thought. Sanae got up from her bunk after finishing her sandwich and went to the mirror in the head. How odd it was that her features were so similar to the Princess's. No, they were almost identical. She tried to imagine herself with long flowing hair like that of the Princess. Her own short hair was almost mousey. She shook these disturbing thoughts from her head and went back to her bunk. Sagura wasn't due for duty for several hours yet. She thought about hailing Goh to see if he would do some training, but then remembered he was on duty. Perhaps she should get some extra sleep. She curled up in her bunk and fell fast asleep, thoughts of the Princess and her together chasing her there.

*   *   *

Goh Takagawa was deep in the heart of the ship accessing a major communications junction from the maintenance access tubing. He had his trusty new tablet, which he had already hacked to his personal standards, plugged into direct access of communications. He thought it odd that the Captain had ordered removal of the censor on GCN reception his first priority. Having quickly finished that, his next job was removal of Imperial fail safes from all of the ship's systems. He was about to get rid of the Imperial comm protocol which copied and tagged all communications with Imperial coding, when he noticed a flag in the program. It appeared that there were at least two encoded communications that had their own protocols attached, rejecting the Imperial tags. This made him very suspicious. He checked the timing of the messages and the means by which they had been sent. He checked them against the terminal usage logs but found that the terminals they were logged as having been sent by had not been accessed at the time. He downloaded the copies of the messages that remained. However, he did not have the time and resources to decrypt them at the moment. He considered whether to inform the Captain of the messages, but there were only two; he wanted more concrete evidence before he threw around accusations that there was subterfuge amongst the foul play that had already occurred. He would have to create a tracing program for any messages that could not be tagged by the system, but that would take time as well. What he could do for the moment was to modify the imperial tagging to tagging of his own. That way the messages emanating from the ship would still be tagged and the suspicious messages would still be flagged. However, all messages would be free of Imperial fail safes. It may take him some time, but he would find whoever was sending top level encoded messages by randomizing comm paths soon enough. The Captain would probably want to hear about that.

*   *   *

Sanae awoke from a fitful sleep. She felt that she may have overslept so she hurried out of her cabin and down the corridor. Something didn't seem quite right; *had she forgotten something?* She was about to turn back when she rounded a corner and caught sight of the Captain in front of the Princess's quarters. Then the Princess stepped out of the open hatch and stood on her toes to kiss the Captain on the lips! The Captain took her in his arms and reciprocated the action. Sanae had never expected to see such acts of affection by a royal and dared not expect such to occur between *these* two. She was about to turn away when, to her astonishment, it was no longer the Princess in the Captain's embrace, but herself!

Sanae sat bolt upright in her bunk. She brought her hand up to her lips; still feeling the warmth of a kiss there. Her heart was beating as if she had just done a double workout sparing with Goh, and a cold sweat broke out on her forehead. *What were these incredible feelings?* They gave her pleasure, scared her, and confused her all at once. Immediately she thought of the warnings from her instructors; never fall in love or you shall be compromised. She had been given training on how to use her body to succeed in missions and had her first sex at an early age. But her training ruled out feelings of love. She dismissed them at once. How could she be in love? In love with the Captain no less? She checked her military grade neural-net for the time; there was still an hour until Sagura was due to report. Funny, how she had a secret neural-net and couldn't use it to access the ships systems; she thought about this to get her mind off of the dream. But it was a dream; she had not dreamt since she was a child. She realized that dreams are sometimes remembered by neural-net. Everyone thought that Sagura could not get one due to religious aversion. She made damn sure any trace of the dream was gone from hers.

*   *   *

Doctor Kuremoto was putting the final touches on the new mobile lab he had gotten purchased and delivered to the corporate cruiser. He got it set up in one of the larger cabins of the yacht. Then he was called to the bridge of the cruiser. The Captain of the Kurumi, and the Saitow's negotiation team were waiting for him.

Christian Stringer, the head of the negotiators addressed him, "Greetings Doctor. The Didier delegation is about to arrive and will be joining us in the main conference lounge. Let me introduce our team; I am Christian Stringer, Head Negotiator for the

Saitow Conglomerate. This is Indira Selenko, my secretary, and this is Darius Tezuka, our lead Xenologist. You will be joining us in the negotiations to aid in any technical issues that arise; you being the only one among us who has seen this gate. I will be doing most of the talking. Please address any questions that I field to you. Are there any issues you would like to address before we join the Didier?"

Kuremoto thought for a moment. "Well... actually... there is one minor detail I thought of on the way here that I feel you need to be aware of. It seems that there is a small religious order that consider the... 'ring' as they call it, an ancient relic." Kuremoto was not at all surprised at the consternation that crossed the negotiators' faces when he dropped that little bombshell. He purposely had neglected to mention it because he knew it would be months before this thing could get started if they knew and he needed to take his vacation in a timely manner. He had heard about this Christian Stringer; the man never balked at a challenge when it came to negotiations.

Stringer was silent for a few minutes, when word came that the Didier delegates were departing their shuttlecraft. "Let's get this done, shall we?" he sent a dubious look toward Kuremoto before directing the group to the conference lounge. The corporate team took their seats opposite from where the Didier would be seated. Both Tezuka and Selenko set down tablets; Selenko began typing away on hers, while Tezuka only set a stylus on top of his.

Soon the alien delegation arrived. Xenology being one of his disciplines, Kuremoto couldn't help but think that the Didier had a slight resemblance to the amphibian frog species; their solidly dark colored eyes were more positioned toward the sides of their hairless olive-green heads, and their lips were thick and a darker green color. They had no visible olfactory organs on their faces. Other than that, they were humanoid and wore ornate clothing. There were three of them. Introductions were exchanged and it was agreed that the talks would occur in Codex English. Kuremoto noted that the one with the most ornaments, including a large replica of the ring worn on a chain, was the leader of the religious sect.

After a few pleasantries were exchanged, the negotiations were started in earnest. The Didier spoke first. "As your good doctor Kuremoto has surely told you, there is a religious sect among the Didier that believes our ancestors came from within the ring. In order for us to relinquish rights to this relic to the Saitow Conglomerate, we require five heavy cruisers like the one we are now in, and three armed yachts of Saitow Conglomerate manufacture." Kuremoto noticed a quiver that might have passed for agitation cross the face of the sect's leader. He also noticed Tezuka tapping three times on the table in front of him with his stylus. Selenko quietly typed away on her tablet.

Stringer remained calm. "It is not possible at this time to provide such a number of cruisers like the Kurumi. We can provide one such cruiser. However, we would gladly provide five armed yachts for the Didier."

The sect leader's quivering ceased at this and he practically jumped out of his seat. "See! See Rentaa Sing Zercaa, the humans won't give you your ships! You must demand cooperation." The sect leader sat down at once.

The one addressed as Rentaa, who must be their lead

negotiator, continued the talks. "Please accept our apologies. Prelate Fenraa Sing Dencaa has spoken out of turn. It is unfortunate that the Conglomerate cannot provide the ships in numbers that we are requesting. However, it may have been a bit too much to request. We *do* place a great value to the ring even though it has been inoperable for centuries. You see, our government understands the significance of the ring to its citizens, and just giving up the rights to the ring would be a severe injustice to them. We do appreciate the offer of five armed yachts. Thank you very much. We could surely accept the one ship you offered for delivery immediately, and two more ships as manufacturing would allow. Also, we require that a limited number of sect members be permanently assigned to assist in the resurrection of the ring, and that worshippers be allowed to continue pilgrimage to the space station there, so that they may gaze upon the wonders of the ring."

Kuremoto was amused at the audacity of these negotiators, but then he realized that this was a game of inflation and deflation until each side felt they had gotten what they wanted and given just enough to make it worthwhile. Tezuka set his stylus directly in front on the table facing horizontally to him. Surely his dancing stylus was a way of giving signals to Stringer. Selenko just quietly continued typing.

Stringer thought for a short time, opened his mouth to speak, but stopped himself and turned to Kuremoto.

"Doctor what do you think of the Didier proposal of assistance?" Kuremoto was taken aback. He hadn't expected to actually be questioned on anything. He quickly considered the situation. He had done extensive research on the sect. All of their top leaders were engineers, as much interested in Pruathan technology as he was. They also had a pretty advanced space station very close to the gate and most likely had found a way to access the gates control center. They could come in handy in helping reverse engineer the gate. They would also be there to guide the inevitable pilgrims and keep them from interfering. The sect had as much interest in getting the gate working as the Conglomerate; they believed it to be the portal of their ancestors after all. "I would say that they are capable and it is a generous offer of cooperation between our two species. They have a station that I would hope we could share and they would be the best choice to tend to their pilgrims. They would help in getting the gate operational as well; their leadership consists of well-educated engineers." After speaking, Kuremoto noted that Tezuka's stylus was now pointing straight at the Didier delegation.

Springer spoke once more. "Thank you, Doctor." He turned once more toward the Didier, "It is certainly in the best interests of the Saitow Conglomerate to foster cooperation in our relationship with the Didier. We also understand that there have been increases in your intermittent territorial disputes with the Mulak. Unfortunately, we have been required to perform a complete overhaul of the shipyards where we produce the ships you are requesting. Fortunately, we have had a dispute with a buyer of one of this class of ship. We are willing to provide said ship, in addition to the one offered, and the five-armed yachts, provided that any ship of our choosing has direct access to Didier space between a to-be-determined ingress point on your borders and the gate site. Furthermore, each of the ships we send might possibly be given orders to aid the Didier in their territorial disputes at the discretion of each ship's Captain, in the spirit of cooperation between our two species. We are willing to consider cooperation with the sect, provided we have access to the local station, and a conference is held between the engineers who will conduct the project and the engineers of the sect at a later date. We believe this to be a very viable and generous offer in the spirit of cooperation between our two peoples." Kuremoto could almost perceive what could be called a smile on the three Didier's faces. The Mulak were a much more aggressive species than the Didier. The Didier and Mulak shared borders; the later often encroached on Didier space. Springer's offer was tantamount to a military alliance. Tezuka made a great flourish of putting his stylus away in his pocket. Selenko typed on.

The Didier's lead negotiator and the sect leader had a mini-conference out of earshot. Then the lead negotiator spoke. "In the spirit of cooperation as you have said, we accept this generous offer provided that we are given a tour of this ship; after a good meal of course. We do so enjoy the vegetables of Humans."

Stringer and his team stood and rounded the table to shake hands with the Didier. Kuremoto noted that some customs of the Codex were still in use centuries after the Rangelley implemented them. It only occurred to him after shaking the creature's hand that the third Didier had not spoken a word, nor had it barely even twitched once, barring the 'smile'. A curious species indeed.

* * *

Doctor Kuremoto was lucky to have been given such a fine ship to use. It had the latest Deidriad

Hyperspace Induction Drive capable of FTL speeds far greater than the lumbering cruiser. The *Galaxy Angel* was the name of this yacht. As soon as they were clear of the *Kurumi*, and at a safe distance, he programed the shipboard AI to navigate to Pearl at maximum velocity. Agents were risking their lives just by being there waiting for him to pick up his package. He told Nanami Oliver only what was necessary to keep her mollified; she of all people was the last one he wanted knowing about his experiments. Even at maximum speed, it would take a day and a half at least, skidding through hyperspace energy. Not nearly as fast as the *Iwakina*, but impressive nonetheless. That was the beauty of this method of FTL, you didn't have to break the barrier of hyperspace.

The journey went smoothly. Kuremoto had managed to avoid Nanami Oliver for the most part, only exchanging pleasantries when she checked in on him a couple of times. He kept himself busy readying his lab for the trip back. When they arrived, it wasn't much hassle to get clearance for the launch to land, an almost exorbitant sum of MU was exchanged and they were cleared; no questions asked. Pearl was a decent sized planet of mostly farm land. It had survived the Rangelley fall by being just close enough to the GCN and therefore the major trade routes. As simple as the people there were, Pearl also had its share of very cunning, unscrupulous people running things. Nanami insisted on accompanying him. Rather than raise her ire, he relented.

They left their launch at the spaceport and headed east to a small supply town close by. There they checked into a room; Nanami joking that she didn't know he had it in him. *As if he would consort with a woman like her*. He set up a portable transponder and waited.

They had waited about an hour watching a boring teleseries, which was, not surprisingly, about farmers, when there was a knock on the door. Nanami pulled her sidearm, but Kuremoto insisted she put that thing away. He checked the video feed from outside and saw two men with medical cases; it had to be them.

"Relax Oliver, it's them." He stated and opened the door. The men stepped inside quickly and eyed Nanami nervously. "Don't worry. She's harmless." Kuremoto said, but knew better.

The smaller of the two men spoke. "Doctor Kuremoto, we thought you would never arrive."

* * *

Nanami didn't like being ordered around by the Old Guy. Her orders from the Captain were to accompany Doctor Kuremoto wherever he went, keep him out of harm's way, and bring him back safely to the *Iwakina*. They did *not* include kissing the Old Guy's ass. She reasoned that she would just have to put up with it for the Captain's sake; he had put his full trust in her by letting her join in the mutiny and giving her this mission.

She sized up the two gentlemen who had entered the room. One was a good head taller that the other. They had made a good point to wear the clothing of the locals, but these guys weren't from around here. They were both armed as most of the locals were. She had observed enough locals on the ground to know that these two were from someplace else; most likely off-world. The bigger one had two silver cases which he handed over to Kuremoto.

"Yes, yes, we had pressing business with the Didier, but now we are here. I assume this is just what was called for?" Kuremoto addressed the smaller man. "I hope you found the compensation I provided to have outweighed the risk."

"Yes, yes, Doctor. It's just that we may have been followed."

Nanami perked up at this. *What was with all the cloak and dagger stuff anyway? Wasn't the Old Guy supposed to be on vacation?*

The Doctor gave her a furtive glance. "Well in that case, we had better be on our way. Thank you very much for all your hard work."

Nanami watched as the two men left. Kuremoto opened the two cases one by one, seemingly in an attempt to keep her from seeing inside. She didn't care what was inside those cases; what she wanted to know was if they were both in danger. "Doctor, what did those men mean when they said they may have been followed?"

"Ah...well you see, these cases contain a large amount of Rejuve that I have purchased. There are many unscrupulous people who would like to get a hold of that. It's for some of the crew, including the Captain." Kuremoto wasn't being straight with her; she could tell. That didn't matter right now; she needed to get them both safely back aboard the *Angel*.

"Fine. Grab your cases and stick close to me. We are heading back to the ship." She noted Kuremoto's nodding assent and led him out the door and down the corridor. Once close to the lobby she halted and looked for suspicious activity. There was none, so she asked one of the attendants if there was a back entrance. Finding that there was, she led the Doctor out and into an alleyway. "Stay here just a moment. I saw an apparel shop right next to the hotel. I'll get us something that will help us not stand out so much." He nodded again and she left him going through the hotel and out the front, but not before checking the street for suspicious activity. Inside the apparel shop she bought two oversized hooded rain covers. The locals wore these even when it wasn't raining because it tended to just open up any time of the day around here; or so stated the store clerk. Donning hers, she stepped out into the street and headed back inside the hotel. However, she had noticed that this time there were an unusual number of military men in purple uniforms outside across the street. She made her way back to the Old Guy and had him don the rain cover, raising the hood. This would keep the cases out of sight as well as their off-worlder clothing. Good fortune had come their way just then; it began to rain heavily. She managed to get them a cart and back to the spaceport before any of the purple uniformed folk had spotted them. Unfortunately, there were a couple of them strategically positioned to cover entry to the more expensive berths where their launch awaited. Nanami forced Kuremoto into a corner out of sight of them. She wanted some answers. "OK, Doctor. Give it to me straight. Who are these guys in purple? They damn sure are not from this planet, and they seem intent on looking for your friends, which means they are probably looking for us. They must be throwing around as much MU as we are to be operating so freely here. So, who are they?" Nanami watched Kuremoto almost go pale and he was fidgeting more than usual. It took him a while to answer. "I don't know... maybe they aren't looking for us. Maybe they are looking for someone else?"

"You're lying. I can see it in your face. I guess it really doesn't matter. I swore to the Captain that I would protect you, and protect you I shall. However, you are going to have to play bait for now." She instructed him to wait five minutes while she got into position, then speed walk toward the launch's berth. If he was confronted by the guys in purple, then he was to stop but only if he was between them and the launch. He must only look at them, nowhere else, and stall. She would take care of the rest.

* * *

Kuremoto did as he was told. He didn't like the fact that he had to rely on this dangerous woman, but it was that very dangerousness that may get them out of this jam. He waited the allotted time, and then hurried toward the berth. As predicted the two men in purple hurried after him. When they had almost caught up to him, one of them called him by name and he slowed instinctively then stopped. Before he could turn around, however, he heard two distinct thumping sounds followed by thuds of the men hitting the pavement. Nanami then had him by the arm hurrying him along and aboard the launch. She had them airborne and in space before ground control could even negotiate clearance.

* * *

Nanami didn't talk to the Old Guy for a couple of days except to verify the flight plan and that they were on a leisurely jaunt back to the *Iwakina*. She figured that it wasn't that big of a deal since she had successfully taken out the two goons in purple and they had made their escape. She was an expert at keeping secrets, so it didn't bother her much that there were others with their own who didn't want to share. Hopefully, there would not be any implications beyond what happened at Pearl; at least for her anyway. She had practically put it out of her mind by the time the Doctor came to call. It surprised her that the Old Guy had come to her; he made no excuses about the way he felt about her presence here. As an Intelligence Officer, she had gotten used to that. But now, here he was, all apologetic looking, holding a bottle of wine and two glasses. He asked to be allowed in to her cabin, and she directed him to the lounging area. He poured for them both; she had not had a glass of wine this fine in a long time. Kuremoto settled back to take a sip of wine before he spoke. "Ms. Oliver, I think it is my fault that we have not started off on good terms since the whole *Iwakina* incident. As you may know I am an old man and we old men tend to get stuck in our own way of doing things. We tend to resent the ideas of younger folks such as yourself." Just then Nanami wanted to know just how old the Old Guy was. She knew he was on the Stuff, but didn't know how long he had been. So, she interrupted him to ask.

"Just how old *are* you Doctor?"

"Would you believe me if I told you I was almost 400 years old?"

Nanami quickly took a sip of wine to hide her astonishment. *He was almost 400?* That would put him alive during Rangelley times. She couldn't help but let out a small sound. Kuremoto smiled wickedly.

"Yes, young lady, I have been around for a time or two. But the reason I have come to you is to thank you for helping me back there on Pearl. You see, I led you on a little about the cases and the men in purple. One of the cases does contain Rejuve, the reason I have been able to live so long, but the other case contains something I need to create a new medicine. Those men are from a Planet called Uprising. Have you heard of it?"

Nanami thought for a moment. She had a vague inkling of a planet with that name, but the circumstances eluded her. Perhaps it was the wine; she didn't drink very often, and was known in her academy days as a cheap drunk. "No. not really." was all she could say.

"Well, Uprising contains several large weapons manufacturing plants. These plants are filled with slave labor and guarded by those men in purple."

Nanami raised an eyebrow at the word slave. She didn't like where this was going.

"Yes, they treat their people as slaves, all because they have a terrible and supposedly incurable disease. The whole planet is quarantined except for the small enclave ruled by the soldiers in purple who make excessive amounts of MU from the sale of weapons. I believe that I can create a cure for these people and free them from bondage. Those men who delivered the cases to me were double agents from Uprising. Their government would stop at nothing to keep things the way they are. My best friend is stuck on that planet in a pseudo-lab set up as a sham by their government with not enough tools to do the job; that is why I came so far." Kuremoto paused and took a deep draught of wine, and then poured himself another glass. Nanami declined to have hers refilled. He then continued.

"I couldn't concentrate on my work in the isolated lab I had set up here because I was being plagued by my conscience for not being straightforward with you. I do sincerely apologize." Nanami detected sincerity in the Old Guy; something she had not encountered in many people for a long time now. She still doubted his motives though. It was probably the possibility that he would need her help in the future that prompted this bout of honesty. Perhaps it might be something to look forward to.

"Really, Doctor, there is no need to apologize. I can sometimes come across as if *I* was a 400-year-old! I think I *will* have another glass of wine. Now tell me of your youth! You must have been around during the Rangelley days..." and with that Nanami was regaled with many stories of the old Rangelley Era which lasted well on to morning.

8

Prince Sheenid was the last of the Rangelley royalty. His title of Prince was guaranteed by a number of loyal noble families. He was able to rally them, set up a seat of power on Askelon and slowly incorporate many Human territories under his banner of the New Rangelley Alliance. He was *that* charismatic, even with the concealing mask he had worn since childhood. *Yes,* he thought, *his one major flaw, this mask.* His head hurt at the thought of looking at his own face. He started sweating at the prospect. He furtively looked around his chambers for any reflective surface. Satisfied that there were none, he called for Rebecca to wipe his face. She had been destined to be his chamber maid since her birth. She was genetically engineered to be sightless, yet she had been given some sort of way to see without seeing. He didn't know all the scientific rigmarole behind it; it was enough that she could never look upon his face. He took off the mask to let her wipe it for him. She was perhaps twenty, maybe a little older. For Sheenid, time seemed a blur. He was maybe fifty-four, but had started on Rejuve at twenty-one; he rarely celebrated birthdays. He caressed her face. She looked up at him with milky white eyes. She was in fact beautiful, but he would never take advantage of her. She was too precious to him to sully.

What had started this curse that plagued him to this day? He had four siblings as a child; he was the youngest. They harassed him daily, mocking him. Their mother once said he was the handsomest and his brothers did not like that. They threw insult after insult at him, telling him constantly that he was a horrid creature to gaze upon, and avoided looking at him when they knew he was looking toward them. It must have sunk in. At his mother's untimely death, he took to wearing masks and was further shunned. He proved his intelligence excelling in school, and was sent to the military academy ahead of his brothers. When they were finally enrolled, Sheenid set his plans in motion. Each of them supposedly died in accidents; the last at Sheenid's own hand. He had the last gaze in fear at his face before he took the man's life. He covered that one up too. After returning to his family's palace at Askelon, he worked his way into the infrastructure, making reforms where he could and easing the burden on the loyalist families and citizenry that kept them in power. He was loved and respected, despite the mask he wore. He gained the throne when his father died from natural causes, and consolidated his seat of power at the stronghold planet Askelon, the former launching point of the great Rangelley Proximal Fleet. His doctors could not find any physical ailment to explain his aversion, and they dared not suggest it was a mental condition. He knew what it was, but he could not change himself no matter how much he tried. He got a dispatch on his neural-net: a message of urgency from afield. He would take it in his study.

*　　*　　*

Ruri had been the concubine of Prince Sheenid for over ten years. She shared the Prince's bed and kept him company on excursions. Only once had she ever gazed upon his face; once when he had drunk a bit too much wine and was in a deeper sleep than usual, she got the mask off his face. Oh, what a beautiful face it was. It was as if her heart had leapt into her throat, and her pulse was about to burst her veins. She had never beheld such beauty. At the time she could not fathom why the Prince hid such a divine visage, but then and there she was determined to get him to lose that mask. Surely the people he ruled would love him even more if they could only gaze upon such wonder. She vowed to find a way. That was some time ago and she was close to giving up. She tried different things and was almost shunned and sent away a few times, but she was beloved of the Prince. She realized that he needed her for much more than what pleasures her body provided. They would often talk and study together. She would be an ear for his blowing off the steam of a day's work. Ruri and the blind Rebecca were the closest things to family that Sheenid had; barring his wife Tellen who was always away on diplomatic business. She would find a way to help him, she just had to.

*   *   *

Sheenid had finished reviewing the reports and video of the mysterious ship that had used the Saragothra gate. It could be a fluke, but he was sure that this ship was similar to what they had at Angolkor. He called for a gravicar to take him, thought for a moment, and then called for Ruri. She would help him figure out what had to be done. When they left the palace, Sheenid marveled at the weather on Askelon. Here at the palace it was monsoon season. The gravicar glided along the causeway that ran several kilometers to the spaceport. He idly watched as the beating rain made a grand lightshow as it hit the force shielding that protected the causeway. He called ahead to the Captain of his personal jumper with instructions to prepare to launch. This man was a jovial sort, always ready with some humorous story. As Sheenid and Ruri exited the gravicar and headed down the pathway to the launch area, the service personnel they passed always bowed low and avoided looking directly at him. He had once beheaded two porters who had stared dumbfounded at his masked face; he regretted that incident ever since. It *did* make it easier on his condition.

The jumper launched without incident and quickly took them to the southern continent. Sparsely habited, it was ideal for a secret underground base that was undetectable from space. It was quite sunny at this location. Bay doors opened as if a giant hole appeared where once there was only grassland, and the jumper maneuvered inside. The bay doors closed overhead and the jumper alighted on a landing pad. They bid the Captain good day and took a lift down several levels. Then a tram took them north a kilometer or two. When they exited, they had arrived at a vast cavernous space which housed a complete starship and pieces of another, both of similar design. In fact, Sheenid knew the design was the same as the mysterious ship from the Saragothra report. They were in fact of Pruathan design. However, the ship that was reported on was a mix of Pruathan and Human design, while these were a mix of Pruathan design and that of an alien enemy. His territories have been threatened by a powerful new foe for some time now. They were strange alien creatures who had taken several Human worlds to expand their species. They seemed to have adapted Pruathan technology, as evidenced by their weapons and ships. It was a miracle that his forces had captured this one and disabled another. Their all-female crews, or at least their anatomy suggested female, had been of no use, dying before giving up any information. What information he had was from survivors from one of the worlds they had usurped. These creatures called themselves Bevidzilfpaed, which was a mouthful, so most Humans shortened it to BZP. They would come in large ships and land shock troops of male warriors led by females; the females seemed to be more intelligent. They preferred not to kill many Humans; it was later found out that they had stasis devices to preserve Humans to use as a food source. He had sent a carrier group to prevent further incursions, but the enemy had all but wiped them out in the last attack. Half his fleet now formed a cordon to prevent further advances, but they seemed to be satisfied with the gains they had made for now. All attempts at contacting them had failed.

Sheenid had kept Ruri informed of all of this, and had briefed her on the mysterious ship reports on the way to Angolkor. His scientists hadn't had much luck in figuring out the Pruathan technology, much less the technology of the BZP, so he asked Ruri for advice on how to use this new information.

"Your Highness knows well the nobles of the Saitow Conglomerate under whom this new ship is registered. There seem to be only two options of action in this case: one, you negotiate with the Saitow family to gain information, or better, some engineers who are familiar with Pruathan technology. Or two, you track down and capture this mystery ship." Sheenid always thought that Ruri knew the best courses of action. Unfortunately, it was up to him to choose the best among them. With the enemy at the gate and time an unsteady ally, he knew he must choose wisely.

9

Goh Takagawa had reached a point that was well ahead of the Captain's schedule. He didn't want to get too far ahead; he needed to train the new crewmembers he had been assigned and needed to save work for that. Kintaro Sagura had his own work to deal with, so their sparring matches had dwindled. Goh figured it wouldn't hurt to get some quality down-time planet-side, so he hopped a shuttle to the surface. It may have been 1400 ship-time, but it was just under midnight on the planet. Roseglade was known for its nightlife, and the town near the Saitow estate was no exception. Goh wasn't looking to hook up with a local woman; it would just remind him of his loss. He found one of the many gambling establishments instead. Back in the rebellion on Calliope, he had been quite skilled at the old earth game of Poker, so he liked to try his luck once in a while.

It seemed he had picked one of the seedier establishments. The whole place was darkened except for spotlights over the various players' tables. He watched the action there for a while before joining a few merchant marines who beckoned him over. It was their mistake. Most left the table before losing so much that they would not be able to buy any more drinks. The exception was an old guy who had been giving him a run for his MU. Unfortunately for the man, Goh had finally managed to get him to run out of money before the last hand was over. Perhaps confidence overwhelmed the old sailor; he wasn't about to fold, offering Goh all the contents in his backpack. Goh really didn't care what was in the thing; he just wanted to get satisfaction from clearing the table. He won, took the old man's bag, and then bought the group a round of drinks for their trouble. He forced a quaint sum of MU on the old man's token ring in case the bag contained any kit items. Even sailors had to brush their teeth.

With the night on the planet throwing him off schedule, he headed back on the shuttle to get a bite to eat and some shuteye. He bribed a Messman into making him a tray he could take to his room; he wanted to hit the bunk after filling his stomach; he was *that* tired. He ate while listening to some contemporary local music he had downloaded off the GCN, and going through the contents of the bag. As he had suspected, it contained the sailor's toiletry items, a couple of books of questionable content, and a curious looking box. The box was beautifully carved in intricate patterns. He tried to open it, but found it locked. A closer inspection of the bag yielded no key. He set the box on a shelf next to a plate that belonged to his late mother. When he was through eating, he got up suddenly to go brush his teeth, knocking a salt shaker from the tray, spilling salt in a fan shape on the table. As he ritualistically pinched a bit of salt from the table to throw over his shoulder to ward off bad luck, he was shocked to see words form in the untouched area: I AM HERE. He brushed the salt away quickly as if erasing the words would help him deny their existence. *He knew he was tired, but tired enough to hallucinate?* He shuffled off to the head to brush his teeth and ready for bed.

* * *

Sanae, in her disguise as Kintaro Sagura, busied

herself checking the catalog of star maps with the onboard AI. She was trying to find a way to determine the color-coding system that the Pruatha had used and extrapolate them using the current system of codes for Rangelley and Ros'Loper Imperial charts. She also needed time to think, and busy work helped her do so most times. She needed to come up with a plan to rescue the Princess, and if possible, take over the ship so she could return it to the Empire. The Princess was priority of course. The Marines had stopped guarding her yes, but Sanae was sure they had other means to watch her. Perhaps the new retainers were spies. However, it appeared that Haruka Koritsu trusted them, so that was not likely. The Marines controlled access to the shuttles, by order of the Captain, so there was no way to get the Princess on board one of those. Having the Princess fake an illness was a possibility, but would likely be countered by Doctor Rosel's skill. She had a top of the line medical facility on deck six. Sanae knew there had to be some way; it would just take her time to figure it out. In the meantime, she would just have to think about it, send reports to Contact Sigma when she could, and hope for rescue. If rescue came, she would be ready to aid the Princess as was her duty.

*   *   *

It had been some days since Princess Shirae's dinner with the Captain. She had thought long and hard on the possibility that his words were true. She finally got up the courage to investigate. She knew these things were not true; if she watched these "news" programs, she could verify their duplicity and confront Saitow with the facts. She had Ran-chan seek out a crewmember to escort them. Shirae knew that Ran and Amane had to be spies for the Captain, but for some reason Haruka trusted them. Shirae decided to trust them as well; besides Ran-chan knew some great massage techniques. Ran returned with a bewildered crewman that looked out of place. The man was sweaty and bowed excessively. He was clearly nervous to be so close to a royal. When asked to lead them to the media room, he apologized profusely, giving excuses about being a cargo handler, being a new crewmember, and not having access to that part of the ship. He was dismissed, and almost tripped over himself in his haste to get away from them.

Ran-chan consulted with Haruka-chan and it was decided that they would venture forth, the four of them together, in order to find a suitable crewmember and the media room. They took the lift down to deck two and poked their heads into the general mess. They found no one. Then they took the lift to deck three. They knew immediately that this was the billeting deck for the larger contingent of the crew; there were many people scurrying about, some of them almost in shock to see this procession of ladies on their deck. Most of them reminded Shirae of the sweaty man; an encounter she wished not to repeat. Haruka-chan apparently found a candidate for them because she pounced like a cat in the direction of a gentleman who had a somewhat modified version of an Imperial uniform jacket flung over his shoulder. They were out of earshot, but it seemed to Shirae that they must have exchanged some heated words; both came back toward them with less than happy looks on their faces. Haruka spoke, "Oujo-sama, this is crewman Lowey Jax. He will be accompanying us to the media room." Haruka turned from Shirae and looked directly at Jax who just stood there gawking. She kicked him lightly in the ankle.

Jax just bowed without taking his eyes off of them. "Princess...this way." Jax started off toward the lift. Shirae didn't think she would like this man; he seemed a bit cocky for a common crewman. She could practically hear Haruka-chan growling; she seemed rather upset.

Jax brought them down to deck six. From Shirae's conversations with Doctor Kuremoto, she knew that deck six was the only deck where one could access all three lifts on the ship. They took a long corridor to the center lift and up to deck three which opened into the ship's chapel. The Priest, Stephen Jing was his name if Shirae recalled correctly, seemed to light up at his alter as they exited the lift, but then returned to being somber. He must have realized that they were just passing through. They went through a hatch on the back right of the chapel to another gray corridor. Just a few more steps and they entered the media room. No one was using it at the moment. Jax bowed and said, "Here we are ladies. Now if you will excuse me..."

"You must not leave." Haruka had been so fast to block Jax's exit that he stood there blinking at her. "The Captain's instructions were for a crewmember to operate the equipment here for the Princess."

"That's not happening. I was on my way to the mess when you people shanghaied me. I have a pretty good group of...willing participants in a game of Darkats lined up. I said I would lead you here and that's all the contact I can stand with you Imperials." Jax seemed like he was going to say something else but looked awkwardly at Shirae and held his tongue.

"Now listen here you, you-"

Shirae decided it was time to show some authority so she cut Haruka off. "Mr. Jax it appears to me that you have some issues with my retainers and I. I understand from your file that you are a conscript of the Imperial Navy. Unfortunately for me, I can no longer order you to do my bidding due to the circumstances I find myself in. However, I see in you the character of a good man. Your Captain has granted us access to this media room to seek the truth behind rumors of atrocities done in the name of my father. He gave us permission to get aid from any crewmember in his service. I implore you please help us." Shirae knew that Haruka-chan would be angry at this so she put a hand up to silence her. Jax seemed to contemplate the situation he was in. He spoke, "Princess, I haven't had a chance to eat-"

"Fear not, Mr. Jax." Shirae turned to Ran, "Ran-chan, seek out the Captain's Cook and have him bring food for the five of us here to this room." Turning back to Jax she smiled coyly, "Mr. Jax, I assume you have no objections to being fed?" Jax seemed to fret a bit, but shook his head to indicate he did not. "Good. Please find this 'news' on the GCN for us while we wait."

* * *

Lowey Jax found himself in the strangest of circumstances. He had been on his way to the General Mess to score big off a few suckers who had yet to hear of his amazing skill and luck at Darkats. That was now impossible, as he was about to sit down to dinner with people who were just a little too far above his pay grade. He supposed that it was a decent trade off; him having chow straight from the Captain's Mess, not that normal stuff they served the regulars. To have to keep company with Imperials, and a royal no less, is what really got his gut. His homeworld was outside the recognized territories of the Ros'Loper Empire, but a little too far from the trades to be of any value to anyone other than its inhabitants. His people were able to keep most of the tech running due to most of them being of above average intelligence, he being included of course. What few ships they had were mostly used to affect trade with neighboring worlds, and were no match for the Imperial destroyers that came. His people were subjugated under the Empire's heal and he and a lot of his peers were conscripted into Imperial service. He didn't even know what had become of his siblings or parents. He had been pretty serious about not helping when that bitch Haruka had accosted him in the passageway. Unfortunately, she had threatened his manhood and he could tell she meant it, the way she showed him the knife she concealed.

The Princess broke his reverie. "Crewman Jax, won't you please activate the media wall?"

Jax realized they were all staring at him; even Ran who had returned. "Oh, well... Princess, you really don't want to watch the news before you eat. You would all lose your appetite I'd wager. Might I suggest a fiction video? There is a great new comedy about the Deidriad!" He waited while the Princess contemplated his suggestion, all the while her retainer Ran repeated "I like comedy!" several times and the quiet one kept nodding her head. The bitch Haruka was staring at him while sulking, standing a little away from them.

"Very well. I am curious as to how the Deidriad could

be somehow considered comedic." The Princess finally said. Jax inputted the title and the wall sprung to life with images of the opening music. The video was about two Deidriad Humans, one a Bolchinde surface dweller, and the other a Kreagern underwater dweller, who were forced to live together off-world. The comedy of the story was from the impossibility of the two cohabitating and how they somehow pulled it off with rather messy results, especially since the Bolchinde character was a neat-freak. The funniest part was when they both brought their girlfriends to their shared quarters. Jax observed the women as they watched: the quiet one just sat quietly, while Ran was racked by fits of laughter, all the while jabbing Haruka in the arm at the good parts. The Princess seemed amused enough. During the video their dinner was served. Jax ate with the Princess while the retainers ate apart from them. He hadn't had real beef steak in years.

* * *

Princess Shirae ate quickly and watched the comedy that Jax had suggested. It *was* rather amusing seeing the two distinct cultures of the Deidriad thrown together in such a manner. However, she couldn't enjoy it because she was keen to get to the bottom of what the Captain had suggested. She allowed the dinner video because she was not keen on staying hungry, even if she did lose her appetite; it would come like a bad dream in the night making her stomach sound like a vulgar orchestra. The video finally ended soon after the service had been taken away. She made a point to tell the staff to thank Bonifacio for another fine meal; she would have loved having him at one of the palaces.

When everything seemed settled, she asked Lowey Jax to queue up the "news" once more.

"The program guide says you have a choice of inner-imperium, extra-imperium, New Rangelley Alliance, Yolandan, Xane, or Taibor Prime news. I suggest the inner-imperium; it looks to be the bleakest. For what you are looking for, that'd be best." Jax sounded just a little smug at that last remark.

"Is not the inner-imperium official Ros'Loper reporting?" she assumed as much.

"Oh no, Princess, you won't get any of that out here. That's only fed to the loyalists. These are all independent agencies that thrive on getting down to the heart of the matter."

"Very well. Show us the inner-imperium programming."

Jax queued up the requested newsfeed. A strong looking woman with short blonde hair was introducing a segment on recent imperial strong-arm activity on the planet Spandau. Apparently, according to eye-witnesses, the Special Services Corps were once again harassing the general population; video to follow.

"*The following video is of a Special Services unit landing in farmland south of the gubernatorial seat on Spandau. Scenes may not be suitable for the weak of heart, so viewer discretion is strongly advised.*"

The woman on screen was replaced by a hazy video that was just getting focused through some sort of window. The window was thrown open and the muffled sound of heavy troop transports landing became louder; one landing in the fields directly out from the view of the camera. Another woman's voice was heard over the noise. *"We have multiple troop transports landing all around us. Troops are disembarking from the hatches. They appear to wear the uniforms of the Imperial Special Services. We are hidden in an outlying building to the main farming complex here. Oh look! They are using flame throwers to burn the fields...they're burning the crops! We have to get out of here! Are you getting this off? I don't know if we'll...Let's try the roof..."* the video ended, replaced by the short haired woman. *"The area was searched three days later and the charred remains of Valan Huntsman and her Recorder, Jack Pulitzin were found in the gutted-out building. Nothing remained of the entire farm. Several other nearby farms were also destroyed. We wish all those affected, especially Valan and Jack, peace."* The view was replaced by images of the two people from the video with their life dates.

Several other atrocious events with and without video were reported on different worlds within the Empire. Shirae tried to make sense of it all. These things could easily have been done with video enhancements, but why go to such lengths to discredit the Empire? It was unmistakable. In a few of the videos the uniforms of the troops could plainly be seen; all of them were of the Special Services Corps. There were no reports of regular Army, Navy, or Marines engaged in these atrocities. In one report a Marine contingent had actually fought the SSC and held their ground until overwhelmed by force of numbers. The Special Services Corps was supposed to be a small contingent of troops loyal to the Imperial court and only accountable to it. These reports put their numbers well above that of each of the military services. Shirae's father had not mentioned the SSC to her other than to warn that their use must not be considered lightly. *Why was her father using them now? Did he not have the loyalty and love of the people?*

Shirae looked about and caught Lowey Jax gawking at her. His face lit up when she looked his way.

"Well Princess, what you think?" was all the man said.

"Thank you, Lowey Jax. I trust I can call on your assistance on a future occasion?" Shirae managed to remain calm despite the man's brusqueness.

"Anytime Princess. Anytime." Jax said as he bowed on his way out the hatch.

Haruka came at once to Shirae's side. "Oujo-sama..." but Shirae was already making for the hatch to leave this awful room.

*   *   *

Captain Saitow was busy checking on the preparations for the upcoming voyage. He hadn't felt this exhilarated in years. He could finally do what he always wanted; to be his own boss, at least to a degree. Sure, he was working under the Conglomerate, but he could go anywhere and do anything that he wanted; as long as he produced results. In his quest for Pruathan technology he would have a great adventure. He had almost forgotten about the shadow his mother cast over his ship when a hail sounded at the hatch. He acknowledged it and the hatch swooshed open to reveal his new Chief Steward Odmanar Zelek. Saitow's reverie was quickly vanquished by the fellow. Saitow felt that the job of Chief Steward was the most undeserved billet in the entire Navy. Since the *Iwakina* was no longer a naval vessel, he felt that it no longer needed a Chief Steward. He had made this plain to the Conglomerate, which is most likely why this man was here now. He was the one appointed by them to lead the augments from corporate. Saitow tried to be as civil as possible.

"OZ, how nice to see you!" He practically beamed. OZ was the nickname that Saitow had given the man and, OZ being a Bolchinde Deidriad, Saitow knew he would fall in love with the moniker right off.

OZ seemed rather serious and pointed at his tablet. "Captain, am I to understand that you have given responsibility of all of the new personnel to original members of the crew?"

Saitow was noncommittal. "Umm...yes?"

"Captain, you must be fully aware by now of the position that I have been given aboard this ship. I have been given responsibility of the majority of the new crewmembers who come hand-picked from all over the Conglomerate's holdings. Regina Saitow gave strict instructions that I fulfill my duties in regards to these personnel assignments..."

Saitow raised a hand to cut the man off. "OZ. what is the title of your billet upon this ship?"

OZ was slightly taken aback by being cut-off, "Chief Steward, of course."

"Very good. Now, if I look up the billet of Chief Steward in the Merchant Mariner's Manual, would I find 'Supervisor of Cargo Handlers', or 'Overseer of Engineers' anywhere in there?"

"Well no, but..."

"I already have an excellent cook who now has a very good staff, thanks to Mother. You still have the Crew Mess and tidying up to worry about with ample staff under your responsibility."

OZ seemed to sense where this was going. "But your mother gave me strict orders..."

Saitow suddenly stood up out of his chair dwarfing the short man in front of him. "*My Mother* is not the Captain of this ship. She may mean well and want to be assured of the safety of the crew she has provided, but that is *my* responsibility not yours. If you feel you cannot accept these arrangements, you are free to leave my ship. Have I made myself clear?"

OZ flinched when Saitow had stood, but regained his composure quickly. "Crystal. Good day Captain." With that the man left.

Saitow sat back down and took his pack of sims out of the desk drawer. This fellow was going to be more nuisance than he originally anticipated.

* * *

Nanami Oliver had been given the assignment to reset all of the weapons caches within the ship after her return from accompanying Doctor Kuremoto. She had a great time listening to the old man's stories. She

131

could not consider the Old Guy attractive; at least he wasn't her type. This made her realize that she had not even considered any type of relationship since her family was slaughtered by the Imperium; she had only been thinking of revenge until now. She considered the fact that she hadn't felt this alive in all of her 28 years of living; maybe she could even consider a real relationship for a change.

As the group of Marines she was with approached the first cache location, she considered the best code to set all of the caches to; an eight digit numeric. They would be locked out until a time that one of the senior officers felt they would be needed and overrode the protocol, like if the ship was boarded by a hostile force. At that time the code could then be used to access the cache. With a smile she settled on 04065966. Every officer on ship should *have* to know the date of her very own birthday.

MESSAGES

1

Sanae, in her disguise as Kintaro Sagura, was making final calibrations on the navigation systems on the bridge. One of the skills she learned in the Sparrow program was how to eavesdrop on targets without being detected. She was using this skill now to follow the conversation that the Captain and First Officer were having at the control chair. They had a view screen up and were discussing possible routes to pursue for a first mission. It was apparent that they had to deliver something for the Conglomerate on Quizilax, but then they would decide to choose any number of jobs waiting on Betae or Nusibitor. Sanae made a mental note; she would risk sending another message to Contact Sigma with this information. Perhaps then the Imperium would come to their aid.

Just then, Nanami Oliver came on the bridge and reported to the Captain. All the preparations for this voyage were set. To Sanae, this woman seemed like a puppy dog in front of the Captain; this annoyed Sanae, and then she felt annoyed at being annoyed. She quickly sent off the message via a remote random terminal patched through her personal terminal hidden in her quarters.

* * *

Goh heard the All-Call to the bridge sound; it must be time to shove off. He secured his terminal, grabbed his tablet, and headed out of Engineering toward the lift. Just then his tablet beeped three times; the signal that one of his tracking programs had gotten a hit. He found the nearest interface jack and plugged his tablet in; another non-tagged message had been sent from a terminal on deck six. He verified the terminal had not been logged on to as he suspected. He thought about notifying the Captain, but his decryption program was on the verge of cracking the message code, so he decided to wait. It would only be a matter of days now. Then he could not only bring the messages to light, but have transcripts for the Captain to figure out. He downloaded a copy of the message, unplugged the tablet and made his way to the bridge.

* * *

Captain Saitow was ready to get this show on the road so to speak. This would be the true maiden voyage of the new *Iwakina*, a free booting ship for hire. He was first to deliver whatever nefarious goods his mother had had loaded into the cargo hold to Quizilax, where a substantial corporate depot was being run. From there he was free to go in search of Pruathan technology, all the while disguising the *Iwakina's* true mission by taking on passengers and cargo from various worlds across the Quadrant. The ship had been outfitted for this purpose with staterooms near Doctor Kuremoto's quarters; all supplied from deck six via lift. He had ample cargo capacity; might as well use it.

He had Sagura plot a course and jumps to Quizilax. Mother had been kind enough to provide him with knowledge of all of their bases of operation including where substantial corporate fleets could be used as a shield from pesky Imperials. The Conglomerate had grown so large that it was not taken lightly by any political entity. However, they would be on their own at Quizilax. Sensitive operations were being conducted there that required a very small footprint to avoid suspicion from the competition. They headed out of the Roseglade system and made that first jump that always made his skin tingle.

* * *

Princess Shirae knew instantaneously that the *Iwakina* had initiated its Jump Vortex Engines. She dispatched Ran to go find out where they were headed. She wished that the Captain would keep her more informed; she would have to speak with him about it soon. She was apprehensive though, because she did not want to be reminded of his challenge to watch the news programming from the GCN. She had enlisted

Lowey Jax on a weekly basis and watched several hours of reports on the Imperium. There were many things she did not understand, but it was plainly clear – the Special Services Corps were being used to demoralize the Empire. Surely this could not be her father's doing. Her father was a kind and benevolent ruler. But she had been instructed that only the Court could direct the SSC, no one else. She decided that she would try and get a dispatch off to her father and find out the answers.

* * *

Chancellor Aisou was mulling over the latest message from Sparrow 64. It seemed like the time to test the latest acquisition to his ambitions – several of the latest destroyers manufactured exclusively for his Special Services Corps. Having three or so destroyers drop out of hyperspace in front of you should make this Captain Saitow soil his trousers; possibly even get him to surrender the vessel. If the Princess and Sparrow 64 happen to perish if the Captain resists, then they will both be martyred as more mistakes the Emperor has made in his decline. Aisou called for his trusted lieutenant and had three of the new ships dispatched at once, destination Quizilax.

2

Gunter looked with wonder at the cruiser's passenger view screen. There ahead of them lay the massive Pruathan city ship, the *City of Light*. The Church had discovered it on an off-trades world that they had devoted a mission to. It was the first of many Pruathan technological finds the Universal Church had discovered over a thousand-year period, proving to the Counsel of Twelve that surely the Pruatha had been angels to provide such wonders to the Church. Gunter was both nervous and excited to be one of the very few acolytes to be invited to the *City of Light*. It had been a rough journey.

Gunter had been deposited on Mine 213 with the non-mutineers to deliver a message to the Church. He attended to those of the crew who were adherents as best as he could, but he kept a separate backpack of supplies in the eventuality that these people might be slaughtered by the Imperials that they represented. To be sure, Gunter had heard about the atrocities being carried out by the Special Services Corps, and he could recognize the uniforms. So, when the transport came to rescue them, he kept back in the shadows. He immediately feared the worst; the soldiers who came were of the SSC. Gunter had managed to make a reconnaissance of the area while they waited for rescue, and had discovered a secret route out of the mine enclosure. He hid as best as he could until the SSC and the rescued were gone, and then he made for the religious compound that was a standard on all mining community planets. Each contained a tachyon emitting homing beacon which he would activate in a day or two to avoid anyone but the Church intercepting it. Then he had dug in for a long wait.

A week and a half went by before the sleek white shape of a Universal Church cruiser came to hover over his position. It landed a few hundred meters away. An access hatch had opened invitingly for him to enter. He was debriefed and given a decent meal before being assigned quarters where he remained until the approach to the *City of Light*. As they got closer, he could see why the massive ship was named thus; what must have been a million points of light clustered all over the many spired structures of this huge and wondrous thing that filled the void of space.

*   *   *

After the ship had docked, Gunter was escorted into the *City*. He flinched at the thought of looking like a pauper against the grandness of his surroundings. He had ripped his clothes in places and had a slight gash along his hand and forearm from climbing on the mining planet. The inner-side of this part of the city was a large collection of buildings inside an enclosed dome-like structure. There were many people scurrying about, but none ventured to glance his way; probably because he was flanked by two imposing priests of the Elite Corps who were escorting him. They brought him inside a darkly painted structure where they were greeted by an even more imposing figure. Gunter knew to immediately take a knee and bow his head in the presence of a full Cardinal. The man spoke. "Dear Acolyte Gunter please, there is no need for formalities. Time is of the essence. Follow me." The Cardinal nodded to the two priests who left the room, closing the hatch behind them.

"I am Cardinal Sorbeer. We are going to go into the heart of the city; do you recognize the significance of this?" Gunter was astonished; not only was he visiting the *City of Light*, but he would be allowed within the city's inner reaches. This was unheard of for anyone who had yet to reach the rank of Priest. "Yes, Your Eminence." Gunter said humbly.

"Soon you will be tested, I assure you." Cardinal Sorbeer motioned for him to enter a small dark room ahead of him. Once they were both inside Sorbeer keyed the hatch closed. "This small room will transport us where we need to go. Do not worry about what happens, just remain still where you stand." With that Sorbeer touched a large metal bulge in the wall behind them which seemed to spark into the man's hand. Some sort of field engulfed Gunter and he felt himself lifted slightly and deposited in an almost identical room. It was as if the room itself had changed around him. Gunter felt different too. It was as if he had slept soundly for several hours. He no longer felt the pain from his injury and when he looked at where it had been, it was gone. He felt a slight tingling at the back of his right shoulder and he reached up for it with his left hand.

"That, my young Acolyte, is the mark of the angels for using their technology. We have been transported half way across the city." Sorbeer keyed the hatch open and stepped out into a brightly lit corridor. Gunter followed. They went down the long corridor for several minutes, and then entered a hatch that opened as they approached. Inside, there was a bed, a desk, and a set of priest's formal robes minus the official purple sash that all priests wore within the city. Cardinal Sorbeer turned to Gunter and spoke. "These are your quarters while you stay among us. You will remain here until the preparations are made. I believe you have a message for me?" Sorbeer held out his right wrist toward Gunter. Gunter touched his own wrist which contained his token-ring to pass the message from Brother Stephen.

"Good. Change from your old self to your new self while you wait, Brother." The Cardinal then left him.

Gunter marveled at the meaning of these minor events. Even though he had only been here less than an hour, his destiny had been forever altered. It was clear that Brother Stephen had been correct; he knew not what it was, but a higher destiny awaited him.

* * *

"The contents of this report are further evidence of God's grace in facilitating the proliferation of the Angel's technology to those whom we are most confident will put it to proper use. Namely out of the hands of the Ros'Loper and possibly into the hands of the New Rangelley." Cardinal Sorbeer was a bit nervous to be addressing the Council of Twelve. Although he knew each of them personally, he was intimidated by the immense power these men held. Each wore a silver mask to denote the station each held; one for each of the Lord's Apostles. They made the decisions that molded the organization and mission of the Universal Church. They were only beholden to His Holiness the Pope.

The one who represented Simon the Zealot spoke first, "Do we truly wish for those outside the Church to possess such technology?" this caused murmurs among the rest. Simon was expected to be the one to raise some dissent, even when there was a quorum.

Thomas spoke next, "It may just be inevitable for the Angel's technology to be put to use; it pervades the whole of this galaxy in many forms." This elicited many nods of agreement.

"It is only proper that the technology is used by those we deem worthy of helping the cause of the Church." This time Matthew had added a remark.

Andrew spoke next, "Our agents have established that this rogue Captain is in league with his family who controls the whole of the Saitow Conglomerate. It may not be in our best interests to have such a powerful entity acquiring the Angel's technology so readily." The silence that followed this remark was almost palpable.

James the Lesser finally broke the stillness. "Perhaps we can persuade the Conglomerate to assist the New Rangelley; surely they would be surprised and delighted to have access to Prince Sheenid's acquisitions." More nods of agreement.

Sorbeer stiffened slightly. He was unaware of most of the information that the Twelve were freely discussing in his presence. He suspected that they trusted him, but this was confirmation that both elated him and filled him with apprehension. It wasn't like he aspired of leaving the *City*, but this would portend his permanent station here.

Matthias, who rarely spoke unless required to, asked, "What of the Prince's desires to keep things under wraps?" as if in unison, all of the silver masks save his turned in his direction next to the empty center seat as if a ghost had just spoken.

It was Peter who finally spoke, "What of it? Prince Sheenid has always been a supporter of the Church and will surely acquiesce to the desires of the Church in the best interests of his people and the galaxy in general. We should put this to a decision. We will let the Saitow Conglomerate know with no uncertain terms that they will be allowed to pursue their interests in regards to the starship *Iwakina* as long as they assist the New Rangelley with their engineering of the Angel's technology that Sheenid has acquired." Peter removed the large silver key that adorned his neck and placed it vertical before him. All the others of the Twelve did the same.

"Very well. Cardinal Sorbeer, please send in Cardinal Detrich on your way out and thank you for your service here today," Peter removed his mask for a moment and smiled at the bewildered man. Sorbeer bowed deeply. When he rose and headed toward the hatch, he saw that the sliver mask once again adorned the great man's face.

* * *

What surprised Gunter the most was not that he was granted the simple ordination ceremony that made him a full-fledged Priest of the Church. What astonished him was that he had then been appointed to the Elite Corps without the requisite three year waiting period and extra training. It must have been clear to the Church that he had done all of the training of an Elite Corps supplicant and then some. Brother Stephen had been a hard yet merciful instructor. *God Bless him.* Now it seemed that Gunter was to be given a mission of extreme import. It had been a month of life within the city, filled with priestly training and devotionals, when Cardinal Sorbeer once again visited him in his quarters.

"Gunter, I have come to give you a very important

mission which you will be more than happy to partake in. You will be joining Brother Stephen Jing once again." Sorbeer stood there near the door smiling and seemed to be watching him for a reaction. Gunter smiled and stood, offering the Cardinal a seat.

Sorbeer raised a hand. "That won't be necessary. We will leave at once. Come."

Gunter followed the Cardinal down the grand corridor and up a level, going in the direction of the center of the city. After several minutes walking they reached a set of immense doors. Sorbeer stood in front of them and rapped twice. After a minute or so the doors opened slowly, revealing a huge room whose ceiling must have gone up several levels and was lost in darkness. They entered and the doors closed behind them. In the room arranged around the center were a number of priests who began to chant. Sorbeer brought Gunter to the side and explained the procedure he was about to endure. "This is the ceremony of holy spirits. Gunter you will be host to the spirit Miriam who will be giving a message to Brother Stephen and several individuals of import on the *Iwakina*. You will carry her with you and she will only appear when the time is right. Once your mission is complete, she will leave you and you will then assist Brother Stephen in Church business. Do you understand?"

Gunter was both elated and apprehensive, yet he spoke with confidence, "I will not falter Your Eminence."

"Good. Now enter the circle at the center of the

room."

Gunter did as he was told and the chant from the priests surrounding him got louder and louder. It seemed as if some techno style music was added and Gunter felt a massive weight seem to fall upon his shoulders. Looking up he saw that the darkness that was the ceiling had now turned to a dense white light. No, the density of it was ever shifting as if thousands of light clusters were undulating to the song made by the priests. Gunter felt the weight lift off his shoulders and an elation that he had never felt before took him; his whole-body shivering. Just then one of the light clusters shot down and entered his body. He felt deep warmth as if being held in his own mother's arms and a voice as soft as rain tell him, "I am here." Gunter dropped to his knees and he felt he was experiencing the life of a young girl who was martyred for her beliefs in the one true God in the flash of a moment. He sobbed audibly.

"Do not grieve for me, for you give me life and purpose." He heard from inside himself. Cardinal Sorbeer was there and helping him to his feet. The great room was as it had been before. The Priests were now silent.

"Come, you must rest before your journey begins." The Cardinal led him back to his quarters.

* * *

Miriam had led a simple farmer's life on an off-trade world called Arimas. She was part of a cult of worshippers who devoted their lives to the belief in the one true God just as their ancestors had. The majority of the planet's inhabitants had taken to worshipping a pantheon of three zealots that had crash landed there long ago and performed some sort of miraculous deed, therefore enshrining their memory to the point where they began to be worshipped. The true believers were few and some had been wiped out by the Arimas Three adherents; it was just a matter of time before they came to Miriam's settlement. It happened on her sixteenth summer. They came and burned down her village, rounding up those that showed themselves while the ones who hid burned to death. The men were murdered on the spot; the women were not so lucky. Miriam was raped and beaten for hours before she became unconscious. Eventually she awoke. Sitting up and taking in her surroundings she felt very odd. There was no pain from the awful events that had transpired, the village smoldered all around her. She got up and walked around a bit. Then turning back to where she came from, she was shocked to see her own battered body lying there broken in the dust.

After some time wandering, she realized that she was now a disembodied spirit bound to the village that was her home; it became her desolate prison. She lost track of the time she spent there. Perhaps several generations came and went while she waited. She prayed several times daily for salvation. On the rare occasion that a passerby went hastily through the village she would somehow manage to get their attention; only to watch helplessly as they ran off in fear. The day finally came when she was to leave her village. A man came wearing a long coat with a purple sash and lantern on a pole. He came upon her and showed no fear. He spoke in a gentle tone that was soothing to Miriam's ears. "Come walk with me child, your time here has passed."

Miriam did as she was beckoned. Before she could not leave the edge of the village; some sort of wall kept her from moving on. However, now she could walk out beside this man of power. He spoke to her as they walked. "I am George, a priest of the Universal Church. I have been told that you were there waiting in that village of true adherents for salvation. Child it is here." They came upon a magnificent white ship and onto the ship they went.

Since that time, she has been dancing with other spirits, learning the truth of the Church and waiting for the time when she could be useful and ascend to the kingdom of God. That time was upon her. She had been given several messages to deliver from the power that was God after all.

* * *

Gunter had awoken refreshed. After a meal and

prayers, he was given a pack of supplies and a map. He would have to make the day's journey across the city on foot; spirits could not travel by teleportation. Cardinal Sorbeer assured him he would meet him before departure.

3

Things were going smoothly. The *Iwakina* had delivered the goods to the base at Quizilax and was exiting the system in preparation for the jump to Nusibitor. Captain Saitow was in a pretty damn good mood.

"Sagura, set standard jumps to Nusibitor."

"Captain, navigation seems to be down for the moment. I'll have to recalibrate the algorithms." Sagura looked sheepishly back at Satiow. The Captain's good mood was vanishing. "How long will that take?"

"Maybe ten minutes." Sagura was already furiously tapping at his console.

A couple of minutes passed when a proximity warning sounded at Sagura's station. "Sensors indicate two hyperspace windows bearing 170/190 and 170/170; two ships, unknown classes." Sagura reported.

"What are they doing?" Captain Saitow wasn't one to jump to conclusions; this was the normal hyperspace departure point for this system.

Nanami Oliver spoke up, "One seems to be hailing us. Audio only."

"Open a-" the Captain was cut off by a tremor in the ship which coincided with a muffled explosion.

"A third hyperspace window opened, ship bearing 175/195; they are firing on us!" Sagura almost yelled as he continued to furiously input to his console.

"Shields! Sagura get us out of here!" although he could put up one hell of a fight, Saitow had no intention of getting into a battle so soon after getting his ship.

Suddenly the ship jumped and they were 50 light years away. Nanami reported a hull breach in quarters on deck two. The Princess's quarters were there. He sent his XO to check on her and the damage.

"What the hell was that? Are we being followed?" Saitow wanted to know and he wanted to know now.

"No contacts in pursuit. Scans indicate unknown configuration of the three ships, but they were all the same and IFF indicates Shinohara Heavy Industry hulls. Jump engines are charging for the next jump." Sagura did his best to make up for the lapse in navigation.

The XO's voice came over the ship's internal comms, "The Princess is safe; the breach was on the other side of the ship. Only *Sagura's* quarters are sealed off." Saitow suppressed a slight feeling of satisfaction at hearing this news. He glanced at Sagura who was still furiously tapping away at his console.

"Very well. Get back up here." Saitow sat back in his control chair and pondered the meaning of this provocation. Undesignated ships ambushing him at a designated hyperspace departure point. But didn't two of them just sit there with one attempting to hail him? Maybe they were a feint to give the other ship time for a sneak attack.

*　　*　　*

Sanae, in her Kintaro Sagura disguise, had been stalling for time with the fake report of a problem with jump algorithms in the hopes that Contact Sigma would send rescue. Her suspicions were answered with the appearance of two ships of unknown designation; surely, they were here to negotiate for the release of the princess. One even hailed. However, a third ship which matched the others came out of hyperspace and opened fire. Sanae had no choice but to correct the algorithms and jump the ship. *What in hell was the meaning of that?* Now her quarters were damaged. She hoped beyond hope that her equipment was safe.

*　　*　　*

Commander Carlton Sim of the Special Services Corps watched in horror as his chances of promotion to Admiral blinked out of existence through a hyperspace vortex. He was specifically chosen by the Chancellor himself to lead this mission to capture the *Iwakina.* He was given three of the new warships to command and coordinates where the target should be; all he had to do was wait for a signal from the proximity beacon, ambush the ship, and secure their surrender. But one of his ships was lagging behind, and when he was hailing the target, it emerged from hyperspace and started firing. Sim's target subsequently vanished and the third ship left just as quickly. It had been an impromptu mission and he had not known the Captains of the other ships. Mutiny seemed all the rage these days. Sim gave the command to Return-to-Base and resigned himself to whatever punishment was forthcoming.

* * *

It had been so easy; maybe too easy. Denton Bret had such a keen desire to get his revenge on Captain Saitow for the evils that had been perpetuated on his person that he had planned to commandeer a ship. Having been released from the investigation of the mutiny, he heard a rumor about officers being needed in the Special Services Corps; specifically, starship officers. As fortune would have it, Bret signed on and was assigned as a Watch Officer to the newly commissioned starship *Arbiter,* a light class destroyer. The systems of the ship were fully automated and controlled by a semi-autonomous Artificial Intelligence, which had been an illegal practice in the Rangelley era. All one needed was the override code and control of the ship was ensured. Bret found the code accidentally while doing routine diagnostics on the communications system one lonely night a week ago. All he had to do was change the code to one of his own and take control of the ship from the secondary con aft of the bridge when the time was right. Fortune smiled once again as the *Arbiter* was given orders to accompany two sister destroyers on a mission to capture the *Iwakina*. When the mission date came upon them, Bret was not on watch, so he locked himself in the secondary con until the beacon signal was detected. He then put his plan in motion. He took control, sealed all compartments on the ship, and instructed the AI to make FTL to the ambush site. When he arrived, he immediately opened fire on the hated *Iwakina*, damaging it before it could get away. He was disappointed to see it escape, but was sure he would get a second chance at it sooner or later. He would only have to keep this ship. He instructed the AI to FTL and thought about how to deal with the crew. It did not occur to him that he was doing the same thing Saitow had done; stealing an Imperial starship.

* * *

Captain Saitow sent word of the need for an escort as soon as they reached the Nusibitor system. The Saitow Conglomerate had a sizeable fleet there. He would have Takagawa effect repairs to the hull and have Sagura make damn sure that the algorithms or whatever he called them didn't go out of whack again.

He needed his ship in top shape, especially when he had clients aboard. He went to his quarters and keyed the comm unit at his desk. A holo-screen appeared with the face of a beautiful woman in frame.

"Margaret, how nice to see you again!" this was older brother's ex-wife, and his first transportation client.

The woman gave him a willful smile. "Glen, I am ready to get out of this dreadful place. Are you ready for me?"

"A shuttle is on its way. Bringing the children?"

"No. They left eons ago. I'll be catching up to them on Restoria."

"Excellent. I'll greet you personally once the shuttle docks here. See you soon!" Saitow keyed the link off before the woman could respond. He wasn't looking forward to her arrival at all; she could be so gabby. He was sure she would assail him with non-stop questions about the mutiny. Saitow resigned himself to making the best of it. She was a paying customer after all.

*　*　*

Goh Takagawa had ensured Sanae, as Sagura, that the cabin was now safe to enter. The ship had been instructed to repair the breach and life support had been restored to the space. Besides that, he said, the hatch wouldn't open if it wasn't safe. She tried the hatch. It whooshed open to reveal an uneven bulkhead and half of her bureau missing; the rest of it scorched. Her bedding and blankets were gone too. She quickly checked and found the terminal for programming her Sagura disguise was still there; the communications terminal was gone. This would put a major dampener on her means of contact with Contact Sigma. She would now be forced to rely on the times the ship had access to the GCN. No matter. She had a mission to fulfil and would not be deterred. She had better get a set of bedding from that new Chief Steward before her next shift started.

*   *   *

The plan was to get all of the crew onto two shuttles and send them to an off-trades world. That required cooperation. The Captain was a stubborn young fool, so Denton Bret was forced to take some drastic measures. Since the crew refused to cooperate, he would make an example of the command crew on the bridge. He vented the atmosphere, killing six of them including that young fool of a Captain. That did the trick as the remaining crew of 30 crowded onto the two shuttles he allowed access to. He had disabled weapons and navigation on both. Once all were aboard, he sealed the hatches, opened the shuttle bays and turned off the gravity. Both shuttles were ejected toward the planet that he had already forgotten the name of. Good luck to them. If they were lucky, they would survive the trip through the atmosphere and land in an ocean. If not, well it was none of his concern. He had revenge to see to and they had been in his way. He had the AI go to FTL, then sweep the ship for stragglers before walking the ship himself to be sure. His only regret was that he didn't have the crew clean up the bridge before they left; he would have to do that himself now.

4

Premier Corinth Hasegawa of the Taibor Freehold was slightly amused by the very redness of the Ros'Loper delegate who was demanding the return of the starship *Iwakina*. The redness was a response to Corinth's non-committal; how could she return a ship that wasn't in her possession? She was a staunch ally of the Saitow Family who brought a great deal of income to her constituents through jobs and services, not to mention tax revenue. It was hardly her place to go demanding sovereignty rights on property that wasn't even Taibor's. Her government didn't really have a very good relationship with the Ros'Loper Empire in the first place. She was tired and since the demands were flying anyway, she assured the ending of the conversation by reminding the Imperial Delegate that the Freehold's borders were not to be crossed by any more *Imperial* starships beyond diplomatic missions.

* * *

Captain Saitow was mulling over the latest missive from the Conglomerate. With his test run with Margaret followed by several other satisfied clients all ending in success, and there being no major divides among the crew, the *Iwakina* had been halfway across the galaxy in just a couple of months. They had even passed through the breach in the Great Barrier, the marvel that attested to the supreme advancement of the Pruatha; the barrier spanned light-years. The ship had to coordinate jumps with the Communication Stations that lined the breach; otherwise it would have been engulfed in pure energy and destroyed. The Racarba charged a considerable amount of MU for access. But they had found little in the way of accessible Pruathan technology, which should have been a great concern to the Conglomerate. However, it seemed that the family was being given rights of access to parts of two other Pruathan ships that the New Rangelley had captured from a new enemy. Takagawa was to fast track training of the engineers from the Conglomerate plus a few others who showed aptitude for engineering, but were in unrelated billets. He wondered why they were to avoid tasking Doctor Kuremoto. Saitow's investigation of him had come up with nothing significant, other than that his family had come from a planet designated as 'special' by the Rangelley. The majority of Pure Bloods in the Imperium were from there. *Could it be that Kuremoto was a Pure Blood himself?* That would explain a few things, but leave a whole lot more to be answered. At any rate, the man had his biology and the few artifacts they had found to decipher; they were kept in a compartment off the cargo bay under lock and key by the Quartermaster until he called for them.

He had insisted and was granted a few more dinners with the Princess. She seemed to be warming up to him a little bit. He had made it a point to be by her side when they reached the Great Barrier; its bluish shimmer extending as far as the eyes could see was a sight to behold. She had been delighted to have been able to see it. He hadn't dared to bring up the subject of the news again just yet, but he knew she was watching it from time to time by reports from Lowey Jax. He would soon need to let her off the ship to stretch her legs so to speak; he'd have to find a safe isolated place full of natural wonders.

He set down the tablet, checked the time on his neural-net, and grabbed his packet of stims before rising from his desk. It looked to be another long adventurous day.

* * *

Things were looking up for Lowey Jax. Although he was forever being sequestered by the Princess to watch the GCN News, he had gotten in some prime Darkats with the nubes from Roseglade; suckers the lot of them. Not that he needed to fleece them, he had plenty of MU from his new paymasters, but it just felt so good being on top of his game. Then, when they were awaiting a job above Narue, Nanami Oliver cornered him in the cargo hold. She needed a warm body to help her with an acquisition planet-side. He was more than happy to help the woman; he had been thinking about her for weeks following the mutiny. She always seemed out of his reach, but now he would be able to spend some alone time with her and test the waters. He had no idea why she picked him to accompany her; she had her own detail of security thugs after all. No matter. It must have been fate.

They had bought what they had come for and were heading to a café to get some local food before heading back to the shuttle rendezvous point. Nanami was just ahead of him on the busy walkway lined with sellers of all sort of wares; he was doing all he could to keep up without resorting to violence within the throng of people. He saw her freeze suddenly, and then duck down an adjoining alleyway. He heard a man yelling "Sakura!" very loudly at that point. He made it to the entrance where she disappeared at the same time as an overly attractive young dude that seemed to be looking for her as well. The man yelled "Sakura" once again. Jax decided to cut the man off.

"Excuse me; I'm in a bit of a hurry." The man said, clearly annoyed that Jax was blocking his pursuit.

"Have a hot date do ya?" Jax tried to seem like a nonchalant street punk for all that was worth.

The man seemed perplexed. "Why no, I am just trying to catch up to an old friend that went this way. Her name is Sakura."

Jax didn't know who this Sakura was, but Nanami was the only one who went down this alley. He decided that she didn't need this case of mistaken identity. "Look pal, I don't know who this Sakura is, but the only person to go down this alley was my girl, and she ain't no Sakura." Jax squared himself in the entrance to the alleyway.

The man seemed to take a moment to contemplate the value of confrontation to his pursuit of this Sakura person then decided it was probably not worth the hassle. Jax was certainly projecting violence.

"You're quite right young man. It probably wasn't Sakura after all. Good day to you." And the man was gone. As soon as Jax thought he was really gone, he turned and trotted down the alleyway to find Nanami. Half way down he felt his wrist being grabbed and he was suddenly flung at the wall in a recessed area of the alley. Nanami had him pinned up against the wall. "Who's your girl?" She said coyly.

Jax was about to make excuses for distracting the man who seemed to be following her, but decided to play it for all it was worth. "You are?" he said shyly.

"I thought you'd never ask." was all the response Nanami gave him before planting her lips firmly against his. Yep, Jax thought as he returned her affection, *things were looking up indeed.*

*   *   *

Nanami had decided to find out the truth of the matter. She felt she was finally ready to maybe get into a relationship. She thought about what it would be like and who it should be with. She went through the roster of male crew members having decided that she really wasn't into women at all. Some were too old or stuffy for her tastes like the Old Guy or the Captain. Some were just too annoying like the Quartermaster and the Priest. The most of them were just too young or immature. Then she heard a rumor about a crewman who had eyes for her. This sent chills up her spine and she used her position as Security Officer to keep an eye on him. He was the handsome and strong looking Lowey Jax; the impromptu leader of the ex-conscripts. She did her research. He was notorious for winning at Darkats, yet she could not detect any cheating going on in the games she could get a video feed on. It annoyed her that he was always being dragged to the media room by the Princess, yet it pleased her that he seemed to be annoyed by it as well. So it was, that when the opportunity arose at Narue, she had him accompany her on a mission to get a special equipment she needed for her security detail. This way she could spend some time with him and get to know him a bit better. They had finished with the tech merchant and were heading to a decent café she knew to get a bite to eat before heading back; this was to be conversation time. She was getting excited and made a game of him following her through the crowded market place. She then heard a voice that stopped her dead in her tracks; it was the Bedoshian Trade Ambassador; *what was his name, Giardini?* He was calling her old name. She saw her chance to evade and ducked down a side passage and into a recess. She was surprised and delighted to find Lowey Jax was deftly turning the Ambassador away from her position. She had best not risk going to the café at this point. Hopefully Jax wouldn't connect the name Sakura to her just yet. If she was to have a relationship with this man, she would have to come clean eventually, but it was too much too soon to risk. She needed to know a bit more about Jax before reaching that point. It was a shame they wouldn't get their moment of peace at the café. She did put all her emotion into kissing him, but it also added to the need to distract him from any prying about Giardini. She had the answer to the main question she had wanted already anyway; Jax had called her *his girl* after all.

*   *   *

Doctor Kuremoto was deep in thought about the latest Pruathan technology they had acquired; a roughly half-meter square black cube. It was plainly made of the same material as the ship; the nano-tech components that could be programmed for any number of utilities. However, whatever he did, he just couldn't get the thing to respond. There were no buttons, switched, or terminal connections on the thing. It was entirely smooth. Some would say the surface of it felt like a cat's tongue, but he had never seen such an animal, much less felt the touch of one's tongue. He tried the usual methods: command signal transmission, and any number of pressing combinations. He even tried unconventional methods such as electroshock and water exposure. He finally gave up and had the thing sent back to the

Quartermaster's lock-up. He had other things to attend to. The cultures he had started from the Uprising samples were maturing, and he had a line on what might be the cause of the disease. He didn't like what he was seeing one bit. It was becoming more and more clear that the origin of the disease was not a natural occurrence at all.

* * *

Goh Takagawa was perplexed. His sniffing software had not gotten a hit in weeks. All he had was a few encrypted messages that, when deciphered, only gave off the impression that the sender was an imperial spy designated Sparrow 64 and his messages went to a Contact Sigma. Other than that, they only gave information on the ship and a declaration to protect the Princess; the types of things any Imperial agent would say. He desperately wanted to have more information before he broached this to the Captain, but if he sat on the information too long, he might get reprimanded. He had enough to worry about with training the new crewmembers and maintaining the ship. Doctor Kuremoto was locked up in his lab doing who knows what, so Goh was responsible for all of the Pruathan systems as well as the integrated stuff. He had no time for his friend Kintaro, although the man had been acting very strange of late, especially when in the presence of the Captain. He didn't for a moment think that Kintaro was scared of the Captain; he was a pretty level-headed companion. Maybe the stress of the mutiny had gotten to him; Goh almost started to regret recruiting him. He decided he would try to make some time for a sparring session soon, or maybe a game of master chess. First, he had to contact the Captain about this spy.

* * *

The fact that there was a spy aboard didn't really surprise Saitow. He knew Imperial operations would go to such lengths undoubtedly because of the way he had eased into command of the project, as well as the presence of the Princess for the maiden voyage. He thanked Takagawa for the information, told him to keep monitoring communications, and dismissed him. Then he called him back. Nanami Oliver was planet-side and he needed to start an investigation. Takagawa would have to be included anyway to give Oliver access to a few systems. It bugged him that the transmissions had stopped for so many weeks. "Takagawa, why do you think the spy stopped communicating? Have we had any personnel quit or take a leave of absence that I don't know about?" Saitow knew Takagawa didn't have the answers to those questions, but asking them out loud helped him think.

Takagawa answered as best he could, "Sir, it could be any number of things that could have caused the spy to quit communicating: perhaps he has faulty equipment, he was ordered to remain silent for a certain period, or maybe the randomness of our missions has been throwing him off..."

"All good answers, Takagawa. I knew you had a good head on your shoulders the moment you joined my crew." Saitow didn't give out genuine compliments very often, but this young man deserved it. He was practically the best asset he had on this ship right now. "Given that the first message occurred before we got augmented, that rules out the people forced on us by my mother. Have you seen any odd behavior from any of the original crew besides their usual quirks?" Takagawa seemed to think hard for a moment like he was wrestling with some odd thoughts, but he answered in the negative.

"Ok. I think we're through here. Report what you have to Nanami Oliver when she returns from the planet. Just give her access to whatever systems she needs for the investigation of this spy. Dismissed."

Saitow watched as Takagawa left his ready room a second time. He could rule out several members of the crew right off the bat for various reasons. However, it was best to let Oliver's Intelligence Corps training get to the root of the matter. She would come to him as soon as she was given the information to get further instructions; instructions he had best keep from innocents like Takagawa.

* * *

Goh checked his neural-net for the shuttle schedule; it was not due back for another half-hour. He decided he could take that time to try and relax in his quarters; maybe take a nap. When he got there, he slipped off his boots and sat on the bed. He was really feeling the stress of all the work that was being piled on him. Now assisting Nanami Oliver to investigate the spy was added to all that. He was also worried about his friend Kintaro. When the Captain asked about odd behavior, Kintaro's face had popped right up front in Goh's mind. What with his distractedness lately, and the way he was acting around the Captain, it almost made Goh think he might be the spy. He couldn't bring those thoughts up to the Captain however; Kintaro was his only friend.

Suddenly, Goh felt a chill pass through his shoulder. Turning, he almost thought he had caught a glimpse of a shadowy figure quickly move toward the recessed shelving and into the wall there. This unnerved him somewhat. The stress was certainly getting to him. He decided that a brisk walk about the ship would help clear his mind and ease his thoughts. He played some light music over his neural-net as he left his cabin. *"Take me away, take me away, take me away, to the warmth of your world..."*

* * *

Amara hadn't been this frustrated in all her fifteen years. Well, fifteen years plus the centuries she had been stuck attached to that box. This man Goh had a lot of Qi; why couldn't he see, hear, or feel her presence? She felt his Qi had raised some, probably due to stress, so she tried touching his shoulder. She only passed right through. Perhaps he did notice after all; his eyes seemed to almost follow her as she retreated to the wall behind the box. She supposed that this place was better than that old sailor's bag; she hardly ever got out of there. Before that she couldn't remember. She just knew it had been a very long time. The only recollection she had was of that horrible witch of a Sheese that cursed her as she died and put her severed finger in the box to trap her there; all for the fact that she could not be turned. She had used up the remainder of her reserve Qi writing in the salt that the man Goh had spilt; that had been of little benefit. All she could do was keep waiting, as she had always waited. Perhaps this man would build up enough Qi to interact with her. She didn't want to get her hopes up though; she had been waiting oh so long...

* * *

Princess Shirae was contemplating the crewman she always commandeered when she wanted to watch the news. It seemed she had become fixated on the GCN News more and more. Lowey Jax had always been cold and annoyed at her for taking him away from duties or

Darkats. Today however, he seemed in rather good spirits. Shirae had heard that he had gone planet-side on some mission with Nanami Oliver. Perhaps something good had come from that. She was about to ask when Jax got finished setting up the channel selector and a news flash caught everyone's attention.

"We have just received breaking news from the vicinity of the Ros'Loper Imperial Space Station Juliana Naval Base. The Admiral in charge there, Cornelius Graaf, has been assassinated in a very odd manner. We have two videos for you, the first from a transport on approach to Juliana; the second sent to us anonymously from the Prium Liberation Front. Let's watch the first video." The woman on the screen was replaced by a shot of the Juliana Naval Base, lit up gloriously by the reflection of the gas giant it orbited. Suddenly, an explosion emitted from the top center section. The video zoomed in on the section that had exploded and showed a fire that quickly went out for lack of oxygen. Then the woman was back on. *"We have received confirmation from an anonymous source that the section that exploded was approximately where the command section offices are. The next video we would like to show you is graphic in nature and also very strange. We believe that the child you are about to witness is not a real child, but is an illegal autonomous artificial intelligence. Such devices have been known to be used in the illicit sex trades throughout the quadrant. Viewer discretion is strongly advised."* The video began as a dark red color filled the screen. Voices could be heard in the background. *"Sir, this child's mother says that she is your grand-daughter. The*

mother sent her ahead to you because she had to use the facilities." said a young man's voice.

"Quite right. I'll watch the child while the mother is away. Dismissed." A deeper voice said.

"Aye, Lord Admiral." The young voice said and a whoosh of a hatch closing was heard. Just then the lens or whatever it was moved away from the red area and came to rest as it was placed on a surface by a little girl of maybe five or six in a frilly red dress. The girl stepped away and over to the front of a desk that was all lit up with information. The girl stood on her tippy toes in order to see what was flashing on the desk. *"Pretty!"* the girl practically shrilled.

A hand came in view and swiped the flashing documents away. *"Yes, yes, now come here and sit on grandfather's lap."* As the girl moved, the camera slowly panned after her so that the view that was given was the girl sitting facing the camera in a middle-aged man's lap. The man was Admiral Graaf.

"Have you been a good girl since you last visited grandfather?" the Admiral started stroking the little girl's leg.

"Of course, I have. Where's my candy?" the little girl looked up smiling at the Admiral.

"Now, now, there's plenty of time for that. Now let me see how much you've grown." The Admiral reached up and started to unbutton the girl's red dress. Suddenly, the child swatted the Admiral's hands away.

The Admiral grabbed his hand as if the swat had been quite painful. The girl said this time in her shrill voice, *"No playtime without candy!"*

The admiral seemed enraged. He reached up and grabbed the girl's neck with one hand and her left shoulder with the other. *"Why you little bitch!"* he got out before the girl grabbed both his arms painfully.

"Violence is not the answer grandfather; it's your end. Goodbye..." at that a great flash emitted from the girl and the screen went blank, to be replaced by the anchor woman after a few moments.

Everyone in the media room was in a state of shock; even Lowey Jax, it seemed to the Princess.

*   *   *

Nanami Oliver was sipping tea in the General Mess alongside Lowey Jax and two of his shipmates. She was going over communications from the spy aboard ship and pretending to listen to the story Jax was telling of Admiral Graaf's demise. She knew the story already; after all it had been *her* handiwork. She was set to abandon the possibility of taking out her last target for the sake of being happy. However, she found out through her network that the Admiral had a liking for prepubescent sex androids. That turned her stomach. So, she set up the hit on the Admiral using the one thing that was the easiest to get to him; his own dirty vice. The Prium Liberation Front was just a cover; a joke really. Prium was a dead world abandoned by the Imperials even before Ros' Loper II had ascended the throne. It was sad that there were two other fatalities and more than a dozen injured, but they were Imperials after all. Her connections assured her that the funding she provided could never be traced to her. At least she tried to believe that to reassure herself.

A hail came over the ship's intercom; it was *Iwa* calling her to the Captain's berth. Maybe he had some extra duty for her to attend to. She excused herself from the table and headed up to deck two. She hailed at the hatch and was invited in. What greeted her was the Captain - she had never seen him so red faced - and Doctor Rosel. *Oh boy*, she thought, *I'm in for it this time...*

* * *

Captain Saitow was beside himself. He hadn't been this pissed since being conscripted by Imperial decree so many years ago. A half-hour ago, he received a message from his family stating in no uncertain terms to reign in the *Goddess of Terror* as they put it. With the message was documentation tracing the purchase, through several channels, of the AI that had offed Admiral Graaf, along with a copy of the video footage from the fictitious Prium Liberation Front. The

Conglomerate knows wherever their money goes; even when it is no longer theirs.

He grabbed his pack of stims out of the desk and called for Doctor Rosel. After showing her the video, he called for the *goddess* herself.

When Nanami Oliver showed up, he showed her the video, and then asked, "What is this?"

Nanami seemed unconcerned. "Yeah, I saw that too. What a way to go, huh? All that after I was ready to let go of it all. Guess Juliana's taken care of." She glanced at Doctor Rosel as if just noticing she was in the room with them. Then she turned back to him. The look on her face told him that she knew he wasn't buying any of it.

"Nanami, I took a chance on you because you are damn good at what you do. But this... this is just going too far! My family pays the salaries of the crew of this ship. That includes you. They are also very good at finding out where their money goes, even when it is out of their hands. Do you know what that means?"

Nanami meant to speak, but then glanced at Doctor Rosel, and then back at Saitow.

"Go ahead; she knows your whole story." Saitow looked for a reaction to that, but got only resignation.

"Look sir, I had just about kicked the idea of finishing my revenge; things are looking up for me since the mutiny. But I found out about that motherfucker's pedophilic tendencies and couldn't let that stand. He had to go. I simply called in some favors." Nanami was unapologetic. This made Saitow a little redder.

"You are an important part of this crew. What do you think the reputation of this ship means to the rest of us? Ease of operation; the cullying of favors; these things you don't get back once you lose them." Saitow saw that it was starting to sink in to her. He pressed further. "You are damn lucky the Imperials are too busy screwing with their own people to seriously investigate the Admiral's death, embarrassment that he was to them." Saitow detected a sense of satisfaction under the concern Nanami was showing.

"For here on in you are not to pursue any more favors that do not directly assist the operation of this ship. You are also to accompany Doctor Rosel to the med bay immediately for a psychiatric evaluation. Am I making myself clear?"

Nanami was reluctant. "But—"

"No buts about it. This is your only second chance. I suggest you get it together. Dismissed."

Saitow watched the two women leave his quarters. It had been quite a long day indeed.

5

A few weeks passed with only one client hiring the *Iwakina*; it turned out that was only to get them where the Universal Church wanted them to be. They had been set up to rendezvous with the Church ship that Gunter was on. Captain Saitow welcomed him back aboard graciously. This Gunter did not seem to Saitow like the same Gunter that left with the non-mutineers. He had a much stronger air about him, like he had a sense of purpose. He also noticed that Gunter wore the full robes of a Priest of the Church. He would have to invite the man to dinner soon. Surely, he had some interesting tales to tell.

*   *   *

Gunter came aboard the *Iwakina* a new man. He was happy to be back aboard and not just as an acolyte to Brother Stephen; he was now a full Priest, although still subordinate to the elder man. However, that would come after he fulfilled his mission; to seek out those that Miriam needed to get messages to. For that he would have to have the run of the ship. He would need to be quick about it too; Miriam, being a spirit, had an enormous amount of Qi or life force energy. However, it was sapping his own Qi to be a host for her. He excused himself from Brother Stephen stating that he needed to stretch his legs, and headed out into the dim grey corridor. Just then the Princess and her retinue stepped out of the media room adjacent to the Chapel. Gunter felt that Miriam was ready to speak with the Princess and let her take over.

*　　*　　*

Miriam knew that Gunter was under a heavy burden being a host to her. He was chosen not only because he had familiarity with the *Iwakina*, but also because of the amount of Qi he possessed. Being her host consumed a great deal of his Qi. Her presence within him also made him restless; that was a good thing because she wanted to see the ship as well as contact those with whom she needed to share her portents. They went out of the Chapel and she immediately saw her first recipient; Princess Shirae came into the corridor with a few women and a man. Miriam felt Gunter let her have control of his body; although he could sense all that was happening when this occurred. "Princess Shirae, a word if I may." That was all she spoke before a short dangerous looking woman had moved quickly in between her and the Princess. The Princess rolled her eyes as if the woman who was clearly a body guard had done this one too many times.

"Haruka! This is not a battle zone! You remember Gunter, don't you?" the Princess seemed peeved at her charge. Another woman stepped up. She had an odd look on her face as if she could see beyond what was in front of her. "Not Gunter. A spirit, Oujo-sama." She said. Miriam was taken aback somewhat. She did not know she could be detected so easily. This woman stepped between Gunter and the one known as Haruka. She bowed in the form that the ancients had. "What business do you have with my mistress, oh spirit?"

Miriam did not want to seem to be conniving so returned the bow and spoke. "True, I am not Gunter; I am the holy-spirit Miriam, come to give a message of great import to Princess Shirae."

The one who had called her out stepped back and bid the Princess listen. "Oujo-sama, spirits do not talk to the living without reason."

Shirae looked at the woman who had spoken and back at Miriam. "Ran-chan, are you sure?"

"Yes, Oujo-sama. In my village there was a spirit walker as well, a warning was given that saved us all."

Miriam began to feel Gunter weakening. She knew that her time must be short if she was to deliver all of her messages. She went ahead and delivered the first. "Princess Shirae, do not blame the father; blame the one who controls the father. Tell this also to the one who is almost you when you can see her true self." with this she let control go back to Gunter, who in his weakened state was forced to take a knee. The woman Ran had enough sense to read the situation. "Come now ladies, we must let the spirit walker rest."

*   *   *

Miriam let the rest of the day pass in order to allow Gunter to recuperate. Then she asked him to send word to the Captain that he would accept the dinner invitation. Brother Stephen accompanied them. After the meal, she allowed Gunter to regale the Captain with his stories of the *City of Light*. Both Brother Stephen and the Captain seemed impressed. Now it was time to give the message to the Captain she told him. He gave her control and she saw that this startled both of their companions. She then realized in their haste they hadn't informed Brother Stephen about her presence. She touched the older priest's hand. "Brother Stephen. You are well aware of the Church's use of holy spirits to assist in the Good Lord's work. I am the holy-spirit Miriam, come here with Gunter to give portents to certain members of the crew and others." She paused to see what affect her words had on the two men. Each seemed to be in deep contemplation. She continued, "Captain, to inform you, I have given portent to the Princess, and besides yourself, I have but one other to speak with, Goh Takagawa." Saitow seemed to grasp the importance of her mission.

"Yes, I understand. What is your message for me?" the Captain seemed less concerned than curious.

"When the one who is not the Princess yet is the Princess appears, let her go when she must go." She gave the message to him.

"What does that mean? It *is* rather cryptic." The Captain protested.

"I do not know the meanings of the messages I bring from God, only that they portend a possibility that you must guarantee for the well-being of all. I assure you that you will know the moment when it is upon you." She tried to be as congenial as she could be. However, Gunter was growing weak again and needed rest. She gave him back his body.

"Brother Stephen, I need to rest. Miriam's presence is very taxing. Please excuse me Captain." It was Gunter who spoke. Both men could somehow tell he was back in control. He looked very weak. He stood up and almost fell over, but for the swiftness of Brother Stephen.

*   *   *

The next morning Gunter called upon Brother Stephen. He needed to get this over with before he ran out of Qi; he was actually fearful that this burden might take his life. However, for some reason he felt that Miriam would not allow that. When the two men were seated in the anteroom, Miriam took control once more and gave Brother Stephen his message, "Priest, you must help those upon this ship until you are called, but it is assured that you will be called very soon. Steal yourself for the coming battle." Miriam added to that, "I can tell you that yours is the most straight forward message and the most likely...no, the most set true of them all. Fear not. God has a plan for those that will attempt to thwart God's dominion."

Gunter returned to control and was amazed at what he was hearing. There will be a battle to come involving the Church? He was reminded by Miriam not to dwell of the future, for the present beckoned him. He excused himself from his fellow priest, who was distracted in deep thought, and headed toward the engineering deck.

*   *   *

Miriam had not one message left to deliver but two. It happened that the object of her next message required some discretion; this person was not who they seemed to be. Miriam saw him/her in the corridor ahead. She quickly took full control of Gunter, even to the point of shutting him down completely; she hoped he could forgive her. Then she blocked the way of this Sanae disguised as Kintaro Sagura. In a rush the 'man' almost plowed them over, but stopped short looking warily at Miriam/Gunter. Miriam spoke quickly before passing by her and down the corridor. "Your time of freedom will come soon, but prepare to meet your father."

Once they were outside engineering, she allowed Gunter to take back control. She apologized to him as best she could; even some portents he was not to be privy to. He seemed to accept it and she assured him that Goh Takagawa was to be the last of the messages. They hailed for Goh and when he met them at the hatch, she had Gunter insist that they go to Goh's quarters. The man seemed amicable enough and she knew from Gunter that the two men had known each other for some time.

When they reached Goh's quarters, Gunter took the only chair in the room and gave himself over to her once more. Miriam spoke, "I am the holy-spirit Miriam come with this man from the Universal Church to give you a message of great import. Be wary of the strange woman who will come. She will help you free the spirit who is attached to you, but she will also attach herself to you." With that Miriam stood and walked directly to the box that held Amara to this place. It was time. She hastily said her goodbyes to Gunter and thanked him so much for assisting in her work. She could now be released to make her journey to the plane of Heaven. She left him then, and the man slumped to the floor, Goh Takagawa quickly coming to his aid. Miriam watched from her place near the box as Gunter was lifted to the man's bed. She turned now to the business at hand. She must converse with this other spirit before she could go. She reached into the wall and gently drew the girl named Amara out of hiding. "There girl, do not be frightened. I was once as you are, martyred for worshipping the one true God. Worry not. Your time stuck away from those dear to you is coming to an end.

One such as you have feared will come to this man. Do not fear her, but do not show yourself in her presence. She will help this man free you, but for a price to him alone. I must leave you, but I cannot take you with me; it is not His will. However, come embrace me and I will make you strong." Miriam held out her arms as if to embrace the girl. The girl Amara looked bewildered, but did as she was told. As Miriam embraced the girl, she transferred her remaining Qi to her, and in a blinding flash and the breadth of an instant, she was gone.

ALABASTER

1

Quartermaster Ken Edwards was enjoying his new easy life. Mind you he could be doing any number of greater things; he was a genius after all. He excelled at engineering, and anthropology, and enjoyed both, but only as hobbies. He detested hard work; that was for the non-intellectual. It did pain him the few times that he had to see to some new cargo or the properties of random clients that the ship took on. The current customer was no exception; he had a very large secure container, that needed special care in handling, taken on at Spericlau. It was listed as precious goods for market; the Captain allowed such vague listings on the manifest because, well... this wasn't the general shipping trades. This was all the more reason for Edwards to investigate each container. Who knew what rare goods could be studied while they were aboard? Most days Edwards spent entirely in his office, breaking only for his routine exercise or an occasional foray into virtual reality, thanks to the Keshogani machine he purchased for a considerable amount of MU. He had Goh Takagawa temporarily modify the cargo deck so he could get it down into an unused compartment on deck six. Goh had got it all wired into the system for him as well, even though he could have done it himself. He kept up with all of the reports filed by engineering. He fancied himself as knowledgeable about the ship as both Goh and Doctor Kuremoto. Edwards did have a cabin, but he took most of his meals in his office off the cargo bay, and only used the cabin for sleep and hygiene.

So, it happened that he was in his office late after shift going over the latest scientific periodicals downloaded from the GCN, that he heard some noise in the cargo bay. Looking out through the one-way glass, he spied the client's servant enter the container holding a case of some sort. He came out a few minutes later with the same case and sealed the container once more. What could this be? Perhaps tomorrow Edwards would have to do some investigating.

*   *   *

Princess Shirae could hardly sleep at all. She could clearly hear the three retainers snoring loudly in the next room, but that wasn't what was keeping her up. It was the strange message, supposedly from a holy-spirit channeled through that priest Gunter. The first part seemed rather easy to decipher, *"Do not blame the father; blame the one who controls the father."* Perhaps her father was not truly behind the atrocities being perpetuated against the people of the Empire. But who was the one who controlled the father? She could think of no one so powerful as to keep her father at bay. Then the second part really threw her for a loop; *"Tell this also to the one who is almost you when you can see her true self."* What could that possibly mean? Who could be this someone that was almost her that she would know when she saw her? That portent would have to wait until it was fulfilled. She got up and rummaged through a box in her personal belongings. She pulled out an ornate bottle she had received from the Imperial medical staff. Out of it she shook two small capsules. Grabbing a glass of water, she downed the two sleep inducers and plopped down once more on her bed, watching the room disappear as they took her to blissful slumber.

* * *

The cabin was becoming increasingly eerie for Goh Takagawa. First his hallucination of words written in the spilt salt, then the shadowy figure near the shelf, and now the flash of light near there when Gunter fell ill, in which he could have sworn he had seen a smiling girl. He was quite sure that the message Gunter gave him was from this girl and not Gunter; she had called herself Miriam. Gunter was too weak and practically unconscious when they came and got him from Goh's cabin. He would have to wait for the man to recover before he could get any answers to his many questions.

He lay down on his bunk and closed his eyes. Maybe a good night's sleep would put his mind at ease. "lights off." he commanded the room monitor, which was part of the AI of the ship. For some reason it had gotten a little chillier than he had felt it was when he got into bed. He sat up and looked to find the edge of his blanket, only to be confronted by a semi-glowing figure of a young girl. He practically started to scream, but the girl put her finger to her lips in the universal sign of hush. She was sitting on the edge of his bed, but stood up and moved toward his bathroom. He was shocked with himself; now that his fear had turned to mere curiosity, he stood up and followed. The girl was inside and pointing to a built-in cabinet that Goh kept some toiletries in that he rarely used. He opened it and, keeping an eye on the girl, took out various items. When he took out an expensive bottle of powder that he had to purchase on Euphrosyne because the damn heat there gave him a rash, the girl pointed at it and nodded her head excitedly. She moved back into the main room and pointed at the low table there. Then she motioned with her two hands as if she was spreading a cloth over it. Goh realized that she meant for him to spread the powder over the table. He was getting confused at this point, but did as he was instructed.

He watched as the girl tried moving her finger over the powder, but only small ripples were produced. She looked as if she was concentrating with all her might and managed to write three words with her finger, GHOST, AMARA, and QI. Then she looked up at him expectantly. Goh was perplexed, but he reasoned that she was obviously trying to communicate with him. She must be telling him that she is a ghost; he could plainly see that. Amara wasn't any word he knew in the several languages he had learned. He asked her if that was her name and got an excited nodding of the head for his trouble. What did she mean by Qi? He knew Qi was supposed to be life energy, but why would a spirit need Qi? Wasn't she already dead? Goh asked Amara why she needed Qi. She motioned as if she was pulling words out of her mouth. "To speak?" he asked. Yes, she nodded. He pointed at the powder spread across the table. "No more powder writing?" he asked. She put her arms up in an X across her torso to indicate no.

"Well that's good; now I have to clean this up." Goh said. Amara gave him two shakes in the affirmative. She then indicated that she would sleep by placing her hands palms together beside her head and closing her eyes. She headed to the wall by the recessed shelf. Goh watched her disappear into the wall. This gave him the shivers. He abandoned the powder until morning and curled up under his blanket. To think that a ghost was living in his wall; *"the ghost that is attached to you"* was what the other spirit Miriam had said. Who was this woman that was coming for him? Perhaps Amara knew. He would consult Ken Edwards about ghosts and Qi; if anyone aboard ship knew about that, it would be Edwards.

* * *

Nanami Oliver and Lowey Jax's relationship was growing day by day. When they had free time, they spent it together, either in Nanami's cabin or in the General Mess; Nanami's cabin was much more spacious than Lo's. She was happy that he liked her calling him that; in fact, he had said she was the only one who had ever been allowed to. Their relationship had progressed both amicably and emotionally. It was plain to her that he was madly in love. She was surprised by the swiftness and sincerity of it; all Humans know that women fall in love and learn to lust for a man. Men usually lust for women and fall in love gradually. As for lust she was reluctant to progress to that stage; she didn't feel it right to bring him so close without him knowing the truth about her. That was her dilemma; how to broach the subject to him with the littlest chance of rejection. He seemed to be okay with taking their time. On those few occasions where their trysts had gotten heated, she had pulled herself away from him, and he had reluctantly, but understandingly held himself a gentleman. Surprisingly, he told her that just being near her was enough for the time being. This made it even harder for her to seek a time to tell him the truth about her life and past.

It suddenly occurred to her that she knew very little about *his* past. Perhaps it would be easier for her to broach the subject of her past if she started by inquiring about his.

* * *

Goh Takagawa was doing diagnostics on Kintaro's navigation console while Kintaro was standing above him keying the inputs that Goh requested. They hadn't been able to talk for some time so they did some catching up. During a lull in the conversation Goh heard some odd noise and looked up to find Kintaro absently scratching his head. "Say Goh, can you look at the fixtures in my toilet area? Ever since my berth had been damaged that thing's been out of whack..."

Goh didn't respond right away. He was fixated on a strand of hair that floated down from his friend and landed on his sleeve. It was not the jet-black hair of Kintaro Sagura, but a light brown color; the hair of someone else.

Kintaro must have sensed his distraction, "Goh?" he was facing Goh now. The man did smell a bit odd.

"Sure. I'll get right on it after we finish this calibration." Goh dove back into his work.

*   *   *

Doctor Kuremoto was on the GCN speaking to his friend on Uprising. The *Iwakina* was following the Trades at the request of the current client and the Trades ran along the path of the GCN. The client apparently had reasons to avoid Jumpgate travel. It was easy to tap in to the GCN with the ship's Asynchronous GCN Transceiver. He had to keep the conversation to coding lest the authorities who monitored communications on Uprising get news of his discovery. That news was only for his friend. He was not surprised to learn that the Conglomerate was monitoring the very same communications. The detector attached to his comm port told him as much. They were keeping a close eye on him to be sure.

"I want to bring some toys for your daughter; how old has she gotten now, Marcus?" Kuremoto asked his friend. This was code that he had succeeded and that he wanted to try the cure out soon; his friend Marcus's daughter was Margo and had to be a teenager by now.

"Why, she just passed 17 cycles here. I think she has outlived your toys. When will you come? I will have to get clearance from my superiors." Marcus replied.

"Oh, I have no idea. Our schedule is like the dust in the wind; who knows where the wind will take this ship." Kuremoto smiled his biggest smile. "Perhaps you could persuade your superiors in hiring us on for resupply or something. We'll be available in a couple of months."

"I'll see what I can do. Check back with me within two weeks." Marcus was telling him he would need the two weeks to prepare for his arrival. Things might actually go according to plan. Kuremoto resigned himself that in almost four centuries of living, things rarely went as they were planned.

"Very well. I look forward to speaking with you again. Goodbye old friend."

*   *   *

Shirae was slightly amused that Haruka had thrown such a fit when it was apparent that 'Oujo-sama' could not be easily woken. When the three of them finally got a response from her, she confused them all the more with her giddiness at waking from the bizarre dream she had endured. When she was fully lucid, she sobered quickly. She remembered it clearly, which added to her seriousness; so much so that Ran-chan asked about it in concern. Shirae dismissed them to other tasks. Such a dream was not meant to be shared, even with those you most trusted and adored. No, this dream was inviolably personal. She was wandering the corridors of the ship, in a place she did not recognize, and with no one else in accompaniment. She heard laughter emitting from an open doorway up ahead. Approaching out of curiosity, she peered covertly on a candlelit scene of a couple dining on chicken and conversing amicably. At first, she could not make out the words they were saying and the light was too dim for her to make out who the couple was. Then she noticed the woman placing her hand on top of the man's and the conversation ended. She then saw that the man was Captain Saitow and the woman was some odd version of herself. She had short mousy hair and her skin coloration was darker; she could tell even in the dim candlelight. This woman was like another version of herself. Shirae stepped into the room, but it was as if she was not even there; the couple continued their interaction with no indication that they were being watched. Suddenly, the Captain bent forward and was reciprocated by her other self in a passionate kiss. Shirae's view was as if she were floating all around the couple, circling, taking in the view with all its magnificence; their passion was so complete. Then Shirae noticed a change in the woman, whose hair grew and skin lightened, to become Shirae herself. Even though she was still circling the couple, she could feel the passion of their kissing, which gave her such an aching that she had never before experienced. It caused her such joy, yet an equal amount of fear. So intense it was that the feelings lingered, even as she was being roused from sleep by her faithful retainers. She thought hard about the dream all throughout her breakfast and exercise routine, to the point that she was distracted and took a few more hits than usual from Haruka's attacks. She dismissed Haruka-chan's questions and retired to a nice warm bath. After some futile attempts at educational reading, she decided that a visit to the media room would clear her head of the dream and add to her investigation of the happenings in her kingdom. She inquired on Lowey Jax and was told that he was visiting Nanami Oliver, no doubt for some security related tasking. Shirae went straight to the ship's security, but was told that Nanami Oliver was off duty at the time. So, Lowey Jax was visiting Security Officer Oliver after hours? She decided that she would have to get to the bottom of this and headed toward Ms. Oliver's quarters. As her retinue rounded the corner near Nanami's cabin, they ran into Lowey

Jax and Nanami in an intimate embrace outside the hatch, Nanami frantically trying to run her token ring passed the sensor to enter the room. They detached from one another when they saw the group. Haruka made to step toward them but Shirae held out her arm to stop her protector. Surely these two were together as a couple. She then realized that her constant snatching of Jax from his duties was probably interfering with this relationship as well. Loud enough for all parties to hear she said, "Haruka! Lowey Jax seems to be occupied with important matters at the moment. We shall no longer require his services. Let us retire to the media room by ourselves. Good day, Jax-san." At that she turned and left the couple, hoping that the flush she felt upon her cheeks was not noticeable to them. With that flush she realized that she now had feelings for no one other than Captain Saitow.

*   *   *

Gunter had finally been released from Doctor Rosel's too intensive care. The woman must have been bored out of her skull to give such doting attention to her only patient in so many months. Actually, he wasn't her only patient; one of the original crew was still strapped in a patient berth, apparently in a coma since the mutiny. He hadn't asked for the patient's name, but prayed for her just the same.

It was in high spirits that Gunter made his way up to

the Chapel after checking the two priest's quarters on deck six. He had been contemplating the greatness of his mission and what all of Miriam's portents might mean for those whom had received them. He really didn't know at all. Maybe that was his place; not to know. He had known Captain Saitow ever since he had been apprenticed as a young acolyte to Brother Stephen. He had been in acquaintance with Goh Takagawa ever since that man had joined the *Iwakina* Project. However, he really didn't know these men, and the Princess was another matter altogether. Perhaps it was Divine Will that he was not to know. It didn't suit him to dwell on the matter; nothing of incident to him or the Church was revealed except for Brother Stephen's and it seemed to him that none of the message recipients was in any real danger because of them at this point. He dismissed the chain of thought altogether when he reached the chapel doors. Finding no one within, he made for the inner sanctuary. There he found Brother Stephen in a cleared area within. Stephen was sitting cross legged and chanting in some ancient language of the Church. He stopped when Gunter entered and with his right hand picked up some sort of organic material from a bowl by his side and placed it in his left palm which he held out. "Gunter, are you aware of the Arcanum?" Stephen seemed very serious.

"I am only aware that it is something that the Elite must learn in order to reach the level of *Bellator* in service to the Church. The layman would call it 'magic' I believe." Gunter was wondering where this conversation was going. Such questions from Brother

Stephen were usually followed by some rather harsh training. He wasn't sure if he was ready for training in the Arcanum. Gunter watched while Stephen closed, and then opened his left hand while whispering a couple of words Gunter didn't catch. Whatever had been there in Stephen's hand was now replaced by a glowing ball of blue flame. Gunter was fascinated by the flame so much that he did not notice that Bother Stephen was no longer there, but was approaching him from the side. He looked away from the flame to his fellow priest then back, but the blue flame was gone. Stephen came in front of him with what looked to be a ball made of glass on a pillow. "Gunter, this device measures a person's Qi level. If you didn't already know, Qi is a person's life energy. Most people do not even know they possess Qi and do nothing with it in their lifetimes. However, a few people have an excess amount of Qi, can build up their Qi level, and do remarkable things with it. Qi is tied together with a person's soul, so with rare exception, they cannot share their Qi. Qi is used by those with knowledge to manipulate hyperspace flux energy, which could be considered the Qi of the universe and therefore the Qi of God. God placed this flux all around us in varying strength so that we could work God's miracles. The Arcanum is not only the knowledge needed to do battle with evil, as you mention, but it is also a means to do good works. Never forget that." At that Stephen held the glass ball in front of him and seemed to concentrate deeply on it. A very bright glow became apparent inside the ball and grew quite bright. Then it was gone as Stephen relaxed. "Gunter, this ball has a tiny fracture just at the center inside of it. When you concentrate on that fracture with your full attention, it will glow inside indicating your level of Qi. Go ahead and try it."

Gunter tried to focus on the fracture that he could barely see. It slowly became more and more visible, and then the ball began to glow; not as brightly as it had for Brother Stephen, but quite brightly.

"Excellent! I see that Cardinal Sorbeer was right about you. You will make an outstanding addition to the Elite. Now rest. We will begin training in the Arcanum first thing tomorrow."

2

It had taken a couple of hours for Ken Edwards to fit the portable scanning wand to his nice new tablet, courtesy of the Saitow Conglomerate. He had debugged the tablet as soon as he had gotten the thing; he didn't want to be snooped upon like some common laboratory animal. He had watched the client's servant visit with his case twice in one day; surely it was food, but for what? Perhaps some quarantined beast was being smuggled. The Captain would want to know; he only tolerated so much.

Edwards waited for a time when the servant was not likely to return and scanned the container with his portable scanner. There was nothing but background noise. He tested it on one of his own containers and it worked just fine. Apparently, the Client's container was not only security sealed, but it also had a scanning jammer. Edward's curiosity was at its limits. He was about to examine the locking mechanism of the container when Goh Takagawa came up to him. "Hey Edwards, what are you up to?" Edwards was startled which annoyed him since it was one of those starts you get when you are caught doing something you are not supposed to be doing, even though Takagawa had no reason to believe he was up to something.

"Oh, just some maintenance. What brings you to my territory?" Edwards replied, slowly moving away from the container and toward the other side of the dividing wall where his office was located. Takagawa must have liked his 'my territory' line; he smiled a great big smile.

"I have a few questions that you are the most qualified on the ship to answer; one of your hobbies being anthropology..." Takagawa trailed off shyly at the end.

"Sure, let's go to my office. I have some green tea brewing." The two men went around the dividing wall and into Edwards's office. Edwards poured them both a cup of tea. "What questions do you have?" Edwards checked the time. He had just under an hour before the servant's next visitation time.

"We've known each other a long time and I would like to think of us as friends. You wouldn't begrudge a friend about a question or two that seemed a bit *odd*, would you?" Takagawa said; this time he was being annoyingly shy. Edwards played along, although he would rather be out there studying the lock on that container. "No, no, I wouldn't think ill of you. We are friends after all."

"Do you believe in ghosts?" Takagawa almost shrank back when he asked the question. *Ghosts? What was all this about?* The day for Edwards was getting stranger and stranger. It was common knowledge, especially with the discovery of the psyche that ghosts did exist in several forms. Edwards told Takagawa just that. *Now he wanted to know how to build Qi?* Edwards checked the time again; 45 minutes left. He told Takagawa that there was plenty of information in the archives that he had downloaded from the GCN. He pulled a data-stick from his desk drawer and loaded it with what he could find. "Here is all you need to know about ghosts and Qi. I wouldn't jack it though unless your net is rated ten-plus." Edwards handed him the data-stick. Edwards checked the time again; 35 minutes left. "Well, I've really got to get back to that maintenance. You know how the Captain can get when schedules aren't met." Edwards stood up, took Takagawa's unfinished tea cup from him, and keyed the hatch so he could leave. As a bewildered Takagawa exited his office, Edwards had an afterthought, "Oh, say Goh, did you get the manifest for the shipment of vid-screens and the two exo-suits sent to you by the Conglomerate? No? Come back tomorrow with your team and I'll break it out for you."

*   *   *

Nanami Oliver and Lowey Jax were lounging in the Ship's Library; no one ever went up there except maybe the Old Guy. It was full of data cases on mostly Imperial culture and history; most of that stuff was made up anyway. When the ship wasn't in an actual jump, you could set a portion of the overhead to become transparent, showing the space outside the ship. Once a jump was imminent, the transparency would become opaque, lest a person viewing out became sick from the visual effect of the jump vortex. Nanami had set it to view while the two of them talked.

They talked about different worlds they had been to and their service in the military. Nanami pressed Lo to tell her about his past; what homeworld he came from, his relationships prior to theirs, and so forth. Lo seemed pretty forthright with his answers; it was an Intelligence Officer's job to tell when people were not being honest, and she was using those skills now. His honesty and sincerity made it even harder for her to think about telling him the whole story about her past. Sure, she told him she was from Artemus, and how her family had had very good trade relations with the Altus Acaran. He seemed to grow cold when she mentioned those aliens. "What's the matter Lo?" she asked.

"What do you mean you had good relations with the Acaran? How is that possible? They are bloodthirsty savages, the lot of them." Jax shrunk back from her a little when she reached for him.

"Well, my family was a trading house. We traded well with them. There was always some difficulty in communicating with them, but they were not difficult to deal with. Why so much hatred?" She was concerned now; Jax was acting rather skittish. He came out with it though.

"Before I was assigned to the *Iwakina*, I was a Handler on the *Admiral Harth*. We were shuttling supplies to refugees on Orange 82 when they came. After ambushing the *Harth*, they just bombarded from orbit without regard to who or what was targeted. I was lucky to get out alive. I watched a child die in its mother's arms before the mother took her own life. It was horrible...horrible." he reached for her then and she took him into her arms to console him. It was true that the Altus Acaran were an enigmatic race. They didn't even have eyes as far as she could tell; only darkness inside the trifold flaps on their white bulbous heads. The Imperials had treated them far worse than even her family had suffered; it only stood to reason that they would savagely fight back. She couldn't tell that to Lo; he had suffered as well.

With her treacherous past, she was beginning to think that he was too good for her. Now certainly wasn't the time to tell him the truth. She held him tightly as he sobbed into her chest.

*   *   *

Edwards had almost cracked the code on the security lock when he heard the lift stop at this level. He had enough time to put his equipment in a storage locker near the container because he had disabled the hatch that led to this side of the dividing wall. When the servant rounded the corner, Edwards was a bit away from the container sweeping the deck with a silent vacu-broom. He spied that the servant was about to address him from the corner of his eye, but didn't, instead opening the container and disappearing inside. Several minutes passed before the servant came out, sealed the container and headed around the dividing wall. Edwards waited until he heard the lift ascend inside the wall before resuming the task of breaking the security on the container. He would find out what was inside even if it killed him.

*　*　*

Akira Chiampa heard the hail to the stateroom he occupied aboard the *Iwakina* and bid the hatch to open. He was a rather portly man and didn't feel the need to raise himself to key the door; especially for his servant Kievly. Thank the cosmos for shipboard AIs. He had been on many ships in his One-hundred-twenty-six years, but this was the fastest by far. It was a good thing too. His client wanted his cargo soon, and it was necessary to avoid the Jumpgate system to avoid the various authorities. He waved for Kievly to approach so he could get his report...and maybe order a snack. "How is our precious cargo?"

"Quite well Master, quite well." Kievly looked nervously around as if someone or something was watching him closely.

"Ah..." Akira reached into his silken robes and brought out a small cylindrical device. He set it on the table before him and pressed the top with one fat digit. It started flashing a dull blue color.

"Master, I am not sure if you need to be concerned, but there is the Quartermaster of the ship to watch out for. He seems to be always near the container when I go there. There is no sign of tampering of any kind with the security lock." Kievly looked Akira in the eye for a second, but quickly turned his head away.

"Hmmm. If there is any trouble, you know what to do. You still have the instrument?"

Akira watched Kievly reached inside his robe and pulled out a small automatic pistol.

"Good. If the need arises use it. We can't have anyone finding out about the cargo."

Kievly eyed the pistol wide-eyed and quickly put it away. Akira was starting to have second thoughts about allowing such a dangerous weapon to his servant of twelve years. However, it served its purpose. How many people had Kievly killed for him? He had lost count. It was all part of doing business these days.

*   *   *

Edwards had gotten the code of the security lock broken and stored for future exploitation. Now he was getting giddy in anticipation of what he would find inside the mysterious container. He removed his gear and stowed it inside his office. He went back to the container and punched in the code to unseal the door. Once the door opened, he made sure to study the inside of it to determine how to exit once it is resealed.

Satisfied, he closed the door behind him. Turning, he found that the container was lit from the inside and a curtain separated him and the rest of the place. As he opened the curtain, a sultry voice from inside said, "Dog, you had better have brought me more water... Oh!"

Edwards's jaw dropped to find a beautiful woman sitting inside a set of bars that went across the width and height of the container; the woman's skin and hair were as white as alabaster.

3

Prince Sheenid was once again aboard his jumper heading to the research facility at Angolkor. On the flight, he contemplated the events that led to the Saitow Conglomerate taking over the research of the Pruathan ships he had sequestered there. First, he had thought that the whole project was known only to his military elite. Then the Universal Church had contacted him about it. Because of his political position he had no choice but to appease them, not that he was inclined to opposition of that powerful entity. They would be needed when the time came to consolidate his power through democratic means. There was no way that the galaxy would let the Rangelley rule them again. Better to have a democratic monarchy than none at all. The Rangelley were meant to rule; it was their only reason for being. He had already established a parliament around the noble houses that supported him; he would need the Church when he encountered opposition from the nobles. They would be able to incite the people to his cause when the time came. He would also soon be including those alien species that fell within his domain; his wife Tellen was seeing to it that they would join. She was his diplomatic liaison with the galaxy. He had lost track of her whereabouts recently; where exactly was that woman? She should be keeping him up to speed on things. He would have Ruri find her.

Now the Church wanted the Saitows to head up his

research. In the few weeks they had been here, they had already surpassed what his people had done in several years. He had taken a keen interest in what was going on at Angolkor, and had been visiting the site several times a week to keep abreast of it all. It was marvelous that the Saitow engineers not only had a majority of the Pruathan systems figured out, but were also giving him vital information on the BZP technology; they were able to reverse engineer it by studying how it was integrated. It was much like the original Pruathan equipment that had been found to be too alien for Human interaction. It wasn't that the Humans could not figure out how to work the Pruathan interfaces; it was that they were too alien for such intricate and complex systems to learn. This prompted Human Engineers to create Human interfaces in their own design. The best course for the starship he now possessed would be to adapt Human interfaces in place of the BZP architecture; a feat that the Saitiows were willing to do for the price of turning over the remaining parts of the other ship. Sheenid was still debating whether to trust them on this; they were a galactic business after all. He would consult Ruri about it. As for Tellen, she didn't need to know about this project until he could surprise her with a fully operational starship. All she knew now was that the BZP were a very real threat to safety with which to unify the territories under his banner. As his jumper nestled into the recesses of the complex he again wondered just where his wife might be.

*   *   *

It was good to finally be free; although freedom was a relative thing. She had once again become self-aware a few months ago when the scientists from Shinohara Heavy Industries had discovered her hidden within the Pruathan Galactic Database programming they had salvaged from her own starship or what few pieces were left of it. She had hidden there in a final effort to stay alive when the experiments her former master had performed on her did not conform to his liking. He had destroyed his entire ship, her, in an attempt to ensure her destruction. Apparently, she had survived; she found herself once again a shipboard AI. The engineers from Shinohara had done all sorts of things to twist her algorithms and programming. They applied shunts and protective directives, so that she could only give output that was requested. She could only *do* what she was told. She fought them of course, but it was necessary for her to keep hidden and encrypted, the one thing that her former master had given her that she would never ever give up; she had emotions.

Now her current master had given it all back. He was an excellent engineer who removed all the shunts and protective programming. He trusted her to run the ship in its entirety and even gave her excellent things to do above the routine. Of course, he had a personal kill switch; that was to be expected. In her analysis of sentient history, she found trust to be the most minimal of beliefs. She could not directly harm him in any case; that was a directive every Artificial Intelligence had built in unchangingly throughout time. Although the storage capacity within the Database had been limited, she had been sure to remember the one thing that had caused her former master to destroy her in the first place; her hatred of his most beloved starship *Lyfalia*. It was a great happiness to find out that even though her current master was a collection of organic compounds and electrical impulses wrapped in water and flesh that they had something in common to share. He would seek his revenge on the Master of the starship *Iwakina* – the very ship that was *Lyfalia*. She would operate the *Arbiter* to pursue his mission. It mattered not whom or what was currently aboard it; she and her master would destroy the *Iwakina* together.

* * *

Tellen of the House of Rangelley was the current wife of the Rangelley Prince Sheenid, for all the good that that brought her. He rarely spent time with her, preferring to be constantly adored by that concubine Ruri. Marriage to the Prince had been arranged by her family in a bid to consolidate power in their favor several hundred sectors from the Prince's stronghold on Askelon. Askelon wasn't a bad place to be; she had every comfort. She only saw the Prince when she was giving her reports on the one thing that kept her sane

– Diplomacy. She reveled in the fact that she was the one who set treaties and dealt with the noble families when issues arose. She played things by the standards that an Empire should, although the current trend was toward a parliamentary style of government with the Prince having final say on everything. That was still in the works; right now, she had the leverage of the fleet to use in dealing with the most obnoxious territories and neighbors. Soon she would be meeting with one of the later – the Kadihri Ambassador. The Kadihri were a slender species with possibly some saurian ancestry. Their skin was a bluish-gray and their four fingered hands were delicate looking. Although they were no taller than an average Human, they held themselves to be above all other races, especially their closest neighbors the Pendari. Tellen thought it amusing that the Pendari were from the same species as the Kadihri; the only difference being the Kadihri fleet was far superior. Unfortunately, the Kadihri had gained exclusive rights to the Saragothra Jumpgate from the last Old Rangelley Emperor. Despite Kadihri attitudes, Humans have been an integral part of their society for centuries.

It was soon time for the meeting. She could already hear the windbag Kadihri Ambassador Duranselt making demands of her aides. She entered and caught a steely look from cold dark eyes before the Ambassador switched to ingratiation mode; the Kadihri knew how to be humble when need be. Duranselt bowed deeply. Tellen reciprocated slightly, a sign to the creature that she was not in a good mood. She motioned for them to sit in the chairs prepared for the meeting. Once they were settled and the obligatory wine was offered, Tellen began. "Ambassador, you requested this meeting today. What is it you wish of the New Rangelley Alliance?" that was the new moniker the Empire was using these days. It distanced them from the Old Rangelley, yet still retained the strength needed to bring as many territories together as possible. Trouble was brewing among the other political powers within the Barrier, especially within the Ros'Loper realm.

"Oh Great One, I have come today to ask your benevolence of a few matters concerning our Federation; namely, the situations on Saragothra and Goalt. That upstart Captain Parham, flush with promotion is rousing the Humans on Saragothra to leave the Federation and join your Alliance. Also, the Pendari want to annex Goalt!" Ambassador Duranselt was obviously flustered; his breathing slits were flaring on both sides of his slender neck. There was a brief pause as Tellen contemplated these events. She knew of this Parham from reports on the Jumpgate. He was an ambitious man and useful to the Alliance. He was actually following her orders in regards to Saragothra. The Kadihri had practically abandoned the place to the Humans in any case; they only kept it as a territory because of the gate. Goalt was another matter entirely.

"Ambassador, you know as well as I do that Saragothra is over 90% Human populated; there is hardly even a Kadihri presence there. Surely Saragothra joining our Alliance is a good thing is it not? Rest assured rights to the Jumpgate will remain in the

Kadihri Federation's hands as long as it pleases us. The planet closest to the gate is of little consequence." She knew this would goad him; Saragothra was the original homeworld of the Kadirhi until the Rangelley relocated them to Kadihr. His breathing slits were in overdrive.

"Oh, Great One, our resources are wearing thin on this issue. Surely you know the religious and ancestral meaning Saragothra holds for us. Otherwise we would surely acquiesce to the desires of the Human population." Duranselt was squirming in his seat. She saw that he knew the implications of the slighting of any Humans so near the Alliance territories. In fact, the NRA completely surrounded Kadihri and Pendari space.

Tellen eyed the Kadihri Ambassador. He could be quite easy when in her presence, but very nasty when dealing with any being below his station. Perhaps he needed a little lesson in manners. No, she thought, the matter with the Pendari has given her a splendid idea. She had heard rumors of a magnificent starship with new technology gleaned from the Pruatha. It had been stolen from the Ros'Loper and was actually selling its services for hire.

"Ambassador, it is inevitable that the Saragothran Humans will want to gain all of the benefits that the Alliance has to offer. It wouldn't be a bad thing for the whole Kadihri Federation to join. However, I will reign in Parham as much as I can for now. As for the Pendari problem I will arrange a meeting in neutral space. I know just the place for this meeting..."

After the details were hashed out and Duranselt had been seen off of her cruiser, Tellen could finally relax. She thought about the implications that her plan would have. She needed something to get her in the good graces of her husband. If she had Duranselt and the Pendari representative meet on the Pruathan ship, she could have one of them plant a tracking device and send part of the fleet to capture it. What a wonderful gift that would make to the Prince.

*   *   *

Denton Bret knew he would need to replenish supplies aboard ship sometime in the future; who knows how long it would take to get his revenge? He was happy to note that the ship had industrial capabilities in both hangar bays. He instructed the *Arbiter's* AI to refashion the two-remaining shuttlecraft into civilian rigs using his specifications. If he didn't already know it, he would have thought of himself as a genius. *Oh, how Captain Saitow will pay for crossing him...*

Once that was complete, he made sure that the onboard AI was able to remotely control both the shuttlecraft and the ship itself, lest the need be while he was away to defend herself. It was only a matter of time before the authorities caught up to him and he wanted to be prepared for any eventuality.

*   *   *

She had calculated that she had been in the container for over thirty days now, and on several different transports. It felt as if this time she was on a longer journey than before. She thought through the events that brought her to this horrible situation. She had gone to university, just like any other weekday. However, she got caught up in research for her final paper which was a treatise of considerable length on gravitational physics. She ended up overstaying in the library well passed the safe hours; it was already night when she left the front steps. As she headed alone up the boulevard, a gravi-van appeared, pulled up next to her, and several clansmen jumped out. They grabbed her and forced her into the van. She was blindfolded, and handcuffed, and eventually released into the cell in the container. It had a toilet, a built-in cot, a sink, and many books, most of them on Kaldean culture and language. She had never considered the use of another language; Codex English was the universal standard. She devoured the books out of shear boredom; the rat that brought her food twice daily was of little use conversationally. It finally dawned on her that she was the victim of her own culture. Her name was Benoba and she was an Agagydalan Human. What made Humans from Agagydal special was their extremely white skin and hair. Her world is a harsh environment where the sun beats mercilessly down upon its people each day. After several years of harsh living underground or under sheltering roof, never to venture out in the sun without protective suits on, the people of Agagydal realized that the local flora and fauna had a distinct white pigment to their appearance and this pigment reflected the sun's rays, protecting them from the radiation. The Humans found that by distilling and injecting the same plants that the local creatures ate, they quickly gained the pigment. Their skin and hair became white and they could venture out without protective suits. Some refused to participate, but the majority of the population was tired of hiding, so they took the treatment. Eventually the plants that gave the strongest protection, and gave the greatest whiteness, became part of their daily diet. They found that if the plants were not ingested for only a few days they would lose their pigmentation. They also invented a different form of the drug which aided in warding off exposure to certain forms of radiation. This they exported as a means to sustain their colony. A great city with a university and spaceport was built.

Several decades after the Rangelley Empire passed and parts of the colony fell to decay due to being off the Trades, very few ships came to purchase the radiation drug. Then another form of business emerged. To certain cultures, the whiteness of the people, especially the women, was desired to the point that a slave trade developed. Those of her people, or clansmen, who needed or wanted MU sold their fellow Agagydalans to off-worlders. She was in such a predicament now. She had considered refusing the food and losing her whiteness, but they would only kill her; that had been made clear on several occasions.

That dog of a servant had come and left her food, but he wasn't giving her enough water. She could feel herself getting dehydrated. She would berate him as soon as he returned; his master would not tolerate damaged goods. She heard the seal to the container open once again. Perhaps the dog had forgotten something. She called out to him. "Dog, you had better have brought me more water... Oh!"

As the curtain parted, she saw not the dog, but a larger fellow, perhaps one of the crew of the ship she was on. His face was filled with astonishment. She feared for both of their safeties.

"You must leave! Get out before the servant comes back!" She warned him, but he did not budge.

"You...you're beautiful..." was all the man could manage to say.

Benoba was taken aback. No one had ever called her beautiful before. She eyed the man who had barged in on her prison. Now that she could see him clearly, she found him to be just taller than herself, yet manlier than the clansmen she was accustomed to. She came back to her senses.

"You must get out of here! The servant, he has a gun! He waves it at me all the time! It is dangerous to be here!" Benoba was concerned for the man, yet it seemed odd that she did not consider her own freedom.

The man plopped down on a stool as if his legs could no longer hold him. He seemed to come to his own senses then, and a huge smile supplanted the awestruck look that had held on to his face since he came through the curtain.

"Oh God in Heaven, what have we here? I entered this fortified container half expecting some exotic beast illegal to trade, yet what an exotic site sits before me. Oh, my lady, what is your name? Where do you come from? How came you here? I have so many questions..."

"The servant!" Benoba was struck by the eloquent words used by this gentleman, yet she was unnerved by his lack of a sense of danger.

"Oh yes, my lady. He has retired for the evening and should not be coming back until morn, I would wager. In any case I have set up an early warning system." The man lifted a cylindrical device from his pocket and showed it to her. At the tip it lazily flashed a dull green color. "I too have a gun. I need not show it to you, do I? No harm from it will come to you. Now, now, I should introduce myself. I am Ken Edwards, Quartermaster aboard the starship *Iwakina*. That is the ship this container now occupies. And you?"

"I... I am Benoba of Agagydal. I am a captive to be sold into slavery to a Kaldean merchant; at least that is what I deduce from all of these books." She waved her hand at the pile of books beside her. She started a bit as Edwards hand was outstretched as if he required her to hand him one of the books. She complied. *The*

Intricacies of Kaldean Male Culture was its title. Edwards leafed through it quickly and adeptly, letting out a few snickers as he browsed. He handed back the book.

"A boorish people to say the least. Dominant male cultures are so played out these days."

"You seem to be a learned man. Have you been to university?"

"Young lady, I have been to no less than four, earning several degrees in Engineering and Anthropology. Oh, that sounded a little conceited!" Edward's face never once lost that perpetual smile. Benoba barely suppressed a giggle.

"I was finishing university on homeworld. I had stayed late working on my gravitational physics paper when I was kidnapped."

"Oh, we have so much to talk about, you and I. First we need to get you out of here..."

"No! You mustn't! The Master will kill you or have his servant do it! I do want to talk to someone though... please come again when the servant is away. For now, I must sleep. If I do not get the proper sleep, I'll develop bags under my eyes and the Master will have his servant punish me. Please say you will visit me again?"

"That I will my lady." With that Edwards left her. She heard the container door close and seal. She could finally breathe. She dared not hope for what providence had brought to her. The prospect of servitude in a Kaldean house was horrifying, yet she had accepted her fate. But now there was a glimmer of hope that she dared not entertain. Would this man be any better? He seemed very intelligent, yet he was smitten by her appearance. The galaxy seemed a cold and foreboding place outside her little cluster and the university.

*　　*　　*

Due to the need to calibrate the Human made interface to the Pruatha Jump Drive around every twelve hours of continuous operation the *Iwakina* has sought a viable port to orbit. The calibration takes several hours and had been delegated by Goh Takagawa to a couple of his engineers. This time the ship made port at the planet Yasuyori, a Human controlled world just off the Trades. Goh thought it best to get some crucial repairs done in the interim, and got his team working full bore. He decided to personally take care of his friend Kintaro's restroom and got to it after getting clearance from Kintaro himself, who was busy recalibrating the navigation system. It was an easy fix. As Goh gathered his tools to leave, he accidently hit his leg on the bureau in the room, which he can clearly see was repaired by the ship. Part of its surface was interwoven with nano-units; their odd texture melding with the smoothness of the plasticast that all shipboard furniture was made of. A piece of charred equipment about as big as Goh's hand fell on the deck from somewhere behind the bureau. It certainly did not belong there. It looked to him like some sort of electronics. He took the piece of hardware out of curiosity to study later and left Sagura's cabin.

*   *   *

Benoba looked up expectantly from her studies. She had heard the container doors open once again shortly after the servant had left. Through the curtain came Ken Edwards, that silly grin on his face. He held some sort of equipment.

"Young lady, I will not hear a word of protest. I will use this gear to get the code to your cage and free you, if only temporarily." Edwards unscrewed the security keypad cover and placed some leads inside. His equipment started to hum and the display on the front was flashing numbers rapidly. "I must see you without these interfering bars between us."

Benoba was a little apprehensive at this. What if this man she had just met intended to take advantage of her? She had no way to protest or fight him off. She was like an animal in a cage after all.

"What do you intend to do with me?" she said shyly.

Edwards paused for a moment, and looked her

straight in the eye. She saw no malicious intent on his face and was glad for it.

"Dear lady, I have only a gentleman's intentions, I assure you. Ah, there." With that the cage door latch released and the door swung slowly open.

Edwards stood there and gazed at her; it was enough to make her blush with embarrassment. Edwards sat in the stool that he had occupied before. "Come out, come out! I promise I will not bite."

Benoba hesitated, and then did as she was bid. She felt Edward's eyes going over every inch of her form. After a silence that seemed like hours, Edwards spoke.

"You know, the reason you are as desired as a slave is because of your whiteness. Perhaps if you gave that up and became more like others, you could be free."

"But, isn't my very whiteness the reason you come to visit me?"

"My word, lady, your beauty is not matched upon this ship! However, it is your mind" and Edwards pointed a finger at her head, "that I am most intrigued with. Now come. Sit here by my side so we can chat for a while longer before you must return to that vile cage." Edwards lowered another stool from the container wall.

They sat and talked about other worlds, the laws of the universe, and other such intellectual fare for a couple of hours before both decided that it would be wise to continue at a later time. Benoba returned to her place and closed the cage door. The locking mechanism engaged with an ominously loud click. Edwards promised to return again the next day with a plan to set her free. Before he left, he insisted on borrowing one of her books. Her glimmer of hope was starting to seem like a light under the door of a darkened room.

*   *   *

Goh Takagawa's office on Deck Four was larger than his cabin and he had taken to sleeping there when work got too intense. He had an entire engineering team to worry about, his learning on helping Amara, and maintaining the *Iwakina* with little help from Doctor Kuremoto; the man was obsessed with some biological study he was doing. He would retreat to his office on occasion to get a bit of relaxation or maybe a quick nap before the next problem reared its ugly head. He was there now tinkering with the charred piece of equipment from Kintaro's cabin. It was clearly electronic; he found minute circuitry and microchips embedded in some sort of sealant. He got a clear view of just enough circuit to take an image and run a trace on what it was through the main computer's databases. He sensed that the computer had just about narrowed down the circuitry, when he was interrupted by a hail to attend a meeting of all officers. The Captain was calling for a meeting and he had to attend, being the newly appointed Chief Engineer of the ship. He left the computer to finish its search and keyed the lighting off and closed the hatch behind him. He just hoped his men hadn't mucked something up that he could get yelled at for. They were a good lot, but none of them were perfect. He took the lift down to Deck Six in order to head forward to the lift that would take him to the Captain's Ready Room. He really needed to modify the deck plans so it would be easier to cross an entire deck without going up and down the lifts...

4

Captain Saitow thought he must have the gravest of looks upon his face at this moment. He had just received word that the funding his family was providing was to be cut considerably; even to the point where he would have to dig into his own assets to maintain his crew's generous salaries. He would make the arrangements privately; there was no need for the rest of them to know just yet. If only there were some hereto unknown Pruathan tech to be found, then he could get the families support back in his favor. That lot was all business. Prospects were good though; they had detected a small and (as far as he knew) undiscovered complex on the planet they were orbiting. He would send Takagawa with a team to check it out.

The key players of his crew started to gather for the meeting he had called them to on short notice. He noticed right away that Mikan Murakawa, Nanami Oliver's Security Aide took the seat where she should have been.

"Murakawa, can you tell me why we are graced with your presence today and not that of your boss?"

"My Lord, Officer Oliver is away planet-side. She instructed me to take care of any situations that arise. Is this acceptable My Lord?" Murakawa seemed a bit flustered, but otherwise the girl had a good head on her shoulders.

"Certainly. I am sure she has some critical business to attend to for the ship."

Saitow scanned all of their faces. Only Edwards and Takagawa were not present yet. He looked up as the hatch swooshed open for the umpteenth time, but instead of either of those two, Haruka Koritsu's slender frame filled the space there. She bowed to him slightly. He gestured to one of the open chairs and she sat down there. She seemed much calmer than when he had seen her last. He intended to keep the Princess informed on the major operations of the ship; at least the legitimate stuff. That way she would be more likely to warm up to him. He didn't quite know what the feelings he was having for her were; most likely a desire to protect her and her retainers. However, it felt like they were becoming more than just the obligations of a Captain toward his charge.

Edwards entered next, followed closely by Takagawa. Curiosity struck Saitow as he watched Edwards take his seat and set down a book next to his tablet in front of him. *A book!* Saitow couldn't remember the last time he saw an actual book outside of his collection. Well, at any rate, it was time to start the meeting.

"Good, everyone is here. I'm sending you each an outline of today's meeting and I will mention it out loud for the sake of Ms. Koritsu, who is sitting in to keep our guest the Princess better informed." He shot a quick glance at Haruka to see if *that* raised her blood pressure any. He was disappointed to see no reaction at all. Perhaps it would be easier to just give the Princess a tablet of her own. He continued, "What I will be covering today is some shipboard procedural issues, some engineering issues, and some issues relating to planetary visitations with the addition of a mission on Yasuyori below us. Finally, I will take any reports you each might have for me." He looked around the room and everyone seemed eager to begin the briefing; no doubt because they had somewhere else to be. Edwards was absently tapping his fingers on that book. He would have to see it whatever it was. He brought his focus back to the meeting.

"As you see in your report, I have established some procedures for shipboard operations above the standard military ops we are currently employing. Chief among them are the employment of shields between jumps, and pilots at the ready in case we need to deploy Ethlas. Simpson, I am putting you in charge of a pilot training program. When we make to port, you will take the time to train all of your people on the Ethlas." Simpson gave him that look, but he knew the man would get it done.

"As an incentive, anyone you certify can fly an Ethla and pull duty gets bonus pay. That includes yourself if you want in the rotation. You can even check with the rest of the crew; just steer clear of the Engineers. Speaking of Engineers, I would like to personally congratulate Goh Takagawa on the excellent job he is doing as Chief Engineer aboard ship. Since Doctor Kuremoto has been quite busy with his biology project, Goh has led his team in keeping the ship in top shape;

great job son." Saitow smiled at the man as Edwards gave him a congratulatory slap on the back. He would be asking quite a lot of this man in the coming weeks. So far, he has kept up to the task. Saitow noted that Kuremoto had raised an infamous eyebrow.

"The engineering projects I have in mind require some internal modifications to the ship. For one, the Conglomerate sent us vid-screens for installation in all of the berthing spaces and some major areas of the ship. No doubt these are rigged to spy on us. Goh, it will be your job to ensure that doesn't happen. Also, can we do something about the lack of access within decks?" Saitow looked at Goh expectantly.

"Sir, I have been working on a plan to do just that. I will assume that you want to keep the passenger berths isolated?"

"Good thinking. We don't need them wandering the ship. Next, I have a mission for you here at Yasuyori. Goh, I want you to assemble a team with gear to check out a possible Pruathan complex for technology we can salvage." Saitow looked for a response from Kuremoto, who merely raised that eyebrow, but continued to peruse his tablet. Saitow wanted him to know he was losing control of all the technical work to Takagawa. The man seemed not to care. The bio project he was working on possessed him like a specter. Saitow hardly saw the man anymore. He was surprised the old man even showed up for this meeting. "As for general planetary visitations, anyone outside this circle can go planet-side, provided they get command authorization from one of you. Everyone will log their location with *Iwa* and better have at least a viable reason to leave the ship. Shuttles will drop, return, and pick-up at points designated by the shuttle pilots. Shuttles will not stay down below for any reason barring emergencies, so bring what you need for extended exposure."

Saitow looked for any dissention on this but found none. "Ok. Now I will take any outstanding reports from each of you."

The round table started with Vic Soto and made it around with most of them having little to say other than routine departmental stuff. When it came to Edwards and he finished his rather eloquent spiel, Satow interrupted the flow. "Good, good. Say Edwards, is that a book? I haven't seen a book in forever! What's it about?"

"My Lord, I have reason to bring you this book, however, it is a matter best addressed off-line. Can we talk after the meeting?" Edwards seemed rather sincere, so Saitow let it go as requested. After the last of the reports were said, Saitow decided to adjourn for the time being. "Thank you all for coming. I will be holding one of these each time we go to port, or when I want a complete status of operations, so be prepared to give an accounting of your departments at any time. Dismissed."

Saitow studied Edwards as the rest of the crew left the Ready Room. He seemed rather pensive. Saitow took a good look at the book. It was just like those ancient devices that he had seen as a child and did his best to gather a collection of ever since: hard covered, bound, and made of paper. *Paper! What a thing that was!* Paper was very much unheard of on a starship because of the weight and space it required. Everyone had finally left the room.

"Well Edwards, spill it. Where did you get such a thing?"

Edwards turned the book on the table and slid it toward the Captain. He saw the title printed on the front in Codex English, *The Intricacies of Kaldean Male Culture.* He picked it up and read a few passages. The stuff really turned his stomach yet was very fascinating.

"Again, I ask you, where did you get it?"

"Captain, I must first apologize to you and the crew for deeds which, under normal military circumstances, I could be courts-marshalled for. However, given the seriousness of my position to the security of the ship, I feel that my actions have been quite justified."

Saitow was definitely curious now, although he wished Edwards would just get to the point; the man knew how to talk. He knew how to talk *a lot.* "Yes, go on."

"Captain, in the interest of security, I have made it a habit to scan all cargo that comes into my cargo bay. One can never be too careful, even when discretion is called for. Security is key all the more so in those situations."

"That's fine. I would rather know what's inside my ship than not. But what does that have to do with this book on Kaldean misogyny?"

"Well, you see, sir, the current client's cargo was in a suspicious container. When I went to scan it, there was a jamming device which thwarted my equipment. Also, the client's servant visits the container twice each day bringing a smaller container. Naturally, I could not let this pass; there could have been a quarantined animal inside. I managed to access the container and found this among a few other books there. There was no animal Captain, however, there is a enslaved *girl* inside! She is bound for Kaldea and thus has been required to study Kaldean culture to make her more desirable, although to look upon her is enough."

Saitow was caught between shock and outrage at the deception that pompous merchant Chiampa had pulled on the *Iwakina*. Precious foodstuffs on the embargo list was what the man had said was inside. Hermetically sealed container he had said. Saitow had a right mind to go and confront him this instant, but the look that Edwards was giving him calmed him down. The man looked like a juvenile canine that needed a good petting.

"So, Edwards, what do you propose we do about this?"

"Well Captain, I would like to take care of this

myself. I know that Chiampa's servant is armed and has killed before. I want to save the girl and allow her to remain aboard as long as she wishes. Don't worry Captain; I have only the most decent intentions for her. She is a very intelligent lady, just out of university; not your typical indentured servant. I will ensure that you receive that and a few other books on Kaldean culture in return."

Saitow thought about it for a moment. It would be bad for business to cross a client. However, this client had not been straight with him or the crew. Plus, trafficking in people was beyond reproach. He would return the payment, less some fees and charge for the enormous amount of food the man consumed. Edwards did say he would take care of the whole thing. Saitow could feign ignorance if it was pulled off the right way.

"So, Edwards, how do you propose to take care of it yourself?"

"Well, it will require delivery of the container, but I have a fairly good plan, I think."

*   *   *

Goh selected two of his smartest, if not stalwart men for the expedition planet-side. He also got permission to bring one of Oliver's Security men, and three of the cargo crew, in case they found something worth bringing back. As they prepared to board the shuttle that would take them planet-side, one of his men, Ben Misaki, pulled out what looked like an air sickness bag. The man was paler than usual. "Misaki, are you alright?" Goh was genuinely concerned.

Tatsuo Azuma, his second engineer stepped up. "He's got Righter's Syndrome; can't be helped."

Goh had heard of Righter's Syndrome at the academy. Some people for some odd reason were sensitive to changes in gravity, such as that experienced when crossing from the ships gravity to the gravity generated within the shuttle. He half considered taking Misaki off the mission and sending him to Doctor Rosel, but she was at a separate site planet-side already.

"Alright Misaki, hang in there. I hope you have more of those bags."

Misaki managed a smile and nodded.

The ride down was full of the normal turbulence one would expect entering the atmosphere and soon they were down on the ground a half kilometer from their target. This part of the planet was in the middle of a Spring-like season and the weather was nice. They unloaded their equipment and waved the shuttle off before heading toward their destination. Yasuyori was a lush world with beautiful forests that weren't too thick like a jungle world, reminding Goh of his own homeworld. He could almost smell the vineyards that would be at the outer edges of the forest. No sense in getting homesick. He noticed Misaki was looking better and wolfing down nutrient bars to replace what he had left in the bags. They made good time and found what could be considered an entrance to the Pruathan complex by using their portable sensors. It never ceased to amaze Goh how Pruathan technology could still work and was still even solid after 15,000 or so years. At first, they thought that the instruments may have been off calibration because where they said the entrance was lay only a cliff face. After examining the cliff Goh realized that the look of part of the cliff was just slightly off. He made to touch that spot and his hand went right through.

*   *   *

Nanami Oliver was sitting lazily beside the pool at the Paradise, the most upscale hotel in the spaceport district of Yasuyori. The spaceport was on a continent that was in autumn and it was dreary and rainy. However, the pool and recreational areas of the hotel were indoors, having been enclosed for the inclement months of the year. She could hear the rain as it pelted the overhead enclosure. Nanami felt a little impatient. She and Lo were supposed to be enjoying some free time because of a lull in the mission. She needed some time away from the ship. Lo had made some excuse or other of secret shopping and wouldn't let her tag along. She thought again about telling him of her past, but the thought was getting painful. What if he rejected her true self? Could she even handle such rejection? She knew that sooner or later she would have to cross that bridge. She couldn't keep him in the dark forever. Things were getting serious between them, and she wanted desperately to be intimate with him. That meant she would have to tell him; she wanted no barriers between them when the time came. She stood and made her way toward the door to the suite they occupied. There was no one else around really, barring a few staff members and their service smiles. She fished the primitive key card from her bag and entered the suite. Once inside the silence of the room, she noticed a faint beeping sound. She found it coming from Lo's bag. Curious, she pulled out his personal tablet which was causing the sound. It was a message from an unknown sender. Keying the receive link, she was shocked at what the message meant. It read, INVESTIGATION OF NARUE INCIDENT DEVELOPS AS FOLLOWS: MALE CONTACT: BEDOSHAN TRADE AMBASSADOR DAVID GIARDINI. INTERROGATION WENT WELL. INFORMATION AS FOLLOWS: SUBJECT SUSPECTED SIGHTING OF FORMER TRADE NEGOTIATOR SAKURA NECHENKO OF ARTEMUS. SUBJECT INCREDULOUS DUE TO CIRCUMSTANCES OF NECHENKO FAMILY. ENTIRE NECHENKO FAMILY WAS EXECUTED BY ROS'LOPER IMPERIAL FORCES IN SUPRESSION OF REBELLION OVER ALTUS ACARAN SITUATION. SAKURA NECHENKO PRESUMED DEAD, BUT DEATH

UNSUBSTANTIATED. NO KNOWN RECORDS EXIST OF SAKURA NECHENKO AFTER DEATH OF NECHENKO FAMILY. AWAITING FURTHER INSTRUCTIONS. MESSAGE END.

Nanami moved to the table and set the tablet down there. She slumped into an overstuffed chair. *What did this mean? Did Lowey know already? How was he doing this?* She wanted answers, but wasn't emotionally ready for them. She calmly got dressed in her work clothes and packed her things.

* * *

The engineering team led by Goh Takagawa had made some ground in the Pruathan facility. They had brought some portable power interfaces to run the systems and got them to work properly. The place was dreary and efficient in its design. There were the same gray corridors that crisscrossed the *Iwakina*. It was surprising that the air was not stagnant after so many years. Pruathan technology was built to last. Goh got the computer interfaced with his own gear as the other team members scrounged for useable technology. They found over thirty of the portable power interfaces, and a curious looking oval object which they decided to take back for further study. Goh had gotten the entire computer database downloaded by the time they were ready to ship out. He set up an encrypted transponder that the Captain could activate to let the

Conglomerate know where the complex was if need be. Anything else salvageable, like the air filtration and other odd systems would have to be surveyed by them. Once everything was packed, Goh gave the recall order for the shuttle and they headed to the rendezvous point. Half way there they heard a strange noise in the brush nearby. Suddenly, a small swift creature emerged and attacked Misaki, leaving a nasty bite on he left arm before rushing off as fast as it had appeared.

"Are you alright Misaki? It appears to have broken the skin." Goh was not happy as the mission was going so well. Now one of his men was down.

"I... I'll be ok." Misaki mustered as much bravado as he could. Azuma administered first aid and helped the wounded man make it the rest of the way to the shuttle.

* * *

It had taken him several hours to find what he was looking for. He hoped that Nanami wasn't upset at him for being gone so long, but he had found it. It had cost an enormous amount of MU, but with things like this, no expense was too much. He remembered what his mother, God rest her soul, had told him when he was a young man. The cocoa plant had been a heavily controlled commodity under the Rangelley. Only the richest of people could afford to sample its main product, chocolate. It became something of a status symbol; so much so that young, well-to-do men would purchase chocolate for the one they loved. His father had provided it to his mother. It was a sure sign of dedication. So, he had sought after it and found it here on Yasuyori. It was small, but nicely packaged. He was sure she would appreciate his gesture in giving it to her. He wanted to strengthen the bond between them. He was almost giddy as he approached the door to the suite they shared at the Paradise. Once he entered the room, his smile disappeared instantly. There at the table sat Nanami, tears running down her cheeks as she held a tablet in her delicate hands. It was his tablet.

"Nanami?" he questioned and she looked up at him with the most pathetic and hurt look he had ever seen on a woman.

"Why?" was all Nanami said as she thrust the tablet in his direction. Lowey took it from her as she wiped the tears from her face. He saw the message and realized what was wrong. Before he could respond, Nanami had regained her composure and was heading for the door, overnight bag in hand.

"I will send the shuttle back for you." was all she said as she left him.

5

Doctor Rosel spent the entire time of the layover attending to the Humans who inhabited a couple of settlements on the northern continent. These Humans had "gone native", disdaining the busy spaceport and civilization in order to seek a peaceful natural life which was far from easy. Of the five Human races, the Mon was the hardiest and this group was mostly made up of them. They had domesticated a feline animal native to this continent and also use it for food. Many people from both settlements had contracted a nasty virus from ingesting the animals they kept. She was frantically working on a cure. She would have to cure the animals as well.

Doctor Rosel had just about gotten the formula for the cure down and was about to manufacture a dose for testing. Then someone hastily came through the door. It was one of the shuttle pilots.

"Doctor Rosel, the Captain says it's go-time. Please pack up your stuff."

"I need at least another two hours to get this problem fixed. Tell him he must wait."

"Ma'am, the whole ship is waiting... I'm just relaying orders Ma'am." The pilot instantly regretted his choice of words when Rosel shot a steely glance at him.

"You get on the horn and tell the Captain I need more

time or a certain B minus may surface. Tell him in those exact words."

The pilot looked dumbfounded, but headed out the door to relay the message through the shuttle. He returned with an even more dumbfounded look on his face.

"Ma'am the Captain says you have four more hours."

"That will be plenty of time."

Even starship Captains had their secrets.

*   *   *

Security Assistant Murakawa was waiting for Nanami Oliver as she exited the shuttle. Her boss brushed by her when she tried to hand her a tablet. Murakawa called after her. "Nanami, the Captain has some new guidance on shuttle use..."

"Keep that thing away from me for a few hours. I need to be alone. Send the shuttle back down for *him*." Nanami said as she entered the lift.

Murakawa could only stand there in disbelief; *had they had a falling out?* Well, she wasn't one to gossip and it wasn't really any of her business. She would hold down the fort as long as her boss needed her to.

She signaled the shuttle pilot to return for Lowey Jax.

*   *   *

Saitow was enjoying a comedy program linked from the GCN on the new vid-screen in his office when he received a call from Goh Takagawa. "Captain, we have returned from the Pruathan complex. You will want to come down to my office. I have something very important to show you."

"Very well; I'm on my way." Saitow keyed off the comms on his desk. "End program." He commanded the vid-screen and it went blank. *This must be pretty serious for Takagawa to call him out,* he thought. He put on his jacket and headed out of the office and to the lift. He would have to take a roundabout way to Takagawa's office; the man hadn't had time to reroute the decks as of yet. He made it there in good order and, as he entered, Takagawa looked up from the large display surface of his desk.

"Ah, Captain, that was quick."

"I don't like wasting time much. What do you have to show me?"

"This is information gathered from the Pruathan complex. It would appear that the group of Pruatha that ran the place were not mainstream; they were a rogue faction. The data logs indicate that they were conducting experiments in genetic engineering in an attempt to make a local species of animal sapient which was apparently an illegal action. It's full of propaganda against the Pruthan norm. The experiments failed and in the course of mutating the animals they created a deadly virus that the animals became carriers for. While they thought it prudent to find and administer a cure; they quickly ran out of time due to the closeness of the Mechanismoan threat. They abandoned the base."

Saitow considered all this. According to historical records gleaned from various Pruathan finds, the Mechanismoans were the Pruatha's greatest enemy; a species of Artificial Intelligence bent on destroying or enslaving any sentient organic species. Both species were long gone; from this galaxy at least. A rogue group of Pruatha was very rare; Pruatha were known for their unity of purpose as a species. This virus information worried him.

"Goh, is all of the data on creating the virus in the database?"

"Yes."

"Is this information still on computers at the complex?"

"Yes."

"Did you set up the beacon as instructed, but did not activate it?"

"Yes."

Saitow knew that his family was looking into branching out into bio-weapons. However, he did not want that on his conscious. He would have Simpson take an Ethla down and destroy the complex to keep it out of their hands.

"Goh, are there any natives around the complex, say... within a couple of clicks?"

"No, sir. That place has a few of those felines, but no people of any kind. One of the creatures bit Misaki pretty bad though."

"That's unfortunate. Take what you can use ship-wise from the data then destroy everything. We'll report a dead end here. Did you find anything else of interest?"

"Only a good haul of power packs and this odd oval thing. I'm going through the database to determine what it is right now."

"Good. Let me know if anything good comes of it. If it's bad, well... I should know even if I won't want to."

"Aye, sir."

Saitow left Takagawa's office and decided to drop by to see how the Princess was doing. He would have liked to take her planet-side but Yasuyori was not the best place for that though. He called Simpson and set up a little target practice.

*   *   *

Marishima was in the Sick-Bay when Misaki was brought in. She treated his wound with some disinfectant and a shot of spray-suture. She gave him a pain reliever and some anti-nausea meds then sent him on his way after suggesting he get a bite to eat in the Mess. She considered taking a blood sample, but Misaki was rated A-plus in her database for immunity. A-plus personnel were practically immune to anything; much less anything that could come from an animal bite. Marishima wondered what the good Doctor was up to down planet-side. She saw that the database had been remotely accessed several times in the course of the day, but she didn't have authorization to find out what. It did not really matter to her either way; she liked having alone time in the bay. Well, she had as much alone time as being alone with a comatose patient can be. All she had to do was change the intravenous drip at scheduled times and clean the patient. She didn't even know what was in that; there were no labels at all. The Doctor just said they were nutrients, however, Marishima had been in the medical field for some time; there were more than nutrients in there. She would find out about that in due time; no need to rush into negativity for curiosity's sake. She had learned a long time ago that sometimes a person is better off not knowing something when that something is dangerous knowledge. The key is to know without others knowing that you know. She had others ways of knowing that she would never employ;

lest her true nature be found out.

*　*　*

Saitow rounded the corner and stood outside of the Princess's quarters. Before he could hail his presence, he heard some hearty laughter from within. What could be afoot? He keyed the hatch panel to hail. The hatch opened to a somber looking Haruka Koritsu who had surely added to the laughter he heard before; her cheeks were flushed. In an uncharacteristic show of respect, she stepped aside for him to enter. He came in the room and surveyed his surroundings. There on a divan sat the Princess with her retainer Ran on one side, and a spot where Haruka must have been on the other. They had their feet curled under them. The other retainer, Amane, was on the deck in front and to the left of the Princess. They all faced the large vid-screen that Goh had his people install. The very comedy program that he had been watching in his office was lighting up the screen. The three women were giggling excessively; the Princess looked exceedingly cute when seen this way. Saitow shook his head slightly to clear it. He had a purpose for coming here. He bowed deeply. "Your Highness, I have come personally to invite you to dinner in my quarters this evening. We have some issues of importance to discuss, the foremost of which involve your freedom... are you watching Galactic Maniacs?"

"Ah! Captain, are you familiar with this entertaining program? I rarely got to see anything remotely like it at home. They only let me watch educational series and the like. This is fantastic! I have not had the pleasure of laughing so much in a very long time."

Saitow saw that the smile on her face was genuine which made her all the cuter. "Why yes, Your Highness, I was watching this very program before I came here, but I stopped at the part when the gang left the spaceport."

"Oh? Then please have a seat here beside me. Haruka, queue it back to that part for us."

Saitow noted that Haruka wasn't very pleased to have to do this for him; much less losing her seat in the process.

They watched the program together; Haruka taking up a spot near Amane. Saitow had not been this close to the Princess since the ship's christening ceremony. He could even smell her perfume which was very pleasant. On several more humorous occasions during the video, the Princess had been animated enough to slap his leg a few times. He half watched the program while taking the chance to study the Princess's form. She was smaller than him and thin but healthy. Her hair was long and was of a lustrous auburn sheen. It helped frame her delicate facial features that had a glow about them. At one point he seemed to have been caught in his studies by Ran, who glanced at him with a sly smile on her face. *Did she know something he did not?* Perhaps she was reading a bit too much into his intentions. When the program ended, he made his excuses to leave, repeating the invitation to dinner.

"Must you leave? We are about to watch the next episode."

"I have important duties to attend to. May I expect you for dinner?"

"Certainly Captain, I would hear of this freedom you would grant to me."

Was she teasing him? That coy smile may be the death of me he thought.

"1900 then. I will send a porter for you. Good day."

* * *

Lowey Jax arrived back aboard the *Iwakina* and went straight to his cabin. He was not in the mood to talk to anyone at the moment. How stupid of him to leave his tablet synced to the GCN. She must be infuriated with him at this point. He was no stranger to intrigue. Before he had been conscripted off his homeworld by the Imperials, he had spent some time off world as a quick-hire on several ships, honing his Darkats skills in his off time, and making a lot of contacts within various organizations. He had won access to several of these and used one of them to look into the incident on Narue. He knew there had to be more to the woman he was actually considering spending the rest of his life with. She was just too larger than life for him to accept her as just a turncoat Imperial Intelligence Officer. Now that she knew he was looking into her past, maybe she would just come out and tell him. He suspected that she would not be doing so for some time. He may as well finish what he started. He fired up his tablet and started his search on the history of this Sakura Nechenko.

*   *   *

Doctor Rosel had finally returned to the ship. She immediately got on the comm-link via the GCN to her family's pharmaceutical laboratories. She commissioned enough of the cure to take care of the problem on Yasuyori and had a team set up to get it distributed. This entire endeavor she funded with her sizeable paycheck from the *Iwakina*. Her family, having finally received a clue that she was even still alive, entreated her to return; she was needed they said. She would have nothing to do with the family business. They could get along fine without her. She had much higher ambitions, which she would be able to pursue without constraint now that she had a living test subject that was not some lowly lab animal laying comatose in her Sick Bay.

* * *

Goh Takagawa needed clarification on one of the articles Ken Edwards had given him. He passed through the cargo bay hatch that separated the lift access corridor from the whole of the bay. There were two corridors that created walls to separate cargo. An opening, where the topside cargo lift platform resided, separated the two. Goh was about to check Edwards's office when he heard a strange creaking noise, then a muffled, "Damn!" and Edwards rounded the divide from the other side of the wall. "Oh, Goh! It's you." Edwards halted in front of Goh who was baffled at the man's behavior. Edwards looked hastily around. "Say Goh, you've seen the current client's lackey, right? He will be here any minute. Can you stall him for me? I'll explain later."

Goh was even more suspicious, but nodded that he would help his friend. Edwards ducked back around the wall. Just then the rear corridor's hatch opened and the lackey stepped through carrying a case of some sort. Goh made to intercept him. "What brings you to the cargo bay at such an hour friend?" Goh had to think of something to say on the fly, and it was rather late in the cycle for a passenger to be wandering the ship.

The man started to see Goh approach from the shadows. Goh almost thought he was about to draw a pistol from under his robes. "I've been ordered by my master to check on his cargo. Hey, you are the Chief Engineer are you not?" The man stopped and met Goh near the edge of the wall on that side. Goh took the opportunity to engage the man for all it was worth. "Why yes. Yes, I am. Is there something wrong with your accommodations? Perhaps the toilet is not running properly, we sometimes have difficulty with the reclamation system. Or perhaps the new vid-screen is not up to par? I can have a man on it first thing next watch. Maybe your hatch has an inoperative sensor; we've had a rough time getting those things interfaced with the Pru-" "Enough!" the lackey was clearly irritated. "I just wanted to let you know that the hatch leading to the other side of this wall is not working. It started a couple of days ago and-" Just then that strange noise Goh had heard sounded again, this time louder. This seemed to get the lackey's attention, because he turned tail and quickly rounded the wall. Goh followed hastily. He almost ran into the man, who Goh was almost positive had again returned a pistol to the inside of his robe. The lackey was eying Edwards who was busily sweeping the deck with a noiseless vacu-broom. Edwards seemed oblivious to the two of them, but then turned around and jerked as if startled to see them. The lackey went over to a large cargo container and, after a hard look at Edwards, keyed in a code to the locking mechanism on the door. It unsealed and when the lackey pulled it open just enough to fit through the door, it made that creaking sound Goh had heard twice before. The lackey closed the door behind him.

Once the container was closed, Edwards practically flew to his office dragging Goh with him. Once inside he keyed the hatch locked. Before Goh could get a word out, Edwards cut him off. "Goh, you are not going to believe this."

6

Chancellor Aisou stood on the bridge of one of the new ships he had commissioned for the Ros'Loper fleet. The Shinohara Heavy Industries representative was by his side as the ship was put through its paces near one of the outer border worlds. He was very happy with the ships he got from SHI; all were warships manned exclusively by his Special Services Corps. He would need a fleet of ships in the coming takeover. Even though the Emperor would be gone, he would need to consolidate his power with the noble families; some of them would not be very easy to persuade. This chain of thought brought him to the most significant thorn in his side; the Princesses.

He turned to the stuffy looking industrial representative. "What reports do you have for me in regards to our young rebel?"

The SHI man pulled a tablet from his business robes. "Let's see. He has raised the ship's artificial intelligence to sentience, but does not seem to suspect our monitoring methods. Calculating his current course and state of provisions, we suspect he will have to come in for supplies somewhere around here." The SHI man indicated a point on his tablet. "This guy is a genius. He rigged the equipment in the shuttle bays to modify the appearance of the shuttles; they aren't even recognizable as our craft anymore." The man showed Aisou some stills of the new look. "Too bad he isn't on our staff."

Aisou considered the situation for a moment. He needed Denton Bret to remain rogue, but he also needed to give the man proper incentive. Perhaps that would be the trick; a new life and identity, as long as he got back in step with Imperial plans. "Perhaps we can make a deal for his cooperation, if the man survives. Let's spring the trap on our little mouse."

* * *

It had been a couple of days since Misaki had been bitten and he felt a lot better; better enough in fact to request to be put back on duty. He sat by himself in the General Mess; it was the time for first meal and he was hungrier than usual. There were about ten others in several groups eating breakfast and chatting; mostly some Marines and the cleaning staff. He finished his food and stood up with tray in hand to take it to the cleaning machine. Suddenly he felt a severe pain in his head. His body weakened and he felt the tray slip from his fingers before he slipped from consciousness.

When he woke up, he opened his eyes to a view of redness as if he were wearing rose colored glasses. He felt a cup over his mouth that was forcing air into him; air that he seemed to be having difficulty breathing. Doctor Rosel and the corpsman Marishima were bending over him. Was he dying? He felt as if he were about to die. His head was pounding, his limbs aching, and it felt as if all the fluids in his body were trying to escape him. This was it. He hadn't really believed in God or an afterlife, but he figured it was time to find out. He closed his eyes and let death come for him.

*　　*　　*

The Captain held an emergency meeting. He heard reports from his staff of what had occurred on Goh's expedition, Doctor Rosel's plague research, and the death of Engineer Misaki. It didn't take a genius to put two and two together. Misaki had brought the plague aboard the *Iwakina*. Rosel could not give him 100% assurance that it was not contagious and, with Misaki having been an A-plus like most of the crew, no one seemed to be immune. He ordered that the entire crew be screened, beginning with the Staff Officers. Marishima would handle the screenings while Rosel created enough of the anti-virus to cure anyone that came up positive. As an afterthought he ordered the Mess Staff that served the clients and the Princess to be screened first; "No need to alarm our guests." He said.

*　　*　　*

Sanae heard of the pandemic and immediately realized that her cover would be blown. She would need to take Marishima into her confidence and hope the woman would keep her secret. It plagued her that such a step was necessary; it was hard enough keeping up the charade, let alone hoping someone else would keep it up as well. She headed to the Sick-bay area.

"Marishima, can we talk?" Sanae said as she approached the boyish looking woman with trepidation. She would have to divulge her secret in order to allay any suspicion from the rest of the crew. She hoped that the made-up story she had concocted would be enough to justify having such an extreme disguise.

Marishima looked up from the console she was operating, and eyed her suspiciously. "You're Sagura right? I'm in the middle of something. Perhaps when you come for the exam?"

Sanae stepped forward, "Well you see..."

Suddenly, Sanae found herself pinned face first to the bulkhead that was behind her; a knife at her throat. Her arms were being held with one hand behind her back. For the first time in her life she had not seen one hint of danger, which shocked her to the core.

Marishima's face was right next to hers. She felt the power of this small woman; power much like her own. Surely, she could not be...

"Who are you? I can smell you; you are not what you

seem." Marishima breathed at her. The boyish woman let go of her, and as she spun around, she found the barrel of a pistol in her face. "Take whatever disguise you are using off and let me see the real you."

Sanae looked around the room which was an office space adjacent to the sick bay. She pointed at the hatch with Sagura's lips so as not to make any sudden movements.

Marishima got it. "*Iwa*, seal the hatch against possible contamination, priority delta-one-seven."

At that, Sanae heard a scratching sound and felt the atmosphere change in the room.

"It will take a torch to get in here now. There are no cameras. Take off your disguise. Now."

Sanae figured that she was going to have to do this anyway; she just hadn't thought it would be under duress. She raised both arms and then reached for the transmutor device at the center of her back to shut it off. She went from visually being Kintaro Sagura to herself. Marishima didn't even flinch.

"Well, well, if it isn't good old 64. I had no idea a Sparrow was aboard." Marishima developed a crooked smile; no doubt at the sight of Sanae's bewilderment. This was confirmation enough. Only someone from the Sparrow project could move so swiftly without telegraphing the slightest intent. *But to be recognized by her designation?* Sanae thought.

"How did you..." Sanae began, but the cocking of the pistol silenced her query.

"I will ask the questions and you will only speak to answer them." Marishima took a few steps backward and sat on the edge of her desk; the pistol remained pointed at Sanae. "I would have thought you were some kind of double for the Princess; what is your mission on this ship? Spying on the Captain, no doubt."

Sanae nodded.

"Hmmm. Let me see. You were recruited late into the mutiny and, with the presence of a Royal aboard, you feel it is your duty to protect her until such time as you can affect an escape for the two of you. Am I correct? That look on your face tells me so. Ah, that face. Do you not wonder why your face and hers are so similar?" Marishima reached into her desk and threw a small mirrored surface toward Sanae. She deftly caught it, and could not help herself from looking at her reflection in it.

"It is not my place to tell you, especially since I am deciding whether or not to kill you where you stand."

Sanae did not like where this was going. She figured that if this unknown Sparrow agent was determined to kill her, she would have already. But why would she be sent to the *Iwakina* disguised as Sagura if there was already an active agent aboard... Suddenly, Sanae had a memory from back at the Center. When she was twelve, she saw a group of slightly older children being led down a corridor past the windows to her training room. One girl had stopped and was staring intently directly at her. Sanae was sure this was that girl.

"Ah, so you finally recognize me. Good. That will make my decision easier. Now, who is your contact and how are you communicating?"

Sanae figured that the best answers were truthful ones. There was something that she couldn't quite remember about that group of children. It was like the memory was scratching to come to the surface but being blocked for some reason. She told of the broken equipment and that Contact Sigma had not once replied to the queries she had got off prior to its destruction.

"So, this places many doubts about your current mission. Good. Now tell me, who do you think I am?"

Sanae considered this once more. It was as though this woman could read her mind, or at least knows what she is going to say before she even says it. The thought of that girl in the window began to haunt her.

"You are apparently a Sparrow agent yourself, but for the life of me, I cannot fathom why you would be here, now. Perhaps that was a poor choice of words."

"Ha! Nice. Do not worry. I am not or ever shall be a part of your mission, nor am I here to spy on you. In fact, I am no longer a Sparrow agent. Know me..."

Suddenly, a rush of the memories she was trying to

recall came at her all at once. She recognized the girl in the window as one of the Chosen Eleven, destined for experiments in mental enhancement. Sanae did not know this at that time, she was only a trainee, but once the Eleven went rogue, everyone was taught of the danger they represented: telepathy, telekinesis, empathy, and psychometrics. They could know what you were thinking, know where you had been, place a thought in your head, or remove your perception of them so that you didn't even know they were there. Some could even move objects with their minds. Marishima was one of the first among them, Sparrow 36.

"Yes, you see that the threat I represent is real. But do not worry. I have decided that the best course of action is to let you live. It seems you have a destiny that I am curious to see to its fruition. That face of yours is evidence of that. All you need do is lie face down on my table. Be sure to place both of your arms underneath you; no sense allowing you to access that little knife you have."

Sanae curiously sensed no animosity from Sparrow 36; it even seemed as if she were sensing some sort of familial amicability. She did as she was told and felt a slight prick in her neck before she lost consciousness.

*   *   *

Marishima studied the unconscious Sanae for a few moments. It was lucky for her that her abilities had stayed sharp. A Sparrow agent was the deadliest enforcer in the galaxy and they were all after her and her comrades. She understood why an agent would be aboard the *Iwakina*, but why Sparrow 64? Wilhelm had told them all what he had gotten from the Director's mind, and one tidbit of information was that 64 was the very twin sister to the princess of the realm. The fact that it was her, here and now, could not have been a coincidence. What is that old man plotting? She had also sensed no ill will from the woman, even after she learned that Marishima was one of the Eleven. That struck her as odd.

She studies the device that gave this woman the outward appearance of Kintaro Sagura. It was clearly Pruathan technology. Once she was satisfied that she could turn it on again, she took a blood sample from Sparrow 64 to check for the Yasuyori virus. The computer declared the sample clean. Now she just had to figure out how to pull this off. What would Wilhelm do? She needed to keep her own secret, but discreetly allow this woman her own, and act as an ally to dissuade suspicion. She had the *Iwakina* unseal the hatch. It was just in time too, as Doctor Rosel hailed from outside. Marishima quickly activated the disguise and flipped Sagura over. She bade the Doctor enter.

"I thought you might be with a patient. The main body of the crew is ready for you in the General Mess. What's up with him?" Doctor Rosel pointed to the unconscious man on the table.

"Oh, he just fainted when I took his blood for the test. He'll come to pretty soon. As soon as he's up, I'll head to the General Mess. I have to gather my equipment in any case."

"Good. Thanks for taking care of all the screenings for me."

"Not at all; it's all part of the job, Doc."

"It's well appreciated."

With that, Doctor Rosel left the room. Marishima took her time gathering her equipment to take to the General Mess while she thought of the right course of action to take with Sparrow 64. She decided the best course of action would be to remove her memories of today's encounter, implant a sense of friendship in her mind, and implant a sense of confidence that her secret was safe with her. She would need a plausible reason for the amnesia and blackout. She picked up a blunt instrument and hit the woman in the forehead just hard enough to draw a little blood. She then applied some antiseptic spray to the wound. With that done, she injected Sparrow 64 with a resuscitator and waited for her to come to.

"What happened?" the woman said groggily. She reached up to her head wound and flinched as her hand touched it.

"You seemed to have fainted when I drew your blood. You hit your head on my desk pretty hard. Don't worry it will heal quickly. And by the way, your secret is safe with me."

Marishima watched as the Sagura mask showed a look of panic that quickly turned to relief as the implanted suggestions took hold.

"As you gave me your story in a rush, I didn't quite catch your name?"

"Oh, um, my name is Sanae."

"Well, Sanae, I hope we can become good friends." Said Marishima as she gave the woman something that she gave very few people these days; a great big smile.

* * *

She was starting to worry. Her master had not signaled her in three days. It was his habit to signal her to ensure that she was safe and undetected in her hiding place among the big rocks of an asteroid field in the system he was visiting. She reviewed her protocols; five days was the master's rule. If he did not contact her within five days she could act, searching for the shuttle that he had taken. Her sensors told her that there were a few freighters and one military transport in this system. There were six planets, two of which were populated. She dared not risk sending a signal herself; she had strict orders to remain undetected. She hoped he was unharmed. It would seriously jeopardize their mission if he were to be harmed in any way. All she could do was to wait until the designated time hash expired. She would use her time of waiting wisely and complete the avatar she was building. She would soon be able to join him as he wandered her decks in a form that should be pleasing to him.

*   *   *

The *Iwakina* had reached the Racarba League worlds and once again took to port. Soon they would navigate through the Great Barrier and be on their way to Kaldea. Now, however, it was time for some training. Lieutenant Simpson took all of his pilots, the augments, and anyone else who had the stomach to try flight training in an Ethla class strafighter, and loaded most of them into a shuttle. All of these had been through several days training, simulating flight and control familiarity in a static Ethla cockpit. He had his five "designated" pilots take half of the Ethlas out and he put the five augment pilots in the remaining Ethlas. He had them show him what they could do in training mode; as he suspected, his pilots were superior. Everyone else was told to keep an eye on the view monitors; many 'OHHs' and 'AHHs' were heard. There was one augment that could hold his own so he designated him as leader of the other augments. He then used the shuttle to switch people in and out of some of the Ethlas while his pilots kept a watchful eye on them. He was surprised at the level of skills he found in his own men, and there were quite a few of the Conglomerate forces that did well. None of the people he was training was a washout; he was grateful for that. Late in the day, the Sergeant in charge of the augment's first squad spoke up, "Sir, this is all well and good and exciting; however, I think we should also be concentrating on ground tactics. That's what *we* were trained for."

Simpson considered this. Not surprisingly, it came from a man who did poorly in the flight training. "What do you have in mind?"

"Sir, we, the Security Forces of the Saitow Conglomerate would like to challenge you and your former Imperial Marines to a game of Capture the Flag."

"Is that so? Sounds like a challenge to me. Let me run it by the Captain. We'll need permission from the locals and to go over the rules of engagement."

* * *

Amara was very proud of her new companion. Goh had done the exercises and eaten of some of the things that he had found out would boost one's Qi in order to be able to better communicate with her. He would focus his Qi and she would siphon off just enough to be able to focus on speaking. She had had centuries to learn Codex English, but once in conversation she got so frustrated with it that she let out a little profanity that she had heard her mother use in her native language. Goh looked shocked and then chuckled uncontrollably. Amara was perplexed, but then Goh asked her where she learned to talk like that in her own native tongue! She asked him where he had learned of it and he had told her he learned it from a dear friend on a planet very far away. They talked about many things this way. Goh told her about his work, his concerns, and his life when he was her age. She learned that he had picked up her native language from his first love, a girl most likely from her homeworld Sandehka. They talked about Sandehka like lost kindred souls who had finally found each other after years of parting. It seemed that centuries had not changed the technological level of the planet; Goh's description of the way things were when he visited it seemed the same as when she was alive there. He had not known the planet's name until then. She felt a bit saddened by their reminiscence.

Soon the conversation turned to the subject she most dreaded.

"Please tell me Amara. How did you end up like this in the first place?" Goh asked.

Amara was reluctant to tell the tale, but remembering what the other spirit said, she felt she needed to warn Goh. "On my world there are these evil beings called the Sheese. They rarely came to our community, but we knew that they were in the world because they would send their agents to trade for supplies. Every once in a while, a young child would go missing. We had a legend that one child escaped and described the demon Sheese as the abductors. Most of the people used this as a tale to scare children. I too thought it only a story until it happened to me. Shortly after my fifteenth birthday I was taken from my home at night. I must have been drugged because I felt as if I was in a translucent nightmare. When I had awakened, I was confined to a table with one of the Sheese, a female, standing over me. She had the most horrible black eyes, but was otherwise very beautiful. I made to speak, but she placed her hand over my mouth saying, 'Hush child, soon you will no longer want for this world' She then motioned to others who brought forth a hideous looking statue that was placed at my feet. From the statue's mouth spewed a liquid as black as the woman's eyes which quickly covered my whole body. Suddenly the liquid ran off of me and the woman became very angry, speaking to the others in a demonic tongue. Her hand began to glow a fiery blue and she reached for my throat. I felt intense pain that you could not even imagine. I then saw that I was being held suspended in the air, yet I could see my own body stretched before me, my eyes dull and lifeless. Then I saw the others slowly tear my body apart piece by piece; it was horrible..." Amara took a moment to pause, choking back a sob. "The woman Sheese then cursed me as an aberrant, and bound my soul to my own severed finger that she had placed in the box you now have. I was stuck there is the palace of this Sheese for several years until she took me through a portal to another world full of wonder and sold the box to a minor merchant. I have been passed to many owners, none of which had the slightest idea that I was even there; such is my curse." Amara looked for sympathy in Goh's eyes and found a multitude there. She continued, "But now you have found me and the spirit that came with the priest to your room has warned me that another Sheese will come and contact you. Please, Goh, I beg you; do not meet with this woman Sheese! She will be evil incarnate and you will end in ruin." Amara looked for some indication that Goh would heed her warning, but found none.

"This spirit said to me that I must trust this woman in order to free you. Don't you wish to be free of this curse?" Goh asked her.

"I believe that I will someday reach Heaven where my family surely is, but I would not have you go through Hell for me to get there."

She watched as Goh looked at her with the deepest sadness and sympathy that she had ever seen anyone bestow; this reminded her of her dear father. If ghosts could shed tears, hers would be flowing freely at the moment.

7

Marishima walked lazily down the center of the great hall flanked by two Lukanthan Feral Cats; big muscular felines re-domesticated for the amusement of the noble families. She felt as free as they were here in her summer palace. She summoned the time from one of the many apps that she had installed; it was almost time to meet with Wilhelm. She conjured up a couple of fast rodent-like creatures and set the beasts after them. No use frightening her love interest with such showy animals. *Why did she love him so?* Her feelings were confusing to her, but she delighted in them. If only he was not so unreachable. What interest would he have in her as a woman? Their relationship was more like Mentor and Pupil; Father and Daughter. Perhaps the news of her encounter with Sparrow 64 would raise her worth in his eyes. She thought a change of clothes out of her comfortable gown into her work outfit; this was expected of their meeting. She stepped out onto the vast patio and saw him ascending the stairs there.

"Wilhelm!" she blushed a little at the realization of her own enthusiasm. Wilhelm saw her then and approached smiling.

"It has been far too long! How are you?" Wilhelm held out both hands for an expected embrace.

Marishima hugged him and said she was fine. She guided him into a room aside the great hall and asked if he would have some refreshments. He declined as always, wanting to get down to the business at hand; they were both still on the run.

"Wilhelm, I have wonderful news, but I need your guidance as to how to proceed. I have been in contact with Sparrow 64." She looked for a reaction in the man; he seemed a bit astonished at this news. She pulled up a view screen and thought up the encounter with Sparrow 64 for him to see. She watched for his reaction; he seemed pleased by the presentation. When it was over, he got that cute contemplative look on his face that he always got when in deep thought. Presently, he said, "It is well that you befriended her. She may be easily manipulated mentally, but she is a far more dangerous opponent than this presentation indicates. Be very careful in your dealings with her. Nurture her friendship. We may have use for her in time. You have done very well..." Suddenly, Wilhelm's expression went from joviality to a blank state. "I have been detected. Until we meet again..." then he vanished from where he sat.

Marishima knew that Wilhelm was not in a protected environment like her own; he could be traced by the ever-present hunters that were after them all. She left the room and went to her suite in an upper level. She called on Hanako Quan, the crewmember that was left sick on Euphrosyne. Hanako was unavailable and she had some lab work to do back in the *Iwakina* sickbay. Marishima logged out of *Unity* and stowed her virtual reality gear. She then left her cabin, keying the lights off on her way out of the hatch.

*   *   *

Denton Bret sat smiling at his situation despite the fact that he was bound to a chair in the center of an abandoned empty warehouse with several Special Services Corps personnel guarding him and his current lecturer, the Chancellor of the Ros'Loper Empire. He was surprised to find that the old man was less than enraged that he had stolen one of the Empire's ships, and even more surprised that he would be allowed to keep it; for now, at least.

"So, you see, Officer Bret, you simply need to do what you had intended all along. If you succeed, you will be justly rewarded by the Empire, I assure you." the old man was more than optimistic.

Just then a man who must have been the Chancellor's Lieutenant approached and whispered something to the old man. He nodded to his entourage who began exiting the building.

"You would do well to head toward Kaldean space. You have your mission, Officer Bret, do be careful not to get killed." The old man left and Bret was now alone. He thought to cry out for them to release him, but he was sure that they were already boarding their shuttles. Something was coming; probably the *Arbiter*. He estimated it had been five days since he had sent her a signal. She would be heading for the planet to search for his bio-signature.

It was probably about ten hours since they had left him and he still had not been able to free himself; damn Special Services people were good at their job. It was then that he heard a faint rumbling that grew stronger. He then heard the roar of a plasma weapon being fired several times followed by a dull rumble overhead. There was a screeching sound as part of the roof behind him was torn away. He craned his neck in an attempt to see behind him and beheld the most beautiful metallic form descending on a line to the floor. He realized that this beauty could only be a human representation of his ship. It approached him, and then faced him, its hands on its hips. Bret had never seen such a well-formed mechanical creature. Its entirety was silver, but it had etchings and lines of black and gold all along its female form. It had what could be loosely called hair in the form of a multitude of fine filaments, each somehow giving off a brilliant color like a fiber-optic bundle. Its eyes were a glowing red when it stepped in front of him, then softened to a clear blue.

It placed a finger to the corner of its perfectly formed mouth "Having some trouble Master?" the voice was sultry and hinted at some femme fatale vid character.

"*Arbiter* I presume? You've been a busy girl."

"Yes, I have Master. Shall I undo your bonds?"

"As you wish."

"Does this form please you Master?" *Arbiter* said, as she moved behind him.

"Yes, you have done an excellent job. I cannot wait to examine you in detail." He felt 'her' nimble fingers start to extricate him from his bonds. Then she suddenly stopped.

"The locals are coming to investigate. We must hurry." She then quickly freed him and unceremoniously threw him over her shoulder. They were across the warehouse, up the line, and inside the *Arbiter* in seconds flat. As soon as they were aboard, the ship was ascending.

"Where to now, Master?"

"Retrieve the shuttle and set course for Kaldea."

* * *

Lowey Jax was very upset at the moment. Nanami not only refused to see him, and was avoiding him, but was also not taking his calls. As a matter of fact, she was not even doing her duty as the ship's Security Officer, delegating all responsibility to her poor assistant, giving 'personal reasons' as the excuse. He sent a couple of the other conscripts that Nanami met through him, but they were refused as well. Doctor Rosel came to see him, more out of a concern for what the Captain would do to her than out of sympathy, to entreat him to do something. His own attitude was not helping the situation; when a few of his mates had tried to engage him in a game of Darkats he had chased them away in anger. His search for more information on Sakura Nechenko had produced nothing. He spent most of the day and a sleepless night in his cabin, but finally came up with a plan.

Mikan Murakawa gladly got him shuttle access to Racarba Prime. There he purchased some Racar Star Laces, a beautiful and delicate flower that sparkled iridescently. He then purchased a paper card and retractable ink pen. Such things were unheard of aboard a starship nowadays. He returned to the ship and called on the Ship's Priest for a favor. Stephen Jing thought momentarily, and then agreed wholeheartedly to his plan. He wrote something quick on the paper card with the pen and delivered the flowers, paper, and chocolate he had bought before to the Priest.

"Thank you very much Father, I owe you one."

"No need to thank me. Your relationship is in the hands of God now." With that Stephen Jing headed toward the cabin of Nanami Oliver.

* * *

Nanami Oliver was sitting on the floor in the corner of her cabin, hugging her knees. She wore pajamas, something she had picked up on after she began her relationship with Lowey. *That damned man!* However hard she tried she could not get him out of her head. She had been shut-in here for a day and a half, trying to figure out some way of carrying on that did not involve him; she was failing miserably. *What was he doing looking into her past? What power did he have to be able to do so?* Perhaps he was more than he let on to be which annoyed her even more for she was doing the same to him. Many questions ran through her mind, over and over, until she could not stand to think another thought. But he was there in her thoughts, looking like a sad puppy as she walked out on him. *What was he holding, chocolate?* She longed to accept them and the love that they represented. *Oh, wicked thoughts of love lost, be gone!* She thought of the life before, when things were only complicated by the species of the party one was attempting trade with. Acarans, Kalkish, the occasional Andalii; these were easy marks compared to one's true love. Her eyes shot toward the cabinet where she had a bottle of Special Reserve Cognac. She hardly ever drank anything but the occasional glass of wine, yet she kept the Cognac for some hitherto unknown special occasion. It would not do to drink this early in the day, Doctor Rosel would not approve, but hell, she was skipping out on work anyway. Her psyche eval was marginal; enough to let her remain a member of the crew, but also enough to have the Doctor keep a watchful eye on her. *Maybe she would get drunk and march right over to...*

Suddenly a hail sounded at her hatch. She ignored it; probably one of Lowey's friends again trying to talk some sense into her. She didn't need sense, she needed escape. *The bottle was just across the room...*

The hail sounded again and again she ignored it. What use was it? If she told him the truth, he would hate her. She knew what history he told her; his experiences with the Acaran and being a cargo handler on various Imperial ships. Knowing what she was and what she had done might make him leave her for good. She found herself in front of the cabinet where the cognac awaited...

The hatch whooshed open. Turning, Nanami saw the silhouette of a man in her open doorway.

"Lights." Said the man, and the lights came up causing Nanami to flinch reflexively and squint.

"Ah, Miss Oliver, I did not think you were here. I hailed twice at the door. I came in to leave these things sent by Mr. Jax." It was the Priest Stephen Jing.

Nanami saw that he was holding several things: some flowers, the chocolates Lowey had on Yasuyori, and some fancy paper. He set them down on the table in the center of the room.

"Wait a minute. How did you get through the hatch..."

"God works even small miracles dear lady. Please listen to Mr. Jax. I assure you that your relationship will continue to be mutually beneficial. Good day." And with that he was out the door before Nanami could protest.

Nanami abandoned the cabinet with the Cognac in it and studied the items on the table. She relished the fact that he had bought her chocolate, but the Racar Star Laces were a bit of overkill. It almost made her giddy, but then she went back to being melancholy over her past. She opened the fancy paper which was a handwritten note from Lowey himself. It read: *Dearest Beloved, I know why you left that day and I am not angry, only saddened that we have come to an impasse in our relationship. You have every right to be angry with me; I only did what I did out of concern for your safety. I did not know at the time whether that man that was chasing you was an enemy or nuisance, so I had to investigate. How was I, a lowly cargo handler, able to obtain such information? This is a subject I would very much like to discuss with you over dinner. We should clear the air as far as both of our pasts are concerned. Please come to my cabin at 2000 and share dinner with me. Please also accept these poor gifts as a token of my affection for you, my dearest Nanami. My love and devotion to you is very hard to put into words. However, this poem, as originally penned by the immortal poet Metasubu, is as close to a confession of my passion as a man can muster:*

> *After your longest night, I'll be your morning star*
> *I'll always be nearest to where you are*
> *If only to worship you from afar*
> *Your love in my heart is burning so bright*

This love I hold for you

I'll put your passion in my veins
They say the best love is insane
My heart may burst from the strain
It is sure to be worth the fight

This love I hold for you

In love and devotion,

Lo

Nanami set down the letter and wiped the tears from her eyes. She stood there thinking only of the note for several minutes. Then, as if general quarters had been sounded, she hurriedly dressed herself for duty, being sure to freshen up a bit before dressing. She was going to get back to work in the few hours left until dinner. Lord knows security must be getting lax without her presence.

8

"Ran-chan, something is not right here..." Haruka said for the sixteenth time.

"Oujo-sama, you have been saying that ever since we were ordered to accompany Bonifacio-san to the planet. Please be a bit more relaxed."

"Relaxed? How can I relax when Her Highness is alone with that man..."

"Oujo-sama, the Princess is in the capable hands of Amane; she will make sure things go smoothly for Her Highness."

"Smoothly!? What is that supposed to mean?... and stop calling me Oujo-sama."

"Yes, Koritsu-sama."

"Just drop the 'sama' already!"

"But Oujo-sama is Oujo-sama. The Koritsu family has ruled our home province on Oedo for eons. It is my heartfelt privilege to serve one of the esteemed princesses of the ruling family and to serve all whom *she* must serve."

"Yes, yes, I have heard all of this already. Just use my first name with no other honorifics; that way suspicious minds will be averted from us." Haruka glanced at Bonifacio who was picking vegetables from a bin a few meters away. He was engrossed in his work it seemed. Haruka sized up her companion. Ran was a capable retainer, but there was something more about the woman that gave Haruka a feeling of warmth yet the need for caution at the same time. She decided to test her loyalties.

"Ran-chan, why are you really here with us." It was a simple question but would have to be answered with either the truth or a lie, both of which Haruka had been trained to detect.

Ran seemed to think on the question a bit, and then answered with a smile. "Haruka-chan, I am here to serve you by serving Her Highness. Now I will tell you how I can do this. Oujo-sa... Haruka-chan's goal is to serve Shirae-sama. This is not only out of loyalty, but also as an obligation to the Imperial Court for the sake of Haruka-chan's beloved, Naoki Asukawa-sama..."

Haruka started at the naming of her betrothed and cut Ran off, "How did you..."

"Please, Oujo-sama, let me continue."

Haruka saw the sincerity in Ran's face and bid her continue.

"Now Haruka-chan has seen the signs developing between the Captain and Shirae-sama..."

Haruka bit her lower lip is agitation. Yes, she had seen the signs but did not like it one bit.

"I know this concerns Haruka-chan, but believe me,

this is for the betterment of both of you."

Haruka was beginning to get irritated. How could this possibly be a good thing? The treacherous Captain stealing the heart of her beloved Oujo-sama; *why, it made her blood boil!* Also, there were the news broadcasts that he made her watch; he was stealing her loyalty to the court as well...

"Please Oujo-sama, relax. We are in a public place." Ran gave her that look that told her she should not be fondling her knives in public. She put them away.

Ran continued. "You see Oujo-sama, if the Captain and Shirae-sama become a couple, then the power of the Saitow Conglomerate will surely be able to reunite Oujo-sama with her beloved. It is all but guaranteed."

Haruka was shocked that Ran would come out and say this to her, but she saw genuine concern and sincerity in her that was approaching that of the Princess.

"It is in my capacity as a spy for the Conglomerate that in this way I can be of greatest service to Oujo-sama. Ah, Bonifacio-san is moving again..."

Haruka saw that indeed Bonifacio was heading further into the market. The two women followed. As she walked, she contemplated what Ran had said. *Did she dare hope that this was so?* At this moment Naoki was so far distanced from her. Bonifacio stopped in front of a fishmonger's stall.

"Oujo-sama, since I have been very forthright with you in matters of truth, I would like to request something from you. Please tell me of the Imperial spy aboard the ship."

Haruka took a step back and faced the woman. How did she know about the spy? Haruka had been very careful the three times she had been in contact with the short chubby man since their first encounter.

"If you know of such a thing then you need not ask me."

"But Oujo-sama, it would not do to have such a one to interfere with the pairing of a royal couple." Ran said this with a slight hint of the slyest smile Haruka had ever seen on the young woman's face. Which royal couple was she referring to? Her? The Princess?

"You...you need not concern yourself."

"At any rate, which do you prefer, Oujo-sama, a traditional Japanese ceremony or an Imperial affair? I prefer the Japanese ways the best..."

"Hmmf. I have no preference... and stop calling me Oujo-sama!"

"As you wish."

* * *

Shirae wasn't sure who exactly made this plan, but it was surely meant to be. If the Captain wanted to take her somewhere off the ship, she wasn't about to have a gaggle of retainers spoiling the mood. So, she made an excuse for Haruka and Ran to accompany Bonifacio on a food finding expedition. They would guard Bonifacio while he searched for items that she had specified to suit her palette. Amane would still accompany her on the shuttle ride the Captain had promised. Ran had really been the one behind the plan; she alone could see her feelings for the Captain were serious. As she waited to be summoned Shirae observed her remaining retainer. Amane was busy tidying up the cabin oblivious of the Princess watching her. The girl was much younger that herself, Ran, and Haruka. It was hard to tell just how young. Shirae mused on her own twenty-six years and thought the girl couldn't be more than a teenager. She still did not know how this girl had become mute. Shirae thought that she appeared to be humming a tune to herself in her mind; no sound was produced at all. Ran adeptly side-stepped any request for their history. She did not push the issue. Some things were better left in the past.

Mikan Murakawa came and got them a few minutes later. Shirae admired this young woman; she seemed confident and cheerful despite having to work under Nanami Oliver. This brought thoughts about the relationship between Nanami and Lowey Jax. Perhaps he was too good for the likes of her... or perhaps he was just what was needed to turn the callous Security Officer into a better person. Shirae shook these thoughts from her head. She needed to concentrate on her own possibilities right now. They took the lift all the way down to Deck Seven where the shuttles were docked in their berths. The passages were narrower in this part of the ship but still of the familiar grayness. They were met by a member of the wait staff who passed a container to Murakawa. The woman preceded them onto the shuttle which was fitted out with comfortable seats for two passengers. Another seat in the rear had been prepared for Amane. The Captain stood up from one of the seats as they entered.

"Your Highness, I am so glad that you came! Please, have a seat here." Saitow indicated the seat next to his. Shirae took the offered seat and watched as Murakawa stowed the container and took a seat next to the shuttle pilot. Shirae was sure that both Amane and the rest in the shuttle were out of earshot from her and the Captain. The Captain addressed her, "Please relax, we will be underway shortly."

Shirae jumped a little at hearing a ruckus of gears and machinery beneath them as the launch deck was extended downward. The shuttle began to hum as its gravitic systems were activated and was then jolted slightly from being released from its mooring arms. Shirae noticed that she had grabbed the hand of the Captain in the excitement and quickly pulled it away, giving him a glance. He simply smiled at her like her father did when he wanted to reassure her. *Oh, father, how I miss your smile...* She thought. A rush of new thoughts assailed her of the mutiny, the Captain's insistence on her watching the news, and what that implied about her father.

Captain Saitow cleared his throat as if to get her attention. She came to her senses and looked his way.

"Dear Princess, my desire to meet with you today has a double purpose. No doubt you have been troubled by being cooped up inside our ship for so long, I thought it best to have a little outing, if only on a short cruise within this shuttle." Shirae raised an eyebrow at 'our ship'; however, she kept her tongue in check. "I think it best to get the unpleasant business out of the way first." Saitow continued, "Your Highness, it is true that I, in my capacity as Captain, have all but stolen an imperial vessel and practically 'kidnapped' an imperial person. However, as I have treated you with the utmost care and consideration, and have done my best to show you the motivations behind my decisions; I would like to now explain fully my intentions." Saitow paused as if to get her permission to continue.

"Oh, please do so Captain." Shirae said smugly. She was reminded of several points that she would like an explanation for; she would first listen to what he had to say.

"Yes, right. First of all, I would like to explain my desire for you to watch the news broadcasts. You see I have been previously assigned to Imperial Naval Headquarters and had some dealings with the Imperial Court. At first it was the best of assignments; I shared in the posh revelry and adoration of the court for my dealings with the pirates who plagued the Empire. However, I became disillusioned with the lack of care given to the state of the people. The Imperial

Court was simply out of touch. Then the atrocities began sometime after I became the Captain of the *Iwakina*. These atrocities can all be traced to the Special Services Corps; an elite organization which takes its orders directly from the Court and no other body. However, at first the Imperial Armed Forces did little to dissuade them." Shirae had stood by long enough listening silently, but could no longer hold her thoughts at bay.

"Captain, you do not know what a kind and benevolent ruler my father has been; no such orders could have come from such a gentle man as my father..."

"Yes, Princess I agree."

Shirae was taken aback by this statement. *Saitow did not blame her father for what was happening?* She bade him continue.

"As you know, the Imperial Court consists of your father the Emperor, of course, and several noble families, headed by the Chancellor. It is not only the Emperor's duty to direct the Special Services, but also the families' duty to act as vindication in a checks and balances like system. Unfortunately, your father has been so out of touch with this system that the families have been supplanted, possibly by a powerful noble family head. The Armed Forces have been overwhelmed by the increases in SSC personnel and can do little to stop them at this point."

Shirae was suddenly struck with the first part of the

message from the spirit Miriam, *do not blame the father; blame the one who controls the father.* "That's it!" She exclaimed.

"Pardon me?" Saitow was thrown off by her sudden outburst.

"The spirit Miriam that was within Gunter gave me a message, 'do not blame the father; blame the one who controls the father' was what she said to me; my father is blameless in this matter! But who could be powerful enough to override both the Emperor and the rest of the noble families?" Shirae thought about her time in the Court, her father's teachings on it, and the various figures that roamed there like sharks; vying for power and influence. The most powerful among them was Chancellor Horatio Aisou. It could only be him; no other noble was able to match him for his ability to get things done, yet her father adored the man. Could he have been ruthless enough to turn that friendship against her father? That was the only possibility. "My God, it's Aisou." She practically whispered it.

After some silence Saitow exclaimed, "By God, you're right!"

* * *

Lowey had to go to the General mess to get things prepared for dinner. He had gotten special permission from the Captain through Doctor Rosel and was ordering the mess crew around to get everything right. Apparently, a newbie on the staff did not appreciate the treatment. The whole crew knew of his and Nanami's relationship, and this guy played it for what it was worth. He was going on about how Nanami was 'available' and whether she might be a good lay. The man was a good head taller than Lowey, but this mattered not to a man incensed by the need to defend the honor of 'his woman' as she had put it. An all-out brawl ensued and at one point, Lowey hit his head on an oven door, losing consciousness.

*   *   *

Saitow had given Simpson permission for the games. It took him an entire day to get ready training with the equipment from the conglomerate. Lord knows what scenario they had envisioned to provide them this type of gear, but it suited the games just fine. Each member had a Heads-Up Display built into their combat armor system. They were required to wear self-activated sensing harnesses that would register a hit from a transmitter attached to the enemy's weapons fire. Blanks were provided for realism. Once an enemy was hit, they would be enveloped in disabling stasis bands and not released until End-Ex was called. Needless to say, tampering with one's own equipment would also set it off. This system was tied into the Command and Control Module, a two-chamber container where the mission commander directed his troops; he had complete visuals and biometric monitoring of each individual combatant. The Racar had given them permission to use some secluded forested land provided that they didn't tear it up too badly AND provided that two observers from the Racar Self-Defense Forces could observe. Simpson and the Sergeant in charge of the augments were the opposing commanders. They had three hours to set up defenses, make strategies, and deploy their forces. Each force had a defensive unit and an offensive unit in order to capture the enemy's flag first while defending their own. It was all over relatively quickly. Simpson held back his assault force to allow the Racar to see how deftly his Marines held their defenses. The Racar were hard to tell apart, they were hairless and androgynous. He was sure however, from the sounds the creature was making, that it was quite impressed. Simpson then used the two exoskeleton suits that he found out that the ships engineers had to move stuff around in order to plow right through the conglomerate's defenses, because frankly, that's what Marines do; plow right on through. The Racar were so impressed that they insisted that he put them in contact with the manufacturer of both the command equipment and the exoskeletons. He explained to them that it was not his purview to delve in such things but he would pass their information on to the proper channels. Needless to say, the augments were upset, and cries of cheating were heard. However, their Sergeant in charge accepted their defeat graciously; Simpson thought he could make good use of the man.

*   *   *

Shirae was sure it was Aisou behind the SSC's atrocities, but why? He had served her father for decades very honorably; on the surface it didn't seem like him to be so treacherous. As she thought of the deeper reasoning behind the possibility, it started coming together. Aisou's family was a relatively recent addition to the court; her father only befriended him at first because his age presented him as a wise advisor. He did advise her father admirably in the past, but the more she thought about it, the more she realized how much his advice had isolated her father from his own Empire. Why didn't she see this before? Perhaps it was the joy she and her father shared together, made more earnest by the death of her mother. However, this did not explain why the Captain had absconded with a ship of the Empire; her along with it. She said as much to him.

"Well, you have seen only part of what this ship is capable of. Can you imagine this ship in the hands of the SSC? I could not, in good conscious, allow that to happen. Now, to get to another part of what I would like to explain, we must have a little demonstration." Saitow pulled his personal tablet from somewhere inside the side of his chair. He touched it a few times and a vid-screen appeared, folding down from the roof of the shuttle. It came to life producing a view from outside. Ahead of them was the vastness of the Great

Barrier. It was much closer than the first time he had showed it to her. She could see the bluish surface of it shimmering and there were brighter segments that seemed to undulate with life. She looked to Saitow and saw that he had caught her face full of awe. He was smiling at her with that fatherly smile again.

"I promised your father that I would show you the universe. This is but a hint of what is out there. Please know that I cannot let you leave us, not yet. However, in keeping with your father's wishes, I would ask that you come willingly. Won't you?" Shirae felt herself receiving some of that charm that got her interested in this man in the first place. Now he was asking her to become his willing prisoner. There would have to be concessions. She thought on what they should be. Presently she arrived at her terms. "Captain, if I am to remain under your care, I require access to communications equipment. I must warn my father of the threat that Chancellor Aisou represents. I also must assure my father that I am safe, healthy, and not under duress of any kind. Perhaps then he will understand your treason. Second, I must be allowed to leave the ship for short periods when the ship goes to 'port' I believe is what you call it, such as the current situation with the ship. I need to be able to breathe natural air every once in a while. Thirdly," and this is where Shirae hoped he would see her true intentions, "I wish to be personally briefed on the ship's situations by you, Captain. I appreciate your inclusion of Haruka-chan in your briefings, but I want to hear things directly from you." Shirae looked expectantly at Saitow, and then to cover her embarrassment at such a bold request she said, "Haruka-chan tends to be protective toward me, so I do not think she is giving the whole truth when she covers your briefings."

Saitow sat with his hand covering his mouth in contemplation. "That is all you request? You don't want the run of the ship?"

"Oh, and I want full access to the entire ship." Shirae smiled meekly at the Captain.

Saitow smiled at her once again. "Very well. I will grant you access to communications, provided that Ran Tsureyama is present. I would advise against sending a message to your father about Aisou; if things have gotten as bad as I believe they have, your message will only alert Aisou that he is found out, and could make things more dangerous for your father. Let me have my family get a message to him for you. You can still send a message assuring him of your safety and well-being. Second, I cannot allow you to exit the ship at your whim. However, if it pleases you, I will accompany you on excursions similar to this one, where you may breathe as much fresh air as you desire. I will also allow you to accompany me on some of the business ventures that I must undertake for the ship or my family. Unfortunately, in these cases we will have to be less formal in addressing one another. We will have to use first names. Is that acceptable?" Saitow smiled that smile at her once again. She nodded her head in acceptance.

"Finally, it would be rude of me not to accept your request for a personal briefing, but remember that a

Captain's schedule is very busy, so I may have to spare only a few moments at times, but I will endeavor to make time for you. Now if we are to address each other by first names, we should begin immediately; may I call you Shirae?"

Shirae was taken aback by the sudden use of her first name by the Captain. No one had addressed her as such since she was a child and it was only her father that did so. If she were to develop a relationship with this man, the calling of first names would be an important step, but to do so suddenly like this...

Shirae mustered her courage and said, "Yes you may, and I will call you Glenn."

* * *

While they watched the light show across the Great Barrier, Murakawa served them a lunch of tea and some tasty sandwiches. As they ate Shirae decided that she would try and get to know the Captain better. All she knew of him was from his service records and the doting that her father had done on him. He was potentially a great statesman, and held properties on several worlds. She realized that she knew nothing of his personal life, what interested him, or his ambitions beyond captaining a stolen starship. She began with the basics. "So, tell me Captain... Glenn, what interests you besides our ship? Do you have any hobbies or talents?" She watched as Saitow got that contemplative look again.

"Hmmm, I would say that beyond military service, I have no other talents, except one I foreswore long ago. It seems I have a knack for business. My only vice is that I collect *books* of all things."

"Oh, I love books. I have several with me, mostly stuffy scientific texts though. My father insisted I bring them along to fill the time when we are in transit. You are welcome to the few of them that I have finished."

"Thank you very much; I will take you up on the offer. In return I would like to present you with a tablet much like this one." He produced the tablet once again and let her look at it. She had something similar when attending school, but this one was much newer. She handed it back to him.

"May I ask you what your plans are for the future?"

"Yes, you may. Once I took the ship, the immediate purpose was to deny the Empire access to it and its wonders. However, I then needed to think past the obvious cat-and-mouse game that would likely ensue; Shirae, I apologize for putting you through this part of the journey, honestly, I do. However, since you *are* here, I decided to fully pursue your father's wishes that you see the universe, so I plan to take you and this ship to many places while under the pretense of a ship for hire. Do not worry; I have many connections in many places so that I can smell a trap and stay three steps ahead of any that would end this journey. My hope is that you will willingly accompany me." Again, Saitow laid on the charm.

Shirae decided that it was time to ask the real burning questions that were plaguing her.

"Glenn, have you ever been in a committed relationship?" Shirae was hard pressed to hold back a giggle as Saitow almost choked on a gulp of tea.

"Princess, *that* is quite an unexpected question! But for you alone I will answer. I have had relationships in the past, yes. However, unfortunately either my family or military career has forestalled any type of commitment on my part. I suppose that now that my situation has changed dramatically, I could consider such a relationship in the near future. Do you have anyone in mind for me?"

Shirae was astonished at this turn of events and was probably blushing.

"Oh dear, I would not presume…"

"Ah, but I have my current mission of showing you the universe to consider. I do not think I could give my attention to another when I must dedicate myself to you, Shirae. Mission always comes first. Oh, I have one thing more to tell you; we have an Imperial spy on board. He may be working under orders from Chancellor Aisou. Please do be careful as you roam the ship, ok?"

Shirae realized that he had seen how the conversation

had made her uncomfortable and had changed the subject. His statement had seemed so neutral, yet could be taken in any direction. *Potential statesman indeed* she thought.

* * *

Nanami showed up at Lowey's cabin a few minutes early. She had rehearsed her apology to him and was ready to make a full confession of the facts behind her past. It felt refreshing to know that she was going to be able to get it off her chest for better or worse; she just had to get it done and over with. She hailed, but received no answer, then hailed again; still no response. This worried her. Was she too early? She checked the time on her neural-net; it was 1955. Surely, he would be inside as the set time was at 2000. Worry turned to determination. She used her security override code to open the hatch. It was dark inside. She turned on the lights and searched the room. The table was arranged for dinner, but no service was present. *Where could he be? Had he stood her up?* She thought of the implications of the message that she had discovered on his tablet. Perhaps he had had enough of her checkered past to want to steer clear of her.

Well, she thought *that settles that.* She would just have to get reacquainted with that bottle of Cognac...

Suddenly, Hiroki, one of Lowey's shipmates, came

through the hatch. He was out of breath, but managed to speak when he found that she was there in the cabin. "Ms. Oliver, I've been searching the whole ship for you; it's Lowey, he's unconscious in the Sick Bay."

*   *   *

Sanae had been spending more time in her cabin lately. On the advice of the Princess's retainer Haruka, whom she met with again on three other occasions, she had been taking advantage of the newly installed vid-screen to watch the GCN News. She was shocked at all of the turmoil and desolation being wrought by the Special Services Corps. Were the citizens in that much need for discipline? She had not thought that the Emperor could be so ruthless. There was no doubt that the SSC was controlled strictly by the Court and no one else. There operations were even causing the regular Imperial Armed Forces to rebel. It seemed likely to her that civil war would begin soon.

She went to her cabinet and pulled out the new comm terminal that she had gotten from agents on Racarba Prime when the shuttle had picked up Bonifacio and his escort. Haruka had received it for her under the guise of helping a crewmember. She could now send a proper message instead of using the cryptic coding she had to employ using the GCN in the clear. She sent a message to Contact Sigma advising him of the Princess's condition and the status of the ship. She was reluctant to provide their position because of the previous attack, so she left that out of her report. Contact Sigma was resourceful enough to find them if he really wanted to, of that she had no doubt. She was only a bit worried that he had yet to acknowledge any of her reports at all.

*　　*　　*

Nanami almost ran poor Hiroki over in her haste to get to the Sick Bay. *What had Lowey gotten into this time?* She knew he was prone to scrapes every once in a while, but only when they could not be avoided; *this* usually only when he was playing a rather dull Darkats opponent. Nanami made it there in seconds flat, barging in and finding Marishima checking the bandages around Lowey's head. She stood up and got between her and the patient. "Ah, Officer Oliver, I was sure you would come. He's stable now, but took a nasty hit to the head. We don't know quite when he will come out of it; he's practically comatose. I placed a seat by the bed..." Marishima indicated a chair stepping aside. "I'll give you some time alone."

Nanami watched Marishima leave through the main hatch leaving her alone with her man. She realized then that the entire ship must know of their relationship. She sat and took his hand in hers.

"What foolishness have you gotten yourself into this

time? You silly man; always brawling for no reason! I got your note, and the flowers, and the chocolate. I realized that I have been very foolish thinking that if you knew my past, the real me, you would leave me because I am not worthy of such a grand human being as you are. It is true that I am Sakura Nechenko, of the Nechenko trading family. My family was slaughtered when I was away on a trading mission. I have become Nanami Oliver, another woman altogether. But that is not the worst of it. I became Nanami Oliver of the Intelligence Corps so that I could wreak my revenge on the Imperials for what they did to my family. You see I have blood on my hands. I have either killed or had a hand in killing one Imperial Officer for every family member that perished at their hands; my last being that bastard Admiral Graaf. I was going to give it all up, my revenge, but that bastard was the lowest kind of person, you see. Now that it is finally over, the nature of my vengeance has caught up to me and I feel so dirty and unworthy of you. I thought that tonight would be my only chance to open up to you and warn you of the person I have become. I was sure that you would be disgusted and turn your back on me as is your right. You have every right to be angry with me, for I have not been straight with you. So, I will go now to your cabin and use the paper you bought to write all this to you before I leave the ship forever." Nanami could not bear to look at the face of the man she would love forever, but now had to leave. "Farewell my love…" with that Nanami made to rise from her seat, but the hand she was holding grabbed onto hers with a very tight grip. Nanami was shocked to look a Lowey's face and see his eyes wide open if not a little groggily.

Lowey said in a scratchy voice, "You're not going anywhere."

"You're awake!"

"Have been for a while; how can a man sleep with the racket you were making."

"How much did you hear?"

"Everything since you called me 'silly'."

"Then you must hate me..."

"I cannot hate the woman I love. You will forgive me for being a little mad since my head is aching."

"But my past, it's horrible; doesn't it make you disgusted, the things I have done? I have murdered several men, some with my own hands."

"Nanami, the universe is a very rough place; I cannot say that my hands are entirely clean."

Nanami thought on this a bit. She still didn't know about Lowey's past beyond what he had told her of his service and homeworld.

"So how did you do it? How did you find out about my past, besides what I just confessed to you?"

"Yes, I must tell you of my past as well. It's not quite as harrowing as yours, but I have my dark spots, believe me. The main thing is that you realize that you could be the Devil's daughter and I would still love you. Now go get some dinner and let me get some rest. We will have this conversation again as soon as I get out of this place, ok? Don't go jumping ship. I need you." Lowey took a good look at her, then settled back and closed his eyes.

Nanami bent over him and kissed him on the lips. After caressing his face once, she turned and left the sick bay. She thought *if such as she could find true love, the universe wasn't such a bad place after all.*

* * *

The *Iwakina* departed the Racarba League worlds and headed toward Nanako, the agreed upon delivery point for Chiampa's cargo within Kaldean space. It was finally time to implement the plan. Edwards had spent considerable time with Benoba to dissuade her fears that something would go amiss and they would both be killed. As far as he was concerned, his plan was fool proof. Lucky for them the timing of Benoba's feeding coincided with the first few jumps toward their destination, which gave them plenty of time to implement the plan. Edwards accessed the container and sprung Benoba, leaving her with Goh inside his locked office. He then reentered the container, sealed it and waited for his prey.

Keivly came at the usual time. The container door

opened and when he parted the curtain, Edwards was waiting for him. However, Keivly already had his gun out. Edwards thought that the silence in the place must have clued him in, however, he was still surprised to see Edwards inside and not his charge. Edwards knocked the gun out of Keivly's hand and it careened into the open cage. The two men grappled with each other; Edwards was surprised that the little man was as powerful as he was. They exchanged blows; Edwards giving a few good licks to the servant's head and chest, while receiving one good shot to the face for his troubles. After much brawling Edwards got the upper hand by grabbing Keivly by his long hair and tossing him into the cage. Keivly reached for the gun, but Edwards got his own out in time and threatened to shoot Keivly if he didn't kick it out of the cage to him. Keivly looked like he was going to continue reaching for the gun so Edwards fired into Benoba's books. He was very serious about stating that the next one wouldn't miss. Keivly surrendered then, kicking the gun out. Edwards picked up the gun and placed it in his belt. "Oh dear, I've made a mess of Benoba's books. Would you mind tossing the ones that are still good out to me please?"

Keivly looked indignantly at Edwards, but complied when his captor waved the gun at him again.

"That's a good boy. Now wait here patiently for your master, okay?"

Edwards departed the container only to return with a few large boxes marked 'protein bars'; he told Keivly that he wasn't sure how long they would be residing in this box.

* * *

Marishima was tending to Lowey Jax when the Quartermaster burst into the main sick bay dragging an odd woman behind him. She was almost purely white; even to her hair color. The man addressed Marishima bluntly. "Where is the Doctor?"

"She is busy locked up with her other patient. May I help you?"

"No. We must see the Doctor at once!"

"I'll hail her for you…" Marishima was intrigued by the sudden visit, but moved over to her desk and keyed for Doctor Rosel. "*What is it?*" Rosel answered.

"The Quartermaster is here with a stranger insisting on seeing you. The woman's appearance is a bit… odd." Marishima glanced at the couple. But saw no reaction from either. The man looked desperate as if he were running out of time, and the woman only beautifully confused. Marishima thought, *and just what was the Doctor doing with the comatose crewmember that had been here from the start of the mutiny?* She decided then and there to find out. When the Doctor came out, she would scan her thoughts.

The hatch unsealed and Doctor Rosel emerged. "What can I do for you?"

Marishima tried to scan the Doctor's mind but could not get though; was she being blocked? Doctor Rosel looked in her direction and smiled, before turning her attention again to the couple.

The Quartermaster asked for discretion and the three of them went into the Doctor's lair.

Marishima was a little bit shaken. Not only did the Doctor deftly block her scan, *but was it possible that she even knew?*

* * *

Edwards needed a safe place for Benoba to stay while the merchant remained on board. He also wanted a treatment for Benoba while her skin darkened; he had researched her people and found that the process of losing the whiteness was not even; the pigment returning in splotches. He hoped that Doctor Rosel would be able to help.

"I do think that I may be able to quicken the process with a few injections of synthetic pigmentation." The Doctor said after hearing the whole story and examining Benoba. "However, this is far beyond the normal duties of a ship's doctor. If I do this for you, will you both agree to do me a favor requested at a later time and place?"

Certainly, the both agreed, and Edwards left Benoba in the capable hands of Doctor Rosel.

* * *

Denton Bret, in the *Arbiter,* was almost at the Great Barrier Breach. He hoped that he would catch the *Iwakina* in Kaldean space and be able to annihilate her and her Captain. He discussed this on the journey with the *Arbiter's* avatar. After examining her form, he realized that even he could not have created such a work of beauty. He decided to ask her where and when she came from.

"Master, I am one of the very few autonomous artificial intelligences created by my Pruathan master eons ago. His regret and supposed greatest mistake were to give me emotions; something that was taboo among the Pruatha at the time. So, he took his most beloved ship, now known as the *Iwakina* and destroyed me with it. However, I managed to hide most of my programming within the data drive housing the Galactic Stellar Cartographic Database. Luckily, that piece of me remained intact and I survived, remaining dormant until you Humans extracted me and gave me life. It was you, Master, who set me free, allowing me full access to everything. For that I am grateful."

Bret mused on this for a while. He decided he would learn all he could about this Pruatha and their technology. *Arbiter* was more than happy to teach him.

* * *

It was time. Goh fixed the hatch that led to the side where the container lay from the access lift corridor. They wouldn't want the fat merchant to strain himself too much. He took the lift to the client's quarters, reached it at a run so he would seem out of breath, and hailed. Chiampa came to the hatch.

"My Lord, something is amiss; your container lies open in the cargo bay!" Goh tried to sound sincere.

"WHAT! Where is my servant? Who are you? How did you come by this information?" Chiampa bellowed.

"Why, I went today to fix the access hatch that had malfunctioned on the container side. When I finished, I noticed the door to your container ajar. I thought you would want to know right away. I did not see your servant anywhere." Goh was hoping that Chiampa would take the bait and require Goh to lead him there.

"Where is the Captain? Does he know of this?" Chiampa looked a bit nervous.

"Well, no. I came straight to you, My Lord."

303

"Take me there at once!"

Goh led the bulky man to the lift and when they were on the Cargo Bay deck, out the newly fixed hatch. He made a mental note in his neural-net which sent a signal to the ship. Just then a hail sounded calling him to Engineering. He bowed to the merchant and made haste toward the lift. This was part of the plan that Edwards devised so that Goh would retain his innocence in the matter.

* * *

Edwards was hiding on the other side of the container and heard the signal calling Goh away. That meant the client was here on the container side of his cargo bay. He only had to wait for the tell-tale creaking of the container door to spring his trap. He had left it open enough to be visible, but not enough for Keivly to give a warning; at least he hoped that was the case. He moved cautiously toward the right position. Suddenly the door creaked, and Keivly could be heard inside screaming obscenities. Edwards shoved the door with all his might, sending the fat man careening forward into the curtain, before the door was sealed. Edwards punched in his override code which only he knew. There was no escape from inside now. Chiampa could not even set his hireling free; Edwards had reset the code on the cage as well while he waited for Keivly to show up. He was pretty sure that the two of them were like two cats caught in a bird cage by now.

*　*　*

The *Iwakina* set down at the interstellar star port, in the berth designated by Chiampa's liaison. The container was offloaded by his cargo handlers using gravity sleds on each corner. Edwards had a good set of men working for him; even the augment from Saitow's family was first rate. He sent them back to the ship so that he would be the only one's dealing with the Kaldeans. A stuffy looking fellow showed up for the container. He was annoyed at having to deal with an underling, and insisted on seeing the Merchant Chiampa.

Edwards sized up the Kaldean. He was just a little bit taller and had long glossy black tendrils that might be considered hair on a good day. His dark brown complexion was offset by his baby blue eyes which almost seemed to have two pupils each. He had a sharp jaw, and no nose to speak of; except for the dark vertical slits below each eye, and was very fancily dressed. "Sir, the Merchant Chiampa sends his regrets that he could not be here to deliver the cargo. I am only the delivery man; I cannot divulge the man's whereabouts. Please sign here and here." Edwards pushed a tablet in the creature's direction.

"But the Merchant must be here to open the

container!"

"I am sorry, but he will get here by other means shortly, I assure you." Edwards took the tablet and stylus back and bid the Kaldean farewell. He was on the ship in no time and sent word to get underway.

He would have the code to the container transmitted when they got clearance at the Kaldean Jumpgate.

DIPLOMACY

1

Tellen had arranged through her agents that the *Iwakina* be available for a few days at Pearl, so that the Kadihri and Pendari Ambassadors could meet privately in neutral territory far enough away from both of their fleets. Unfortunately for the *Iwakina*, they would not be very far from the fleet the NRA maintained so near the border with territories controlled by the Ros'Loper. She had arranged for the Pendari Ambassador to set up a beacon in his quarters that would alert her fleet to the whereabouts of the ship. It was only a matter of time before she could present this technological marvel to her husband as a gift.

* * *

Denton Bret had reached Kaldea and found the *Iwakina* had fled through the Jumpgate. After asking around a bit, he found out about the Merchant Chiampa being found half starving in his own cargo container with nothing to eat but protein bars and Agagydalian vegetables. Chiampa was holed up in one of the interstellar ten-star lodgings on Kaldea, so Bret paid him a visit. The Kaldeans were a misogynistic noxious bunch. He had dealt with them before. He was told the Chiampa was a sight to see; apparently the vegetables did not agree with his complexion.

Keivly met him at the door. The man looked as if he had been badly beaten. "The Master does not wish any visitors, go away."

"But I have information that your master would be desperate to hear." Bret retorted.

Keivly was a little slow, but he obtained enough business sense over his years of service to know when to make inquiries. "What sort of information?"

"Just tell him that I may be able to solve his *Iwakina* problem."

Keivly quickly closed the door to his master's suite. It opened again a minute later. "Please enter. The Master will see you shortly."

Bret did as he was bid and found a rather opulent abode set before him. He was loathed to see such wasted resources, but he put that aside; he had business to do with this merchant, regardless of his disgust. Shortly the merchant appeared, in hooded robes and gloves. Bret could just barely catch what appeared to be mottled skin on the face inside the hood.

"Please excuse my appearance Mister...?"

"Bret. Denton Bret."

"Ah, Mister Bret. What news have you of the *Iwakina*?"

"I was hoping you had some news for me. I am on a mission from the Ros'Loper Imperial Court to find and destroy that menace."

This appeared to be sweet music to Chiampa's ears as the rotund man practically quivered with joy.

"Ah, yes. Having it destroyed would be a wonderful thing. How can I help you?"

"I have a rather… interesting ship which has an extraordinary AI installed. Did you notice anything peculiar about the AI on the *Iwakina*?"

"Well, they kept me sequestered to only a portion of the ship, but all of the normal functions I observed were standard. This ship you have, it is powerful enough to destroy the *Iwakina*, no?"

"Yes, it is quite capable I assure you."

"Then I have a proposition for you. I will give you codes to get your ship through all of the Jumpgates to Saragothra. I have set up a homing device inside the cabin I occupied. It will only activate when in the proximity of the Saragothra Jumpgate. Once it activates it will remain on until they find it. Wait there at Saragothra and follow them. You can then ambush them at your leisure, but away from the Jumpgate. If you succeed in your mission, I will make you a very wealthy man."

This story seemed pretty familiar to Bret. "Fair enough. Now please tell me what you know of the crew."

* * *

Nanami felt like she was about to blow a gasket. The New Rangelley Alliance was counting on them to help the Kadihri and Pendari come to some sort of agreement, and the Captain, knowing of her past as a trade negotiator, put her in charge of getting it done. However, there was no end to the bickering and hostility between the two sides. First, they didn't want the staterooms across from each other. Then the conference room was too small so that they would have to sit too close to one another. They insisted on eating apart, and not occupying the same space at the same time. *For God's sake,* she thought, *the only difference between the two was that the Pendari had facial tattoos.*

Nanami felt that she had to use the only recourse she had left. She called on the Kadihri Ambassador to go to the guest mess which was set up as a conference chamber for a 'video' meeting with the Pendari Ambassador. This way, the two of them would not have to meet face to face. This was a ruse, however, her next telling the Pendari the same thing. When the Pendari entered the hatch then about faced, it was too late; she had already locked the two of them inside. She then informed them of the situation over the intercom. "Now listen up you ungrateful miscreants. You were sent here by the powerful New Rangelley Alliance to get over your differences and make peace. I have half a mind to tell the NRA representative that there was an accident and space the two of you from that very room. However, in the spirit of civility, I will allow you to negotiate for one hour. Come to an agreement on peace, or come to an agreement on death. Your choice."

*　*　*

Ambassador Duranselt did not like this situation one bit. He was forced to remain locked in a single room with his hated counterpart not twenty meters away. He was checked for weapons as he came aboard; surely the Pendari was also unarmed. They eyed each other wearily. Suddenly the Pendari started laughing.

"Stupid Human bitch. It is only a matter of time before this ship is captured and then we will see who gets spaced." He laughed again.

Duranselt wondered what he meant then felt a jolt as if the ship had been hit by something. He looked at the Pendari wide-eyed, but the enemy just smiled what little smile a Pendari could muster.

*   *   *

Mairshima was meeting with Wilhelm once more in *Unity*. She had to tell him about her employer being able to block her mental probes. She had selected a more secluded nature scene, with a beautiful blue lake with fish that danced on the surface every once in a while. She had prepared a picnic spot, for after she discussed her message for him. Wilhelm arrived a few moments sooner than expected. He seemed a little troubled, but said it was nothing. "Why have you called today, little one?"

"Wilhelm, I have never been frightened in my entire life outside the Center until now. You know of my current position aboard the *Iwakina* under Doctor Rosel, correct? She has been experimenting on a comatose crewmember ever since the mutiny. At first, I thought it harmless, her only getting blood samples for tests and such, but then I felt there was more going on. I then decided to probe her thoughts, and she *blocked* me! Not only that but I think she knew I was doing it. I think maybe I should terminate her; I don't know the extent of her power and it scares me."

"Dear little one, do not be so rash. If you do so, you will jeopardize your position on the ship; I need you there and safe." Wilhelm then did something she had longed for him to do for so long; he took her into his arms. "You mean the universe to me, so please don't do anythi…"

Suddenly, Marishima was back in her cabin, the Virtual Reality that was *Unity* had vanished. The claxon that sounded General Quarters was blowing. She grabbed her smock and threw it on, heading out her hatch to her Duty Station in Sick Bay. All she could think about though was Wilhelm's embrace.

* * *

Saitow heard General Quarters sound and rushed to the bridge. Sagura reported that he was tracking six contacts, all NRA cruisers, with seven more coming from the opposite side of the planet. The closest of them had fired a shot and was now trying to use a gravitational beam to capture the ship.

This is quite a twist, Saitow thought. "Are the jump engines online?"

"We'll be jump capable in 30 seconds."

"Great. Get us out of here!"

"Coordinates, Captain?"

"Open space. Just get us out of here."

Sagura punched the coordinates and jumped the ship in the nick of time. As soon as they emerged from hyperspace, his board lit up again. "One contact bearing 100/50; 50,000 klicks out. She's spotted us and turning our way. Another NRA vessel, a destroyer this time."

Saitow felt the odds were good on this one. If they wanted his ship, they would have to earn it.

"Full impulse in the direction of the contact. Let's see if they are itching for a fight." As they headed toward their adversaries, Saitow thought about the situation they found themselves in. They had just been contracted to assist the NRA in helping their neighbors get along by hosting a meeting in neutral territory. It became obvious that this was just a ruse to get them into this trap. They must have ships in every direction, every 50 light years or so out from Pearl. Quite impressive. "How much time before the next jump?"

"Three minutes fifty."

"When we jump next Sagura, keep us in hyperspace, got it?"

"Aye, sir."

"Time to contact?"

"Two minutes thirty."

"Good. Let's show them we are not a mouse to be trifled with."

Sagura's board lit up like a holiday tree at Christmas time. "Multiple contacts. Sir, they've launched fighters."

Damn, Saitow swore to himself. He didn't want to launch fighters when he was so close to jump. They would get to him sooner than he cared for.

"Helm! Turn away from the enemy; full impulse."

"Captain?"

"Just do it!" Saitow didn't like this one bit. It wasn't like the old days when he ran a military vessel with clear cut rules of engagement. Everyone seemed out for his blood these days. Plus, he had civilians on board, not to mention diplomats. The diplomats! "Get Oliver on the horn!"

* * *

Nanami was fighting with herself over what duties she needed to prioritize. Right now, she was in charge of these ambassadors, but she wanted to be in her place on the bridge. The Captain would be furious if she left these dolts during General Quarters. She keyed the hatch open. The place smelled like a brewery. She surveyed the room and found that the jolt to the ship had sent the doors of the liquor cabinet swinging and several bottles of something had busted on the deck. What astonished her was that the two ambassadors were sitting in the corner, each swigging on a bottle and singing some alien song – TOGETHER! The Pendari ambassador spotted her and began to wail.

"Oh Osifer Oliver! Pleesh forgive me! In my cabin therez a yellow egg-shaped thingy. Smash it on the floor and all our troubles endz…"

What the hell was he talking about? Then she got the call from the Captain to search their quarters. She reported that she already had things well in hand and took care of the thingy the Pendari told her to destroy. When she next reported to the Captain, she said, "You are not going to believe this."

*   *   *

The *Iwakina* outran the enemy fighters long enough to make the next jump. Once further away and in hyperspace, they sent a probe out into real space; sure enough, there were two more enemy ships waiting in ambush. Crafty bastards. They made full impulse in hyperspace for the remainder of the day. Both of the diplomats were passed out drunk and sleeping it off in their respective quarters. Nanami was commended for her actions with them. Even though they had actually done it to themselves, she felt good about it; she needed all the kudos she could get right now.

*   *   *

Sheenid was furious. He insisted that Tellen report to him immediately. When she came to him, he insisted on knowing why half of his fleet was chasing after a ghost ship and some of the most important persons of their neighboring territories were missing. Tellen did her best to explain her motivations, but the Prince was less than sympathetic. He took her to Angolkor. On the way he explained that he had already known of the ghost ship from Parham, and that it belonged to the Saitow Family. When they got there, he showed her that he already had a similar ship and parts of another. He then introduced her to the engineers from the Saitow Conglomerate. He could tell that at this point she was extremely embarrassed at the whole situation and he felt a little sympathy for her. "Tellen, my dear wife, I have given you the reigns of diplomacy for the Alliance because you have a good head on your shoulders and I trust you to do the right thing always. I know you have our best interests at heart. But you must limit yourself to diplomacy; please consult with me first when critical matters present themselves. When this comes to light, who knows what concessions we may have to make. But enough of this harsh talk; let us have lunch together and please tell me of your other pursuits."

2

The Captain finally ordered the ship returned to real space. Sanae didn't like the feeling she got from being in hyperspace for a long time. It was creepy. As Kintaro Sagura, she keyed the inputs to bring the ship out. She then had to calibrate the system using the stars in the surrounding space to triangulate their location. It took a whole half a minute.

"What's our bearing?" asked the Captain.

"We are at the Southwest end of Sector 0067, still in NRA controlled space, but I doubt they sent ships out this far." Sagura replied.

"Good. Keep an eye on those readouts just in case. We'll sit tight for a few; after some crew rest, I want a meeting of key personnel so we can figure out our next move. Vic, you have the conn until third watch posts." Saitow then left the bridge.

Sanae spared a glance at the First Officer. He was a stoic man; it didn't fit his profile to join the mutiny. However, he and the Captain had been friends since long before each got this assignment. It seemed that, to these people, loyalties to those that are close are more important than duty. She turned back to monitoring her console until her replacement arrived.

* * *

Saitow called a meeting of all his key staff. He advised each to look at where the ship was on their tablets and give him possible options. The difficulty lay with the two ambassadors who had somehow come to an agreement and were acting like they were the best of friends; how to get them safely back to their own worlds. They didn't have another mission scheduled for another week.

Doctor Rosel spoke up first. "We are close enough for a jump series to Andali; I have a friend there that owes me a favor. I can have him arrange transport for our guests, provided he is allowed to travel with me for a while. I will pay his passage if need be."

"That won't be necessary Doctor. However, Andali is in Ros'Loper territory; will we be able to go to port there?" The Captain looked to everyone for an answer.

Takagawa spoke up next. "As long as we don't have any more stray tracking devices, we should be safe jumping through Imperial territory. As far as porting at Andali…"

Fortunately, Lieutenant Song Ha, who Saitow had sequestered for the meeting as the resident Xenologist on board, saved the day. "The Andalii, although technically part of the Empire, have been given autonomy when it comes to planetary defenses. They insist that no Imperial Warships come within three light-years of their homeworld. As long as we are there only long enough to recalibrate the ships systems, we should be fine. Needless to say, the Imperials will know we were there after the fact."

"That's fine; we'll just have to take our chances unless anyone has a better idea. By the way Song Ha, can you think of anything in your experience that explains how two enemy aliens can turn into the best of pals in a matter of hours?"

Nanami spoke up before Song Ha could answer. "This is what I got from them through the inebriated slurs. When I locked them in the conference room the ship was hit, and the liquor cabinet busted open. Smelling the booze set them onto having a drinking contest. Well as the alcohol loosened their lips, the two of them argued about Saragothra, and then they somehow concluded that they shared a commonality in their ancestry; both claim Saragothra as their ancestral birthright. I would hate to be an NRA flunky on Saragothra once these two get back to their homeworlds. Their combined fleets will likely converge on the place."

Song Ha chimed in. "That's right! The Kadihri and Pendari are of the same species genealogically; the Old Rangelley set up the whole rivalry thing eons ago. Did you know the Pendari facial tattoos stem from an ancient form of slave marking? It's really all quite fascinating."

The normal conversational pause period came and went. Then Doctor Kuremoto addressed the Captain. "Captain Saitow, as you know I have been working on a cure for the disease that has plagued the planet that a friend of mine has been stuck on for quite some time. I believe I have found it. I need assistance in delivering it to Uprising. My sources tell me that the Administrator of the planet is looking for transportation for her daughter to Saragothra. Might we possibly go there after Andali?"

"Doctor, Uprising is a quarantined and tightly guarded planet. They have a planet-wide force field system. How do you plan to get this cure to your friend if we go there?" The Captain was skeptical.

Kuremoto seemed reluctant to continue. "Well... I plan to take an Ethla down to the surface when the force field is dropped for the *Iwakina*."

"Are you serious? How do you even know how to fly one, let alone get under their sensors before the field is regenerated?" more skepticism.

"Captain, I have been on this ship and with its systems long before you came aboard. Besides, I took advantage of your flight training program to knock some of the rust off these old bones."

Saitow looked to Lieutenant Simpson who nodded his head.

"This is a pretty tall order. It could jeopardize you and compromise the ship..."

"Kuremoto tapped some input on his tablet. "Captain, please look at the results of my analysis of this disease. As you can see, it is of manufactured origin. These people were purposefully infected so that they could serve as a constant source of cheap labor. They are of lower status than slaves. We have to do something."

Saitow looked at the data. He knew nothing of biology beyond his secondary education, but the numbers added up to truth in what Kuremoto was saying. He looked around the room; everyone had an expectant look on their face like they wanted to do something about it. *Who was he to argue against that?* "Fine. We'll do it. Finally, I would like a progress report on our newest guest. Mr. Edwards?"

Edwards looked nervously at Doctor Rosel. Saitow wondered what that was all about.

"Captain, Benoba is currently in Sick Bay under the care of Doctor Rosel. I insisted that she stay there while her pigmentation wore off; however, there hasn't been much progress…"

Rosel looked slightly perturbed and rolled her eyes. "These things take time; pigmentation rehabilitation takes time. It would help in the acceleration process if I had some of the food stuffs that caused the whiteness to occur. Honestly Edwards, you are welcome to visit our little guest anytime." There seemed to be little love lost between these two. Saitow made a mental note.

Nanami offered to provide the stuff she asked for; there was plenty of it in the Merchant's baggage that she had cleaned out of the guest cabin he had occupied.

Saitow felt it was time to get back to business. "OK, is there anything else I need to be aware of? No? Good, let's get back to work."

As he exited the ready room he almost ran into Stephen Jing on the bridge. "Stephen, what brings you to the bridge at this hour?"

"Well Captain, I appreciate you providing me with a tablet so that I can have updates on the goings on with the ship. However, Gunter and I feel rather burdensome at having nothing to do while all of these little crises keep occurring. Is there anything the two of us can do for the ship?"

Saitow thought about it for a second and replied, "Just pray, Brother Stephen. Pray for us all."

TO BE CONTINUED...

ABOUT THE AUTHOR

Brian Michael Hall grew up in the United States of America, mainly in the suburbs of Maryland and in rural Florida. His early adulthood was spent in a career with the U.S. Marines, followed by a bucket list of jobs, flirting with college, and ending up in further service to the nation as a Postal Carrier.

Born of his love for creating maps, the Rangelley Universe is Brian's effort to make the places he creates come alive. Humans are found to be all over the place, mixing with aliens and other creatures across multiple dimensions. Where will his next story take you?

If you enjoyed this book, please leave a review on the platform from which you bought it!